South View

Renny deGroot

Also by Renny deGroot

FICTION:
CAPE BRETON MYSTERY SERIES
Garden Girl (Book One)
Sea Child (Book Two)
Heritage House (Book Three)
Night Rose (Book Four)

CANADIAN COTTAGE COUNTRY MYSTERY SERIES
Lakeside Beauty (Book One)

HISTORICAL FICTION:
Family Business
After Paris
Torn Asunder

NON-FICTION:
32 Signal Regiment: Royal Canadian Signal Corps – A History

This is a work of fiction set in Northumberland County, Ontario, Canada. The names, characters, events, and incidents are the products of the author's imagination, other than those noted in the acknowledgements. Any resemblance to actual persons, living or dead, or actual events is purely coincidental. The story is not intended to represent the actual methods and practices of any Canadian Police Service.

Copyright © 2025 Renny deGroot

Regular Print: 978-1-998891-13-9
Large Print: 978-1-998891-14-6
Ebook: 978-1-998891-12-2

All Rights Reserved. No part of this publication may be reproduced, stored in a retrieval system, or transmitted in any form or in any means – by electronic, mechanical, photocopying, recording or otherwise – without prior written permission.

NO AI TRAINING

Toadhollow Publishing 7509 Cavan Rd., Bewdley, Ontario K0L 1E0

Contact Renny at: renny@rennydegroot.com

Dedicated to Rod Doris, my realtor for more than thirty years.

Thank you for always going above and beyond
to get me the perfect home

AND

to Amanda Pellinen, the Sudbury, Ontario real estate broker
who may see some of herself in Shannon Coyne.

Prologue

THE WIND FROM THE lake cut through him. He knew he shouldn't be out on the water so early in the season, and now couldn't even remember how he came to be in this boat on the fifth of May. *I took drugs,* he thought. *My mind's so fuzzy.*

He didn't argue when he was told to take his overcoat off and throw it in the lake. He watched his fine coat float away through bleary sleep-heavy eyes. He stopped shivering in the stiff breeze as his body relaxed into sleep, although he woke up long enough to gasp at the shock when he tipped over into the icy blue-black water of Rice Lake.

He floundered for a few seconds and then gave himself up to the embrace of the lake he had loved for so long.

Chapter One

Saturday, June 3, 2023

IN HER DOWNSTAIRS FLAT of the converted red brick century home in Port Hope, Ontario, Shannon Coyne studied the room and questioned her choice.

She looped her long red hair behind her ear. "Somehow, I thought *Wild Sage* would be greener. It just looks grey to me."

Her best friend Piet Van Loo, who lived in the upstairs flat, squinted and slid his large, square, black-framed glasses further up his nose as he studied the newly painted walls. "It's a silvery green. I like it."

"Do you? I liked the idea of some wildness in the room, but it seems very tame."

"You can't be wild all the time. Sometimes, you need to be quiet and relaxed, and that's what this colour is all about."

Shannon laughed. "As if I'm a wild girl."

Piet raised his eyebrows. "You can be. Have you already forgotten that someone wanted to kill you not so long ago?"

She protested. "That wasn't my fault. I was in the wrong place at the wrong time."

He snorted. "It had nothing to do with your tendency to get a little too involved in other people's business, I suppose. Like the police?"

"You and I both know if the police had listened to me sooner, I wouldn't have been in the wrong place at the wrong time. Now, let's forget about all that. It's long behind us."

She opened her French door to let in her blond cocker spaniel, Dusty. "Are you all done terrorizing that squirrel, madam?" Leaving the door open to invite the early June breeze to fill the room with the fragrance of blossoms, Shannon turned to Piet.

"Tea?"

Piet looked at his watch. "I better not. I just popped down to see how it looked. Now that the painters have finished, I love it. I might think about this colour for my bedroom. It's very calming."

She smiled gratefully. "I can always count on you to make me feel better. It's Saturday. Do you have to work?"

He nodded. "Yes. One of the old dears from the Manse died yesterday. She was 92, so a good age, but still, I'll do my best to make her look as well as I can. It's an open casket, and she has a lot of family around here."

Shannon clicked on the kettle and then walked her friend to the door. "You're so caring. When it's my time, I want you in charge of my funeral."

Piet hugged her quickly and kissed the top of Shannon's head with its cascading red hair. "Silly girl. You're only 28 years old. By the time someone needs to think about that I'll be long retired out of the funeral home business and perhaps gone ahead of you."

"You're three years younger than me. You'll be here."

He waved and left her to climb the stairs to his second-floor flat.

※

After lunch, Shannon decided to take advantage of the perfect spring weather to take Dusty for a walk in downtown Port Hope. "We'll walk down to *My Sister's Closet.*" As she leashed up the spaniel, she kept talking. "I saw a gorgeous plaid handbag in the window the other day. I deserve a new purse, don't I?"

The spaniel wagged her tail enthusiastically as if to agree with her mistress, and Shannon smiled. "You only care about going for a walk, don't you?"

The weather brought people out, pale-skinned after weeks of dreary weather. Shannon waved to her neighbour, busy raking dead leaves from the front garden, and a few minutes later, she stopped in front of *Our Lady of Mercy Church* to chat with two women she knew from the local florist. "Oh, how beautiful. Flowers make the heart glad, don't they?"

The older of the pair, a woman named Ivy, nodded. "They certainly do. Today, a wedding, and on Monday, a funeral. Flowers are good for the soul, no matter the occasion."

"A wedding? How wonderful. Who is getting married? Do I know them?"

"The couple doesn't live in Port Hope, but the bride's parents do, so they decided to have the wedding here in town instead of in Toronto, where they live."

Shannon nodded. "Makes sense. Who are the parents, then?"

"The MacBrides. He used to own the hardware store that was on the corner." Ivy pointed down the block.

"Of course. I remember them. The daughter is younger than me, but I remember she was very good at some sport. Was it track?"

Ivy shook her head. "Skating, I think."

"You could be right. Nice family."

The younger woman, Diane, a former colleague of Shannon's mother, asked how her parents were doing. "The bank was never the same after your mother left. She always made me smile."

Dusty seemed to realize she'd be there for a few moments and lay down on the sun-warmed sidewalk in front of the grand red-brick church with its beautiful statue of 'the Child and His Mother' positioned in front.

Laughing, Shannon agreed. "They're both fine. Mammy's joined the Colborne Rotary Club and is now immersed in some fund-raising projects."

The woman smiled. "That's so Mary. I'm sure they'll be glad to have her. And what about your father?"

"He's good too. It's a busy time of the year, and he's in the second year after planting a new high-density orchard. He's out there every day nurturing his baby trees. He's lucky, though. My oldest sister, Bernadette, and her husband, Danny, have joined him full-time in the business. It's working out well. They seem to enjoy it, and Daddy's very glad to have them by his side."

Diane nodded. "A real family business. And you aren't interested in joining them?"

"Oh, no. I love being a realtor. Finding the right home for a family is so satisfying."

Ivy nodded to the church. "We'd better get these flowers inside and arranged before the wedding guests arrive."

Diane started. "Oh, my, yes. I got all caught up chatting. Give my regards to your mum, Shannon."

With a promise to pass along the greetings of both women, Shannon nudged Dusty, and they carried on along Walton Street.

Shannon looked in several shops in downtown Port Hope but arrived home empty-handed but relaxed and in a good mood at the end of the day. As she set Dusty's dinner down on the floor in the kitchen, she shook her head. "I'll have to wait until I sell a house, Dusty. My budget won't stretch to a new handbag right now." She smiled as she watched her dog lick the dish. "Oh, well. Mammy would tell me I have plenty of handbags already, wouldn't she?"

Dusty looked up, hopefully, but Shannon picked up the empty dish. Instead of filling it with more food, she carried it to the sink to wash.

She had just dried her hands when her phone rang. Checking the caller's identification, she saw the name *Kal Khan*, a detective who worked for her uncle, Bob Miller, in the Northumberland County Police Service. She and Kal had become friends the previous year, and although she wouldn't say they were dating, she wouldn't quite say they weren't, either.

"Kal. This is a nice surprise. What brings you to my phone on a Saturday evening?" She put her phone on speaker and continued to tidy up the kitchen.

His voice was warm, and despite his years in Canada, the slight Indian accent gave him an exotic sound. "Am I disturbing you, Shannon?"

She loved how he was always careful to ensure he wasn't interrupting her. "Not at all. I'm just tidying up, and then I plan to sit in front of the telly and relax with some mindless show. Probably a home renovation thing."

He laughed, and it sounded like music. "My grandmother also calls the television 'the telly.'"

"We have more in common than you thought."

"Indeed." He hesitated and then continued. "The reason I'm calling is that I spent the day today retrieving my motorcycle from storage. I changed the oil and polished it. I am now looking for a destination to take the bike for the first ride of the season tomorrow. I wonder if that might be to visit you."

"A motorbike! I didn't know you rode a motorcycle. Wow! How brave! You'd never get me on one. You're very welcome to visit. I have no plans, but don't imagine I'll get on that thing with you and risk my life whizzing through traffic with nothing between me and the pavement."

"I will enjoy a visit with you. What time is convenient?"

They agreed he should arrive after lunch. somewhere around one o'clock.

☙

When Kal knocked on the door Sunday afternoon, Shannon jumped.

She opened the door to him, and her eyes widened at seeing the cherry red motorcycle parked in her front yard. "I thought I'd hear you roar up in a cloud of smoke and noise."

Kal, dressed in black leather pants and jacket, smiled. "She purrs like a kitten. She doesn't need to roar. Come and see."

She followed him to the machine, whose engine still ticked as it cooled. "It is quite spectacular looking." She ran her fingers across the black leather seats, first the front and then the raised rear seat with its curved backrest. On each seat, a white helmet rested. The bright red body sparkled in the sunlight. "It seems very new."

"No, no. It is a 2017."

"You obviously take very good care of it."

He smiled. "Yes. It is my hobby, I suppose."

As they stood admiring the motorcycle, Piet came bounding from the house. "Oh, wow! What a gorgeous machine! It's a Honda Gold Wing, am I right?"

Kal's teeth flashed white as his grin lit up his face. "Yes. Are you a fan of bikes?"

"I am. I once took a weekend course to learn how to ride a bike but never ended up buying one."

"You are still young. You have plenty of time ahead of you."

Kal showed Piet the various highlights of the motorcycle, who made appreciative sounds as he admired everything.

Kal bobbed his head in his classic shrug-nod movement. "I'm afraid I never lend it to anyone, but if you fancy a short ride, I would be more than happy to take you."

Piet sighed. "I wish I had time, but I need to go to work."

"Another time."

Piet looked at Shannon. "Are you going, Shanny?"

She laughed. "Oh, no. I've already told Kal I wouldn't go."

"Whyever not? Look at this thing. It must be like sitting on your living room sofa."

Kal smiled but let Piet continue to encourage Shannon without his help.

She held up her hands to ward off further comments. "They're dangerous."

Piet shook his head. "Life is dangerous. You need to take chances. You know that. You've done it before. Think of last year when you kept going against every person's advice to get justice for Jason."

"That was different. I didn't think about any danger."

"So don't get hung up on it now. Instead of overthinking things, just go for it." Piet glanced at his watch. "And with that, I have to go."

Kal stood watching Shannon after Piet disappeared back into the house. "I don't want to pressure you, but your friend Piet sounds wise."

Shannon chewed her lip and walked around the bike. "It does look solid."

He nodded. "Yes. I promise to drive carefully if you come for a short ride."

She looked at his dark, serious eyes, magnified by square, black-rimmed glasses. "I can't believe I'm doing this."

Kal grinned. "Does this mean yes?"

"Yes. Let me go put a pair of jeans on instead of these cropped pants. If I want to come home, even if it's only a block away, you'll turn back?"

He held up his hand. "Scout's honour."

"Were you ever a scout?"

"No, but I am honourable."

She smiled. "Yes. I know. All right, come in for a minute while I change."

Ten minutes later, her heart thudding, she sat on the back of Kal's motorcycle, arms tightly locked around him as he raised the kickstand, balanced the machine and pushed the button to start.

Oh my God. What am I doing?

Chapter Two

SHANNON GLANCED UP AS Kal pushed the bike backwards to take them out on the street, and saw Piet standing on his small second-floor veranda, grinning and waving. He wore a white shirt, black funeral jacket, and grey sweatpants bottoms. She didn't dare loosen her grip to wave back, but she was glad he had seen her.

Kal drove down her street and turned right onto Walton, following Highway 2 west and north. After a few moments, he tilted back to call out. "How are you doing?"

"OK."

As they travelled sedately along, Kal sticking to the 60-kilometre-an-hour speed limit, she found herself relaxing. They approached a motorcycle coming the other way, and as the two bikes passed each other, both drivers held out their left hand in a brief salute to each other.

I guess Kal knows people around here. How could he recognize that person in a full visor? Maybe he knows the bike. As she considered Kal's wave, another bike approached, and each rider repeated the ritual.

Shannon was intrigued by the waves, which she soon understood happened every time they passed another bike. Busy thinking about these things, it was several minutes before she realized she wasn't afraid anymore.

She had a moment's panic when she realized they were approaching the on-ramp to the 401 Highway. She must have tightened her grip again because Kal turned his head to say, "We won't go on the highway."

She shouted back. "Thank you."

Aside from those few words, Kal didn't try to engage her in conversation. When they reached the village of Welcome, he continued north along County Road 10, winding along the beautiful country road with its spring-green farm fields and small shady villages. In Garden Hill, Kal pulled into the conservation area and stopped. He kept the bike stable and balanced until Shannon climbed off before letting down the kickstand. Kal dismounted and removed his helmet, helping Shannon unbuckle hers as she struggled to figure out the closing. She shook her head, and the breeze from the pond caught her long red hair.

He smiled. "Your hair is so pretty in the sunlight." He hurried on. "How are you? Were you comfortable? Did you enjoy it?"

Shannon took a deep breath. "I didn't enjoy it."

Kal's face fell.

"I loved it."

"How marvellous. I knew you would. You have an adventurous spirit."

"I must admit that once I got used to it, I felt a sense of freedom I never imagined."

"Just you and the wind." He suggested.

"Yes. Just me and the wind. And you." She smiled.

"I'm so pleased."

"I don't think I'm ready for the 401 or any of the other really fast roads, but this was nice. Truly nice."

Kal nodded to the path leading into the woods. "Shall we walk a little?"

"What about our helmets?"

"I'll lock them to the bike."

They walked for fifteen minutes in the shade of the forest. Kal exclaimed to see several turtles dive from a log into the water next to the trail, and then they made their way back to the bike.

Kal unlocked their helmets. "Are you ready to go back?"

"It's pretty here, but yes, let's go."

He took a different route back to her home. The complete trip was just over an hour, but for Shannon, it felt as though she'd gone on a journey of a lifetime.

🔥

They sat at the kitchen table enjoying tea with some snacks Shannon assembled.

Kal scooped some hummus onto a celery stick. "Women are so talented in creating a feast in minutes."

She picked up a cracker piled with a clump of goat cheese and topped it with a dab of red pepper jelly. "You should see what my mother can do. One minute, there's nothing, and then next, she's got a spread laid out."

Kal smiled. "My mother is the same, and I know she learned that skill from my grandmother. Nani doesn't chop and stir anymore but is very good at giving orders."

Taking a sip of tea, Shannon paused in thought. "I wish I knew my grandparents more. They all stayed in Ireland when my parents came to Canada."

"Have you never gone to visit them?"

"Yes, I've been twice, but as a kid. I was very shy, and they did their best, but everything felt strange to me, so I didn't take advantage of the time to get to know them. Both my grandfathers are gone now, and one grandmother. My mother's mother is still alive and lives with my aunt."

"You have time to go and visit. You are an adult and can go without your parents. Meanwhile, you have an uncle to make up for it."

She laughed. "Yes, I do. I'm sure you and I view my uncle quite differently. For me, he's just my mother's brother. He and my aunt are warm and loving family members. For you, he's your boss. It's funny how people can see the same person differently."

"I can see he is a caring uncle. He was very worried about you last year."

"That's true. And it's also true I can go to Ireland to visit my nana on my own. You're giving me something to think about there. I don't know why I didn't consider it before now. After going on your motorbike today, I think I can do anything. Wait until Mammy hears about that."

"Will she be pleased?"

"Good Lord, no. She'll berate me for risking my life on a 'death trap.' That's what she always calls motorcycles."

"Would you go again?"

"I would if you're driving. I'm not sure everyone is so safe."

He smiled. "I knew you were more courageous than you thought yourself."

Shannon flushed. "Tell me more about your grandmother. She must be courageous to come to a new country like she did."

"Yes. I am very fond of her. She left her whole life behind. Her sisters and her community. When we first came to Canada, she and I shared a room in a tiny flat."

"You must have chafed at that." Shannon thought about the large, rambling farmhouse where she was raised and remembered games of hide and seek with her sisters in its many rooms and alcoves.

"If I did, I don't remember it. She kept me grounded in the old world while school forced me into the new one. It was comforting to have her. She has a sharp tongue, and I feel its lash often, but I love her and would do anything to help her if I can."

She topped up his tea cup. "Families are interesting. I feel close to mine, but there are so many times I feel there are things I don't know. Like about the time before my parents came to Canada or things that happen in the life of my older sister, Bernadette. I want to give them a shake sometimes and say, 'Just tell me.'"

"Everyone needs their secrets, and no amount of prodding from you will change that."

She pouted. "But I *want* to know."

"And do you share everything with them?"

Shannon tilted her head. "Maybe not."

"I suspect not." Kal drained his cup. "And speaking of families, I promised my mother I would return for supper, so it's time to go."

"Thank you for coming. I had such a nice time and didn't think I would."

He bobbed his head. "And thank you for taking the chance to come with me."

She walked him to the door and stood watching as he put on his helmet, flipping open the visor to smile at her before guiding the bike out of the driveway and setting off down her street.

Chapter Three

MARY COYNE REACTED AS Shannon had predicted. "You surely aren't going out on the deathtrap again, are you?"

Shannon smiled as she saw the horrified look on her mother's face on the screen of her phone. "Well, Mammy, I might. We'll have to see. I have to say, I felt very safe."

"Sure, don't you have a lovely car to take you wherever you want to go? Why risk life and limb on a contraption like that?"

"Mammy, there's something liberating about zipping along in the fresh air."

"So, ride a bicycle, then. You'll get more fresh air that way than speeding along on the back of a machine."

Shannon nodded. "You may be right, Mammy."

They went on to talk about other things, including a house Shannon planned to look at the next day for her new clients. She explained it was on the north side of Rice Lake.

Mary nodded. "It's on the water, you say?"

"It is, and it looks like a small beach is part of the property, along with some rocky bits. The rocks will be good to prevent erosion, so it sounds like a nice spot."

"Take some photos and come for dinner afterwards. You can tell us all about it."

"Sounds good, Mammy. I'll see you all tomorrow, then."

※

Shannon was dozing in front of the television at eight-thirty when tapping on her front door woke her.

"Hey, Piet."

He was still dressed in his work clothes. "I heard the television, so I knew you weren't in bed." Dusty spun circles around her friend as Piet followed Shannon inside.

"No, you're fine. Come on in. How was work?"

"Oh, you know—lots of wandering around with a coffee pot and boiling the kettle for cups of tea. At least I'm not hanging up coats. That's done for a few months."

"Was it busy, then?"

"Surprisingly so, considering how old she was. Sometimes it's the opposite. People outlive their friends and sometimes even family, and there's hardly anyone at the visitation. It was good, though. People truly seemed to celebrate her life. One daughter told me, "I'm glad it's over because I know *she's* glad it's over. She was ready to go." He waved a hand dismissively. "Never mind all that. I couldn't wait to hear how the motorbike ride went."

"Fancy a cup of chamomile tea, or are you tea-ed out?"

"Oh, yes, please, if you're having one."

He followed her into the kitchen and leaned against the counter as she filled the kettle, took out two cups and placed a bag into each one.

She turned to him, and when he frowned, she didn't wait any longer. "I loved it."

Piet's face cleared. "Aha! I knew it."

"How come everyone seems to know me better than I know myself? I was sure I'd hate it."

He waited until she poured boiling water over the tea bags, and they each carried a cup back to the living room. "It's the freedom. There's something about being there in the wind and sun that makes you feel free."

She nodded as she dipped the bag in and out of the water in her cup. "Yes, there's that, but I think it was more."

"An adrenalin rush?"

"That too, I guess, but I was so afraid, and then, once we got going, I wasn't anymore, and that felt good."

Piet set his tea bag in a saucer Shannon had provided. "Of course. You faced your fear. You didn't allow your fear to rule you. That's huge and something we all should do more often."

She put her bag in the saucer with his and took a sip of her tea. "You're right. I think I feel stronger somehow for having done this."

"So, will you go again?"

"Assuming Kal invites me again, yes."

He smiled. "He'll invite you."

※

On Monday morning, Shannon was busy with work, responding to emails, reviewing new listings, and checking any changes from the weekend. One house she had considered for her new clients had a conditional offer, so she took that one off her list of potentials. If it fell through, she could still consider it. It was mid-morning when she was ready to look at the house she had mentioned to her mother.

She spoke to the dog sitting at her feet, who looked up hopefully at her. "It's a perfect day for a drive here in Southern Ontario. You coming with me, pup?" She laughed as Dusty ran to the hook where her leash hung. "Yes, all right. I'm coming. You'll have to stay in the car, though."

Shannon pulled her cherry red Toyota RAV4 from its parking spot in front of their house. *Maybe that's why I liked Kal's bike so much. It matches my car.* Her GPS gave her directions, and she settled in for the half-hour drive to the house in Pengally Landing on Rice Lake.

As she drove north on Highway 28, she called the listing agent. "Hi, Rod. It's Shannon Coyne calling. I saw you listed a place this week on Rice Lake. The one east of Bailieboro. Just to let you know I'm on my way there now to take a quick look at it, but I want to make sure that doesn't interfere with anything you've got on."

His warm voice came over her speaker. "Hi, Shannon. You're fine to see it. Do you have the lockbox code?"

"I do, thanks. Anything I should know about the place?"

"It's beautiful from the outside, but the inside needs some work. It's ideal for someone ready to put some love into it to make it their own."

Shannon laughed. "OK. I'm forewarned. I'll let you know if I go ahead and show it to my clients."

"The lot is gorgeous. It's right on the water. The southern exposure means it's bright and sunny. Nice for sitting out with a cold one in summer."

"What's the water frontage again?"

"A hundred feet, and it's two fifty deep."

"OK, thanks. That's a great size."

"Most of the lots along there are large, so you don't feel like you're on top of each other. In fact, with the landscaping, it's super private. Let me know what you think of the place, will you?"

She assured him she would, and hung up, smiling. Looking in the rearview mirror at Dusty curled up on the blanket in the back seat, Shannon said, "Rod sees the best in everything. I'm reserving judgment until we see it ourselves, right Dusty?"

Turning east in Bailieboro, Shannon made a mental note to stop for butter tarts at the village bakery on the way back. *Mammy and Daddy will love them.* She looked forward to spending the evening with her family on the apple farm where she grew up near Colborne.

Shannon slowed down as she examined the properties to her right, along the lake. *Nice area. Rod's right. Large lots. Well spaced out and private with plenty of trees.*

She turned in at the 'For Sale' sign and opened the car windows before switching off the engine. Studying the house from the outside, she admired the old stone structure, which looked like an English cottage. On either side of the lot, cedar trees formed a tall, dark hedge that ran the length of the property to the shore, opening up to a sandy strip of beach.

Shannon turned to wag her finger at Dusty. "Now, don't climb out the window. I won't be long."

Once inside, the realtor in her kicked in. She walked from room to room, making notes in her leather portfolio. Her parents had given her the leather carrier with her initials emblazoned on the front as a birthday gift, and Shannon had never left without it. A narrow staircase led to a second floor where three bedrooms and a small washroom nestled under sloped ceilings. At some point, the main floor was opened up and now served as a great room with sliding doors displaying a view of the lake and leading out to a deck. The pine floors needed refinishing, and the kitchen cabinets showed their age with years of grime and scrapes marring them. *They need replacing. Can't fix those anymore.*

By the time she left, Shannon felt the house had good bones for the right buyer. It showed its years as a well-loved family home though, and the work and investment required to fix it up would frighten many potential clients away. *That's an opportunity for the right people, though.*

She left her business card that proclaimed *Shannon Coyne, Your Cottage Country Specialist,* on the kitchen counter and left the house.

After locking the key back into the lockbox, Shannon opened the back door of her car to let Dusty out. "Come on, sweetie. Let's take a little walk around. Don't go for a swim, though. The water's too cold, and I didn't bring a towel."

The blond American cocker spaniel scampered out of the car and raced around the front yard with her nose to the ground.

"And don't get caught up in any burrs," Shannon called out, even though the small shaggy dog ignored her and belted off into the underbrush before emerging again with twigs stuck in her ears and coat.

"Oh, well. You're going for your spring grooming next week. I guess we might as well get my money's worth."

Dusty suddenly scented something near the water and turned away from the bushes to race down to the water's edge. This time, Shannon called out firmly. "No. Don't go in the water!"

Dusty whined and pranced at the water's edge near some large rocks.

"If it's a dead fish, leave it. Leave It!" Shannon hurried to see what her dog was so keen to pull out of the water.

"Oh, my goodness. It's a coat. OK, get back. Let me pull it out of the water."

Shannon pulled the heavy, sodden black woollen overcoat out of the water where it had wedged itself between two rocks. Tugging it out and up on top of the rocks to allow it to stream water back into the lake, she studied it for a moment. "How strange, Dusty. The coat is in good condition, aside from being mucky and wet. How in the world would someone lose something like this, do you think?"

Dusty stood with her forepaws on the rock and snuffled at the coat before losing interest and exploring the rest of the small beach.

"Come on, Dusty. Let's go. You're going back in the car, and I'm getting a couple of green garbage bags to take this with us. If nothing else, once it's dried off, it might be good enough to donate to someone."

The dog was ready to settle down on her blanket in the back seat again, and she glanced up once before she circled a few times and settled with a grunt. Shannon returned to the dripping coat and tried to press most of the water out before rolling it into two green garbage bags. As she stuffed the soggy garment into the first bag and then the second bag, she noticed the embroidered name on the blue lining. *Malcolm Joseph Walker.* Shannon shook her head. *Who are you? And why is your beautiful winter coat in Rice Lake?*

The house may not suit her clients, but one thing was certain. Shannon Coyne would discover why Mr. Walker's coat was in the lake.

Chapter Four

THE COAT WAS STILL wet, but it had stopped dripping when Piet came down to Shannon's flat to check it out.

He ran his fingers over the embroidered name. "This name is familiar for some reason."

Shannon widened her eyes. "Really? You know him?"

"Oh, no. I don't think so. Just the name."

"You mean he's famous?"

Piet frowned. "I'm not sure. I need to think on it for a bit. It's a beautiful coat, though. I can't see someone tossing it into the lake like garbage."

Shannon nodded. "I put a notice on Facebook to see if anyone knew anything."

He smiled. "All of Facebook? You did a post to all real estate friends, you mean?"

"No, silly. On the group, *Shores of Rice Lake*. I said I found the coat floating in the lake and gave his name, hoping someone might come forward."

"No joy?"

"No. Lots of comments, but nothing to help me find Mr. Walker."

"Let me mull it over for a bit. It'll come to me. Did you Google him?"

She slapped her forehead. "Why didn't I think of that?" Shannon walked over to the kitchen table, where her laptop was running. She sat down, and Piet followed her as he peered over his friend's shoulder.

Shannon clicked on a link. "Maybe this one?"

They both read the obituary, and Shannon sighed. "Is it him, do you think?"

"I'm sure of it. I remember now. We did the funeral about a month ago. I remember hearing that they had a summer place on Rice Lake." He nodded. "I think there was money there."

She studied the obituary as if it might answer more questions than it did. "But even people with money don't throw a beautiful coat into the lake. They might throw flowers or whatever, but not a fine woollen coat."

"Cashmere, my dear."

"Cashmere, then." Shannon closed the laptop. "I'm going to investigate this further. Can you get me the contact details for the widow? I'll get the coat cleaned up and then see if she wants it back."

Piet bit his lip. "I shouldn't, but if you promise not to say where you got it, I'll get it tomorrow when I'm at work."

"Thank you, my friend. You're the best."

After Piet left, Shannon went back to her computer to Google the man whose coat she had hanging in her bathroom. "Good Lord, Dusty. This article says he died in suspicious circumstances, and the investigation is ongoing. That was from six weeks ago, and since then, nothing. I wonder what happened." She looked over at her dog lying stretched out on the sofa. "I wonder if I should call Uncle Bob."

The dog opened her eyes briefly, stretched, turned, and went back to sleep. Shannon smiled. "Yes, you did your part by finding the coat, didn't you?"

※

That evening, everyone wanted to know about Shannon's motorcycle adventure.

"I was afraid at first, but it wasn't long before that went away. It was exciting, and I was glad I had decided to try it."

Her father nodded. "I know your mammy disagrees with me, but I say good for you. I rode a bike when I still lived at home."

Shannon widened her eyes. "Did you, Daddy?"

Her mother interrupted. "You can't compare that small bike with the likes of what Shannon's talking about."

He sniffed. "I know it was just a 125 cc, but it went like the devil."

Shannon, glad for her father's support, defended him. "And on those little roads, I bet it was more dangerous than Kal's great big heavy thing on our wide Canadian roads."

"You're right. You had to keep your wits about you."

Mary Coyne glared at her husband. "We don't need our children to do everything we did when we were young, James. We came here for a better life. A safer life."

He turned away from his wife's piercing gaze to look at Shannon. "Your mammy's right, of course. We want you to stay safe." He straightened his back. "I trust your judgment, though." With that, he hastened to change the subject. "What else have you been up to?"

Happy to change the subject, Shannon told her family about the coat. Her mother crossed herself and muttered, "Jesus, Mary and Joseph."

Her father puffed out his chest. "Would the coat fit me, do you think?"

At the same time, Shannon's mother tsked and said 'James!' while Shannon's sister Bernadette, sitting next to her father, slapped his arm and cried 'Daddy!'"

"What? If it's as fine as Shannon says, it'd be a shame to let the coat go to waste."

Shannon shook her head. "Ah, Daddy. No, it's not your style. Besides, I plan to give it back to the widow."

After that, there was a lively debate about what Shannon should and should not do. Both Bernadette and Shannon's other sister, Meghan, felt she was right and should give it back to the widow.

Shannon turned to her mother. "Mammy, you're very quiet. What do you think?"

"Since you ask, I think you should bundle it back into the garbage bag and send it to the dump. Don't get involved with this. You don't know. Maybe putting his coat into the lake was part of the widow's grieving process. You said they had a home on Rice Lake?"

When Shannon nodded, her mother continued. "Maybe they had a ceremony and all and sent the coat off with prayers. The ancient Egyptians did that. Sent their loved one off with food and clothing. Imagine the horror she'd have if the coat came back to her."

Meghan widened her eyes. "I've changed my mind. I think Mammy's right. The poor woman might feel like her husband is haunting her."

Bernadette nodded. "Imagine if she had a heart attack when she saw it. How would you live with that?"

Shannon finished the last bite of the cabbage and mashed potatoes. "The colcannon was delicious, as always, Mammy. Thank you. And you know, you may be right about giving the coat back. I'll have to find out if it was put in the lake on purpose."

After scraping his plate clean, Bernadette's husband, Danny, spoke for the first time. "I don't mind wearing a dead man's coat. If it fits me better than James, I'll take it."

Bernadette shook her head. "You won't." Everyone at the table knew that was the end of that discussion.

Mary Coyne stood to start collecting the plates but hesitated with a final look at Shannon. "Don't do anything more about it,

Shanny. Bin it and leave it at that. Look what happened last time you got involved in things."

They all took a moment to remember her brush with death, and then Shannon shook her head. "It's nothing like that, Mammy. Don't worry yourself."

Shannon left after a slice of freshly baked apple cake made with stored apples from their own orchard, topped with softly whipped cream. Bernadette and Danny had already gone, and Shannon saw that her mother wanted to turn the conversation to Shannon's love life.

"Dusty and I need to go. You can spend time analyzing Meghan's life instead."

Meghan laughed as she kissed her sister goodbye. "Mammy's exhausted that subject, and she needs to know what you're up to. She quizzes me endlessly about you and whether you're dating the lovely Declan, the exotic Kal Khan or someone else altogether."

Her mother flushed as she hugged Shannon. "I don't. I just take an interest in the lives of my daughters. Sure, what's wrong with that?"

Shannon hugged first her mother and then her father. "I love that my family takes an interest. But right now, there's nothing to report. It's work, work, work."

On the half-hour drive from Colborne back home to Port Hope, Shannon thought not about the men in her life but about Malcolm Walker's life. *Yes, I'll find out more about how it came to be in the lake before I say I have it, but how do I do that without mentioning the coat to the family?*

Chapter Five

EARLY TUESDAY MORNING, SHANNON sent Kal Khan an email note. *I want to thank him anyway, so it's a legitimate excuse for contacting him.*

Hi Kal. Hope all is well with you.

She glanced outside and confirmed the sun was shining, then continued.

> I want to thank you again for taking me out on Sunday. I enjoyed it so much. My mother was horrified, as I knew she would be, but my father seemed pleased. It's such a beautiful day, and I wondered if you felt like meeting for lunch. I noticed that the Buttermilk Café has its patio up and running. Let me know, and if you'd like to get together, propose a time. Have a great day.

She thought now about Declan and knew her parents longed for her to attach herself to the young Irish man. *He is handsome with his wild copper curls and a big grin. So Irish. And he makes me laugh because we have the same sense of humour. But he's so predictable. Kal, on the other hand. I never really know what he's thinking. Spending time with him is always an adventure. He fascinates me.*

Shannon blinked and came out of her reverie when she heard a *ping* and saw a note from Kal.

Good morning, Shannon. What a splendid idea. I can meet you at the Buttermilk Café at 12:30 if that suits you.

Smiling, she wrote back.

Lovely. I'll see you then.

Who says splendid these days? I hope he isn't annoyed when I ask him about Malcolm Walker.

❦

He was there when she arrived, and Kal waved to ensure she saw him.

She sat down across from him and admired how he looked both professional and comfortable at the same time in his crisp, open-necked white shirt and navy-blue suit. So different from Sunday's leathers. "You scored a great table here. Have you been waiting long?"

"No. Not at all. I think more people are inside than prepared to dine al fresco yet, so I didn't need to race anyone for the table."

Shannon smiled. "And here I thought maybe you showed your badge to get someone to move."

"Ah. That's not a practice I have attempted. I'm not sure it would work."

"No, maybe not."

A waitress arrived to give them menus and take their beverage orders—coffee for her and regular orange pekoe tea for him.

He studied the menu. "Have you eaten here before?"

"Oh yes. You haven't?"

"No. I rarely eat out. I'm not averse to it. I don't find pleasure in eating alone in a restaurant."

"You're in for a treat, then. I'm having the Chicken Pazzano with flatbread, but everything is good. Of course, they're famous for the pancakes if you like that."

Kal tilted his head in the way Shannon had come to understand, which meant anything from "yes" to "I hear you" to "no." He turned the page of the menu. "Perhaps I'll try the pancakes another day. That seems more appropriate for breakfast. Today, I'll try the Americano Tartine."

"Oh, good choice."

Shannon sensed that the confidence he exuded when he was on his motorbike eluded him today. "Lunch is my treat. I want to thank you for the adventure on Sunday."

"No need at all. It was my pleasure."

She bit her bottom lip.

The waitress came and took their orders. In the silence that followed, Kal studied her. "Is there something else?"

As they sipped their drinks, Shannon began. She told him about finding the coat as Kal leaned in slightly, focused on her story.

She finished by asking him. "So, I don't want to contact the widow with this coat if it might upset her. Mammy suggested it might have been put in the lake as part of a ceremony."

"I see your dilemma, but not how I can assist."

"Well, there's just a bit more. When I googled the name *Malcolm Walker,* there was a very short news article that his death was being investigated."

"Ahh. By us?"

"Yes, I believe so. I thought if you looked it up and let me know what's happening, it might give me a direction to follow regarding the coat."

He hesitated. "If it's an ongoing investigation…"

She put up her hand to stop him. "Of course, you can't share any confidential information. I understand that completely."

The waitress brought their lunches, and Kal nodded. "Let me see what I can discover, and we will go from there."

They ate lunch and enjoyed a companionable hour, mostly talking about his family. He finished his meal and concluded his family history. "So, you see, I was only five years old when we came to Canada in 1999, and although I grew up here, with the influence of my grandmother and my parents, I feel strong cultural ties with my Indian and Pakistani heritage."

Shannon nodded. "I was born and raised here in Canada, and yet, I, too, feel very strong cultural ties to my Irish heritage. It's natural. Your family shapes who you are."

"So true."

When the bill came, Shannon picked it up.

Kal frowned and then nodded. "I'll get it next time. Thank you."

After she paid, they stood outside the black iron patio fence for a moment.

Kal nodded. Thank you for lunch. "I'll see what I can find out about your Mr. Walker and will be in touch. Have a good afternoon."

🔥

Shannon had just walked in the door and was in the process of giving Dusty a treat when her phone rang. She frowned, tempted to let the call go to her voicemail, and then she shook her head. That's not who she was.

"Hi, Rod. Before you ask, I haven't discussed the property with my clients yet, but I promise I will today."

She heard the disappointment in his voice despite her colleague's effort to put on a bright tone. "No worries. Like all of us, I'm sure you're busy."

"Actually, Rod, I must admit I'm caught up in a mystery that started when I was visiting that property."

"Oh? You have me interested."

"I found a beautiful winter coat in the lake washed up on the shore there at that house. It has a label inside showing that it belonged to a man named Malcolm Walker, and I've been trying to track down the owner ever since."

Rod's laughter was warm. "I can help you there. He was the owner of that house. He died not long ago, though. Very sad."

Shannon put her hand on her forehead. "No way! How did I not know that? Walker isn't the name on the listing, is it?"

"No. The daughter is doing the paperwork on behalf of her mother, so the paperwork shows Jennifer Jones, but in fact, Violet Walker is the actual client."

"Violet Walker. Why is that name familiar? Wait. Violet and Mal. Right? They never called him Malcolm. It was always Violet and Mal."

"That's right. We've known each other for years. I sold their house in Newcastle when they moved up to the house on the lake full-time when he retired twenty years ago."

"This is unreal. I met them when I was in high school and volunteered at The Manse They.came in to help with a couple of the seniors' programs. She played piano, and they ran an afternoon tea dance. Mal was so good. He danced with all those ladies while Violet provided the music. Oh my gosh. I even remember the daughter. She complained about me once to my supervisor."

"Complained about you? What for?"

"She came in once while her folks were running a bingo game, and she was insisting that her father come outside to talk to her, but when I went in to ask Mal to come out, he made a face and said his daughter would have to wait until the bingo was finished. She was irritated when I told her that and claimed I was preventing her from seeing her father. I admit I stood in front of the door to block her from storming in. Many of the residents had dementia, and it didn't take much to upset them, so I was determined to prevent a scene."

"Did you get into trouble?"

"No. My supervisor called me into her office later to hear my side and rolled her eyes. She knew Jennifer, and it didn't go any further. I gather the girl was looking for money from her father. I saw him give her some cash after the bingo was over, and she threw me the vilest look on her way out as if it was my fault she had to wait."

Rod's voice was sympathetic. "I can't say I'm shocked by that story. Jennifer was married briefly, but she's on her own now and living in a basement apartment. I agreed to allow her to be the main contact for this sale, but it's still Violet's house, and I won't do anything firm without talking to her first."

"So, there's no real mystery, then. Somehow, the coat ended up in the lake. Did they have some sort of ceremony and put it there on purpose, do you know?"

"Not that I know of. I went to the funeral, and Violet didn't say anything about that. She's decided she'd like to move to Florida. She wanted that for some time now, but Mal loved it here, so aside from a couple weeks vacation every winter, they stayed put."

"I was going to get it dry cleaned and give it back. Would she like that, I wonder?"

He hesitated. "I doubt it. I'm afraid she has more on her mind right now. I wouldn't take her the coat. In fact, you may want to hold off on getting it cleaned and give it to the police instead."

Chapter Six

WHEN SHANNON DISCONNECTED FROM her conversation with Rod, she sat for a moment, processing what he had said.

"Oh, Dusty. This just can't be right." She stroked her spaniel's head absent-mindedly. "Rod told me that lovely woman is a suspect in her husband's death. The Violet Walker I knew wouldn't be capable of anything like that. Mal was grumpy sometimes, but she and Mal were like Mammy and Daddy. Just *so* together." Shannon sighed. "No wonder Rod is keen to help her sell the house as soon as possible. Paying for a lawyer will eat up any savings she has quickly."

She stood up to take her pup out into the back garden. Dusty scooted through the French doors, and her owner followed, slowly walking the perimeter of the deep, fenced yard. *No. This is just wrong. I must call Kal and tell him I know this woman and it's impossible that she is responsible for this. It must have been an accident. I need to know more.*

Shannon heard Piet call her name from an open window on the second floor.

She looked up and waved. "Hi, Piet! Oh, I have so much to tell you. Are you rushing off to work?"

"No, I have to go back later for an evening viewing, but I have a few hours. I'm coming down."

She went inside to meet her friend, leaving the garden door open for Dusty to come back in at her leisure.

Piet wore black and white plaid flannel pants and a black sweatshirt. Even dressed casually, he looked tidy.

Shannon smiled. "You know that sweatshirt will be covered in long blond hairs as soon as Dusty realizes you're here."

"No worries. I haven't yet found the perfect colour to wear that will hide my Caesar's grey tabby hair and Dusty's blond hair, so I accept it and make sure I never wear my funeral suits for more than five minutes when I get home."

"Wise man. OK. Listen to what I've found out about the whole coat mystery."

"Put the kettle on for a cup of tea, and when you're finished your part, I'll tell you what I know as well."

Piet listened as Shannon told her story, then shook his head. "It's so hard to imagine. She seemed so nice. That daughter, on the other hand, was a piece of work."

"Why do you say that?"

He shrugged. "She seemed to bully her mother. First, it was about all the extras for the funeral. Mrs. Walker kept saying, 'Your father wanted to keep it simple,' but in the end, the daughter got her way, and they had the whole shebang, including the visitor book, bookmarks, memorial pins, and, of course, prayer cards and programs."

Shannon *tsk, tsked*.

"Of course, it's our business, so I can't complain about that, but I felt a little sorry for the woman because her daughter treated her like she was incompetent, which clearly, she isn't. I remember that, at the visitation, I was chatting with her before any visitors arrived, and she told me she loved going to Florida and hoped to move to

Sarasota one day. She has friends there, and she and her husband visited several times. A perfectly normal, innocuous conversation, and then the daughter came over and told her to stop talking about it because it was never going to happen. Mrs. Walker turned red and shut right up."

Shannon shook her head and told Piet about her own experience with Jennifer.

He nodded. "Well, that doesn't surprise me. How the police can imagine that Mrs. Walker had anything to do with her husband's death is beyond me. They need to look at that daughter."

"I agree. I'm going to talk to Kal."

"When you hand over the coat?"

She smiled. "Yes. That's as good a reason as any."

"Here's the other thing I remembered once I saw my notes from that funeral. Remember I said I thought there was money there?"

Shannon nodded. "They sold a house in Newcastle and have the property on Rice Lake."

"Aside from that, he was an antiquities dealer, apparently. I remember having a conversation with his former business partner, a man named Nate Stevens. This Stevens fellow talked about how Walker had extensive Rice Lake memorabilia, including one of the most comprehensive compilations about the Rice Lake sea monster. He told me that Malcolm had recently promised to hand over the whole collection because, technically, it belonged equally to him, Stevens, since they were once business partners."

Shannon raised her eyebrows. "Rice Lake sea monster? Or lake monster, I suppose. Are you serious? Was there any value to this collection?"

Piet shrugged. "Who knows? When I looked at my notes, I saw that Nate Stevens did a eulogy, and when I saw his name, I recalled the conversation."

"Well, that's weird. I never heard of a lake monster before. How much memorabilia could there be? And if it was part of their joint business, why is it still an issue? Since Mal retired long ago, the business assets must be settled by now.

"I don't know, but it seemed like Stevens was bitter about it. I wondered why they didn't have someone who felt more warm and fuzzy about Walker for a eulogy, but it was fine. He didn't say anything that sounded angry, whatever his private feelings were. Maybe he's been trying ever since to get his share, but you know how it goes—possession is nine-tenths of the law. Anyway, that's what I have for you, along with the fact that Mrs. Walker lives at the Manse." With that, he rose to go back up to his flat.

"Thanks, Piet. You're a wealth of information, my friend."

※

After Shannon sent a note to Kal saying she had some information for him, she contacted her clients. "I'm not sure this house is for you since you're looking for turn-key, but if you're game, you might like to look at it. The lot is gorgeous, right on the water, with a beautiful southern exposure. The house has good bones, and I think you'd have an amazing house with some investment."

They agreed to take a drive with her the next day to view the property. Shannon told herself the place may suit the family. They had a toddler, with another child on the way, and while the house needed some work, Shannon estimated it could be completed in about six weeks, leaving them time to enjoy the place for the end of summer and fall and well before the new baby arrived.

She sent Rod a note to let him know she was taking her clients for a viewing the next day.

Shannon sat for a moment, arguing with herself. *What do you think you'll find? If Malcolm's death were suspicious, the police certainly would have searched the place already. They released his body for his funeral, so they must have collected whatever evidence might have been there. But I found his coat. So maybe there's more to find.*

※

Shannon got up and paced the floor. Resisting the temptation to pick up the phone to call Kal, she walked to the door where Dusty's leash hung. "Come on, sweetie. Let's go for a walk." She clicked the leash to her spaniel's collar, irritated when the clasp stuck open. She wriggled at it until it closed enough to loop around the collar ring. "I need to have Daddy look at this clasp, Dusty. It might have some rust on it."

They strolled along Walton and south to the park, where gardeners were busy planting flowers. Shannon thought she heard a text come in and stood in the shade of a tree to pull out her phone. Distracted, she didn't see the squirrel that dashed down the tree trunk beside her, right in front of Dusty's nose. Her dog only weighed thirty pounds, but she was a small powerhouse when she was fueled with adrenalin. Suddenly, Shannon was left holding an empty leash. Her small blond dynamo broke the clasp, and she dashed off in pursuit of the squirrel.

"Dusty, NO. Dusty, COME!"

Shannon's shouts only served to make the gardeners look up and smirk as her dog shot off after the squirrel, ignoring her mistress.

After the squirrel was safely up another tree, chattering down at the impotent dog, Dusty lost interest and trotted off behind the bandshell as Shannon jogged after her. By the time she followed her pup around the back of the stage, Dusty was nowhere in sight. Shannon felt queasy as she swiveled her head searching for the small blond spaniel. She kept calling, knowing how futile it was, but compelled to continue shouting anyway. *How can you have gotten so far?* Shannon peered across Elias Street to Lent Lane, knowing that led out to busy Walton Street. She saw no sign of a disappearing small dog up that direction, so she looked left to Augusta with no sighting there either.

"Dusty. Dusty, come on, sweetheart. I have treats." She shouted.

She stood helplessly wondering what to do when a man came around the north side of the bandshell carrying a squirming Dusty.

"Oh my God. Oh my God, Dusty!" Shannon ran to the man, whom she now recognized as one of the gardeners.

He held out her dog, and Shannon clutched her to her chest, sobbing. "Thank you so much."

He smiled. "I have a Houdini at home myself. I got a GPS for him because I lost him so many times. He's expert at backing out of his harness, and then he's gone. At least now I know where to find him again."

Shannon shook her head. "This is the first time I've lost her like this, and it's the last time. The first step is to get a new leash, and then I'm looking up the GPS thing. I couldn't go through this again."

He nodded. "Ten minutes feels like an hour. I know. Well, back to work."

"Thank you again."

"No problem. She's a friendly little thing. She came around the corner of the stage and headed straight over. She probably thought you'd still be where she left you."

The gardener headed off to return to his work, and Shannon set Dusty down, firmly clutching the dog's collar. Instead of trusting the faulty clasp, she looped the leash through the collar, forcing the small dog to walk directly by her side.

"Oh, Dusty, you nearly gave me heart failure. Don't ever, ever do that again."

They were home in minutes, and Shannon breathed a sigh of relief. It was only after she refilled her dog's water bowl and poured herself a glass of cold sparkling water that she recalled the text. Pulling out her phone, she took the time to read Kal's text.

Are you available for a phone call?

Shannon texted in return, hoping he wasn't tied up by now.

I am now.

In moments, her phone rang.

"Hi, Kal." She answered the phone in speaker mode and sat at the table with her portfolio pad and pen, ready to take notes.

Chapter Seven

KAL KHAN'S VOICE WAS serious. "Hello, Shannon. As promised, I looked into the case of your Malcolm Walker."

Shannon almost interrupted to tell him what she had discovered but held her tongue to listen to Kal.

"You are correct in believing this man is deceased. As far as how his coat came to be in the lake may be answered by the fact that he drowned in Rice Lake."

Shannon nodded. *That's why Rod told me to hand the coat over.* "That's terrible."

"Yes. He may have been wearing the coat when he died."

"How awful. I should give it to you, then."

"Yes. That's why I'm calling. You mentioned you might get it cleaned. I hope you haven't taken it to a dry cleaner yet?"

"No, no. I just left it to dry, and that's all I've done."

"I will come to get it if you don't mind?"

"Of course." She nudged him. "Wasn't it an accident? Why the urgency?"

Kal hesitated. "It's an open investigation, so I can't really discuss it."

"But they've had his funeral already. Surely the cause of death has been determined?"

"They performed the autopsy, freeing the family to hold the funeral. But some questions surrounding his death remain."

"I see. Kal, as I mentioned at lunch, I knew his death was under investigation. Since then, I have spoken with someone who tells me Malcolm's wife, Violet, is under suspicion. I realized then that I knew this family. He always went by Mal. Mal and Violet volunteered at the seniors' centre when I did my high school volunteer hours there. They were such a nice couple and were so good together. Violet could never have done anything to cause her husband's death."

His voice was calmly professional in response. "Shannon, that must have been some time ago. People change, and even when you think you know someone, they only show you one side of themselves."

Shannon shook her head despite knowing he couldn't see her. "It's the daughter you should look at. I don't know what makes the death suspicious, but I knew the daughter Jennifer as well, and she is much more likely to do someone harm. Not Violet."

Kal sighed. "We are looking at all possibilities. We have not yet made an arrest, so we are continuing our investigation."

"But Violet is under suspicion, right? Why? I haven't seen her in a long time, but she must be pretty frail by now. How could she cause her husband to drown?"

"Shannon, I know you are a great champion for justice. I admire that in you, but you must accept that we know what we are doing. If Mrs. Walker is under suspicion, you must trust that we have our reasons for believing that."

She pounced on him. "What possible evidence can you have to make you believe this elderly woman did something so terrible?"

She thought she had dropped the call for a second, but then his voice came through again. "I can't talk here. If you will be home around six o'clock, I'll drop by. I will pick up the coat, and we can talk. I know I can trust your discretion if I explain the situation to you. You won't let it go unless you understand the full picture."

"Thank you, Kal. I'll be home, and of course, you can trust me."

❦

By the time Kal parked in her front courtyard, she had vacuumed the flat, cleaned the bathroom, and set out a platter of veggies and Asiago dip, along with some toasted pita triangles and hummus. It wasn't a meal as such, but it was enough to say *welcome.*

She opened the front door and invited him inside. "I have tea, apple juice, or sparkling water. What can I get you?"

"Apple juice would be refreshing. Thank you."

"Please sit and help yourself to a snack. You're probably peckish. Lunch was a long time ago."

Sitting on the sofa, he smiled and helped himself to a small plate of snacks. "This is very kind and wasn't necessary." He leaned back and glanced around the room. "Have you done something to your flat since I was here? Something is different."

"I've had it painted a couple of weeks ago."

"I should have noticed on Sunday. It's very nice. Very calming."

"The big adventure dazzled you, as I now think of the motorbike ride. The paint colour is called wild sage."

"It seems a small play on words. You have chosen a colour that brings nature's wildness indoors, and you celebrate your inherent wisdom."

Shannon turned to look at him from the kitchen. "I never considered it in those terms. I'm not sure many people would agree with you about my wisdom."

"They should. I respect your sense of judgment."

She set down his juice and a glass of sparkling water for herself and sat across from her guest. "Well, thank you for that. And for coming. I appreciate that you dropped by. And I admit I'm curious to know why you think Violet Walker had anything to do with her husband's death. I don't know much about the circumstances. The news article was so cryptic. It seemed to suggest that it was accidental."

Kal took more veggies and balanced the plate on the arm of the sofa.

"I read the file today when I got back into the office. I know Mr. Walker's death was assumed to be an accident at first. They were staying at their home on Rice Lake, and it appeared that he went for a walk. Mrs. Walker met three friends at a nearby vineyard for lunch. She drove herself. The journey should have taken her only a few moments, but the timing is a little bit off. She had a glass of white wine and claimed she felt slightly light-headed as she started to drive. She decided to pull over for a few moments to get some fresh air. The entire drive from the restaurant to her home should have taken about six minutes, assuming she drove below the speed limit, but with the time she stopped to get out of the car for fresh air, it turned into half an hour. When she resumed her drive and arrived home, it was approximately four p.m., and her husband was not in the house. He often liked to go walking, so she was not worried to start with. When he hadn't returned by six p.m. and wasn't answering his phone, she became alarmed and began calling friends to see if he was visiting with anyone in the neighbourhood. His car was home, so she knew he couldn't have gone far."

Shannon nibbled a piece of pita bread laden with hummus, her eyes glued to Kal Khan as he meticulously recited from memory the background of Malcolm Walker's death.

He took a sip of juice and continued. "After a few calls, the neighbours gathered and organized a search. The sun sets at that time of year before 8:30, so they spread out quickly to take advantage of the last of the daylight. A neighbour also called the police, and Violet herself called her daughter and nephew. The daughter lives in Port Hope while the nephew lives in Peterborough, and both agreed to come as soon as possible."

Shannon imagined the scene. All the neighbours scrambled to locate the elderly man, who may have been injured or worse. She shook her head. "Did they find him quickly?"

Kal did his classic nod, which may have been yes or may have meant no. "It was shortly after nine o'clock. The Marine Unit of the Ontario Provincial Police went out on the water with searchlights and discovered his body a short way offshore."

"That's truly awful."

The only good thing is that rescuers found him relatively soon. Not to be too graphic, but it helped that he carried more fat than muscle."

She held up her hand, not wanting to know more about bodies in lakes. "I'm no wiser on why you feel that poor Violet had something to do with it when she wasn't even there that afternoon. He went for a walk; maybe he went out on the dock and fell in the lake."

Kal nodded. "Indeed, that was the thinking at the time. His sight was apparently very bad, and the investigating officers initially believed he may have stumbled into the water."

Shannon tilted her head. "What changed?"

"This is the confidential part. I should say nothing, of course. My boss would be very upset if he knew I was sharing this information with anyone, especially his niece."

Smiling, she leaned forward. "I won't tell him if you won't."

Kal became serious again. "When the autopsy was conducted, they found drugs in his blood."

She widened her eyes. "Drugs? Cannabis? A lot of people take that now, especially to help relieve pain. Maybe he had arthritis or something?"

"No, not cannabis. He had a significant amount of diazepam in his system."

Shannon sat back and took a deep breath. "Tranquilizers. This sounds more like an accident or, at worst, suicide. He was always such an active man. Maybe he decided he'd had enough and took advantage of his wife being away for the afternoon. I do recall he liked to be in charge. Perhaps he wanted to be in charge of his death? That would be sad but not criminal."

"Yes, these possibilities were also considered. According to the notes the first responders made before handing the case over to us, show that Mrs. Walker was terribly distraught by her husband's death."

"Surely no one believes she faked that?"

"Even people who are responsible for someone's death can be upset about that death at the same time."

Shannon folded her arms across her chest. "You must have found something to question her authenticity. I still say Mal took the drugs himself. She couldn't have jammed them down his throat."

"She may have crushed them and given them to him without his knowledge. It seems he had recently lost his sense of smell and taste, along with his deteriorating vision. He wouldn't have known if it was in his food."

Shannon frowned. "I remember learning about that when I worked at the seniors' home. The residents who had dementia often had no sense of smell and taste and, because of that, had no desire to eat. It was always a struggle to get them to eat their meals, and we, volunteers, often sat one-on-one with those residents to help coax the food into them."

Kal lifted a shoulder in a small shrug. "I have not seen his previous medical records. I only recall the statements. This came from the daughter who said her father was depressed, and this was one of the reasons."

She nodded. "Again, I have to ask what else, then? So far, I'm more and more convinced that Mal may have chosen this death."

From his wife's statement, she absolutely did not accept that he would do this. Mr. Walker's strongly held beliefs prevented him from taking such an action."

"Hunh. OK, but sometimes people do things we don't expect. You don't know what you might do until you're in the situation. I've learned that."

They both smiled, remembering for a moment her perseverance to find the killer of her friend's wife.

Kal took a breath. "What his wife claimed he might or might not do did not determine our conclusion."

"What, then?"

During the autopsy, they discovered a shadow on Mr. Walker's back. They used a technology called photogrammetry to reveal a handprint."

"A handprint? Maybe that came when the responders pulled him from the water?"

"The technology proves the print is ante-mortem."

She gulped. "Meaning before he died?"

Kal nodded. "He was given tranquilizers and then pushed into the water."

"Murder," Shannon whispered.

"Yes. The coroner has ruled Malcolm Walker's death as murder. I know you believe Mrs. Walker to be incapable of such an act, but we recently discovered she purchased a new life insurance policy on her husband's life not long ago. Sure, he signed off on it, but it still raises questions. I'm sorry, Shannon, but we now have the evidence to arrest her for her husband's death."

Chapter Eight

SHANNON WATCHED AS KAL Khan put on latex gloves. Then, he carefully took the now-dry man's coat and placed it into a large paper evidence bag, which he sealed and initialed.

He nodded to her when he finished and peeled off his gloves. "I don't think we will find much on the coat to assist our investigation, but the forensics people can do amazing things."

"Are you on this investigation now?"

"Yes. As soon as I read the reports, I felt it was a case to which I could add value, and Detective Miller, your uncle," he amended, "agreed with me."

Shannon sighed. "I'm glad. At least I know you'll keep an open mind."

"Yes. I hope so. But Shannon, we can't have a repeat of last time. You have done your part by handing in this evidence, and now you must stay away. I'm sure you know that."

She nodded. "I understand what you're saying. Can I ask one question?"

"Go ahead."

"You've read the reports. What was the daughter, Jennifer, doing that afternoon?"

"She was out with friends at a pub."

"Do you remember which one?"

He frowned. "Shannon. Why do you ask?"

She shrugged. "I'm just curious."

He sighed. "Beamish House."

Shannon nodded. "Well, that's pretty solid, then."

Kal walked to the door and stopped for a moment as he opened it. "I know you have an interest in all this, and when I can share information with you, I will. I'll be in touch."

"Thank you. I appreciate that."

One last nod, and he left.

Shannon put the kettle on for a cup of green tea. It had been quite a day: first, losing Dusty, and then finding out the police were about to arrest poor Violet Walker.

When she had her tea and sat with her feet curled under her on the sofa with her dog snoring quietly beside her, she nibbled her way through the remaining hummus and pita. *I know I've been warned to stay out of it, but I can't sit back and do nothing. They don't know Violet like I do. Or did, anyway. My first challenge is to find out about that daughter.*

She needed to think this through and hoped her friend Emma Anderson would help her with that.

Emma answered after two rings. "Hi, Shannon. We didn't see you in the office today."

"I know, but I've been busy. I'm taking the Sullivans up to view the property outside Bailiboro tomorrow."

"The one on the lake?"

"That's it. Where I found the coat."

Emma's voice was sceptical. She wasn't a real estate agent like Shannon, but as the clerk in their agency, she had a good sense of their clients. "Aren't they looking for turn-key? I thought you said that place needed work?"

"Sometimes clients only think they know what they want."

"Well, I'm sure you know what you're doing. How can I help?"

"Oh, it's nothing to do with work. I can't go into all the details, but I think a terrible miscarriage of justice is about to take place, and I need your help, Emma."

Her friend groaned. "Oh no. I refuse to go poking through anyone's garbage."

"No, no. I need your mind. Feel like coming over for a drink later? I have a lovely California Cabernet Sauvignon just waiting to be shared."

"I can't tonight, but maybe tomorrow?"

"Thanks, Emma. By the way, it's your favourite."

"*Josh?*"

"Yup. Say around eight?"

"All right. I'll see you then. I'll bring some snacks to go along with it."

"Thanks, Emma. You're the best."

Shannon spent the rest of the evening making notes with random thoughts she and Emma could talk through when they got together.

She also turned her mind to her clients and the Walker house. *It's a great house. I think they'll like that property.*

※

Shannon settled her dog with a biscuit. "Don't look so disappointed. After yesterday's escapade, I'm not taking you anywhere until I get a new leash for you, madam. Besides, it's work, so I can't take you in, and I can't leave you in the car now that the days are getting so warm."

Dusty jumped up on the green wing chair by the French doors overlooking the garden with her prize and began nibbling the cookie before Shannon was even out the door.

※

Her clients pulled into the driveway and parked behind Shannon. She greeted the couple and waited as Nick Sullivan lifted his three-year-old son out of his car seat. They stood together, looking at the house with the lake visible behind it.

The fieldstone one-and-a-half-storey house glowed warmly in the sunlight. The dark grey roof looked like slate, enhancing the overall English country cottage appearance.

Shannon glanced at their faces. "Well? What do you think?"

Nick smiled. "It sure has character."

Jessie looked more doubtful. "It looks old."

"I can't lie. It needs some work. Come inside and see what you think. I know you said you wanted turn-key, but with some renovation, you can make this your own, and you can't beat the location. On the water, sun all afternoon, and a nice deep, private lot."

Jessie rubbed her baby bump. "Well, we're here now. Let's take a look."

Shannon led them inside. "I know the floors need refinishing, but that's easily done when the house is empty of furniture."

Nick walked to the sliding doors and looked out at the view of the lake. "This is beautiful."

His wife crossed the room to stand beside him. "It is. I'll give you full marks for the view." She turned and studied the room. "I do like these built-ins." The previous owners had fitted oak shelves and cabinets to both sides of the fireplace, leaving the space above the mantel for a large-screen television. Jessie opened one of the closed cabinet doors to see how much storage space was inside, and a piece of paper fluttered out. "Oh, sorry. I guess I shouldn't open things."

Shannon scooped up the page and held onto it. "Not at all. Feel free to look everywhere. That's what these viewings are for."

As Nick and Jessie wandered through to the kitchen area, Shannon glanced at the paper before returning it to the cabinet. She widened her eyes when she realized it was Malcolm Walker's collection inventory. She glanced over to the Sullivans, who were speaking quietly between themselves. "Why don't I give you some privacy to go up and look at the bedrooms upstairs? Take your time. It's a big decision, but make sure you look out at the view from the master bedroom up there."

Nick grinned and led his wife upstairs.

Shannon walked over to put the paper on the kitchen counter and took several photos of the front and back before replacing the document in the cabinet. Then, she made her way up to join the young family.

"Well? What do you think?"

Nick stood gazing out at the view. "I love it. Is the shore gradual enough that kids could play in the water?"

Shannon made a note. "That's a great question. I'll find out. I suspect it is. Rice Lake is a shallow lake; as far as I know, there aren't many deep drop-offs. Any other questions so far?"

Jessie sighed. "I'd want both bathrooms completely redone. What does that cost?"

Shannon nodded. "Why don't you give me a list of the things you think you'd want to do? I can speak to a contractor friend of mine to give you a ballpark number. With that, we could use it as a negotiation tool if you think the house is something that appeals to you."

Jessie bit her lip. "OK. But do you have any other places you can show us? More turn-key?"

"I do have a couple of places in mind. I'll send you the links to see what you think of them, and if they appeal to you, I'll make the arrangements to view them. How does that sound?"

"Yeah. That sounds great. This feels like a lot of work, and I'm not very energetic right now."

Shannon smiled. "Fair enough. Let's walk around the property to give you a feel for the whole place."

They went out through the sliding doors off the deck, and right away, Nick made for the shore. He set his little boy on his feet to walk out on the dock, holding the toddler's hand. For a second, as Shannon watched, she had an image of someone pushing Malcolm Walker off that dock and into the water. She shuddered and shook her head to rid herself of the thought.

After waving the Sullivans off with a promise to check on the water entry and a reminder for them to send her a wish list of their proposed renovations, she went back into the house. Shannon had her photos but wanted to study the original document. She retrieved the Rice Lake Collection list and laid it on the kitchen table. Most entries were typed, but there were a couple of items with a red ink line drawn through them and three additions added to the bottom in a script written with what appeared to be a fountain pen.

The crossed-off items may have been sold or given away. One was described as a framed news article, and the other a photo of Scituate's Mann Hill Beach, Massachusetts. Shannon frowned. *None of this sounds like a collection that would be worth anything. We're not talking about a Rembrandt or something.*

The added lines were more cryptic in their descriptions. One had the letters N.S. beside it, and annotated beside two entries were the letters A.N., but there was no hint if they were the initials for a person's name or a short form for another collectible. Shannon put the document back where it had been, no wiser than she had been, but glad that Piet's comments about a collection had been verified.

Shannon locked up the house and headed back to Port Hope. It was another thing to discuss later with Emma.

I wonder if Violet has this collection in their apartment in the Manse or if it's here in the house.

Chapter Nine

SHANNON SPENT THE AFTERNOON in the office, gathering and sending off the details for the two other cottage listings she had in mind for the Sullivans. Although they were both more move-in ready, the property lots and locations were less desirable. She suspected the trade-off might be worth it to the family, especially for Jessie.

She stopped at the reception desk to talk to Emma when she left the office. "I'll see you later, then."

"You promise you won't ask me to do something dangerous or stinky?"

Shannon laughed. "I promise. We're going to stay in, drink wine and talk. That's it."

Emma beamed at her. "That I can do."

※

When her friend arrived, Shannon had the wine open and breathing and a platter of cheese, crackers, and salted nuts out on the coffee table. Emma handed her a bag, and Shannon added grapes, sun-dried tomatoes, and olives to the platter. "Lovely. Thanks, Emma."

When the two young women were settled comfortably with their wine and small plates of food, Emma tilted her head. "OK, so what's up?"

Shannon felt a pang of guilt when she shared all the information she knew, including what Kal Khan had told her. She reminded Emma, "He told me that in confidence, so please don't say anything to anyone else."

Emma shook her head. "I won't. Who would I tell? Anyone else would think I was a ghoul talking about murder. Don't worry. Your secrets are safe with me, but why are you telling me anyway? If I understand you, the police are about to arrest Mrs. Walker for this awful thing. I know you. You aren't just gossiping with me. That's not who you are, so you're telling me all this for some reason."

Shannon nodded and picked up her portfolio from the couch beside her. "I don't believe she's responsible."

Emma stared, holding a large stuffed olive halfway to her mouth. "Oh, no. I don't even want to say this, but why not?"

"She's just not that sort of person."

Emma popped the olive into her mouth and took a moment to savour it. "Shannon. You said yourself it's been years since you knew these people. Even then, you didn't know them well. People aren't always what they seem."

"I know that. Truly, I do, but still, I don't believe it."

"Did you say that to that handsome Detective Khan?"

"Yes. He said essentially the same as you."

"There you are, then."

"OK, hear me out. I think other people have as much motive or more than Violet Walker."

Emma sighed and took a bunch of grapes. "Go ahead, then."

Shannon told Emma about her history with Jennifer Walker-Jones and added what Piet had said about his experience with the Walker daughter.

Emma nodded. "Sounds like she isn't someone I'd want to be friends with, but it doesn't mean she's a killer."

"I know I don't have any evidence, but I'm not sure the police checked into her very much. I'm going to try to find out from Beamish House what they remember about her from the day of her father's death."

"Good Lord. They probably won't remember a thing. It's weeks ago, and you don't even have a photo to show them, do you?"

Shannon made a note. "That's true. I need to get a photo."

"That's not really what I meant. I meant to show you how impossible it is to try and dig into her alibi. I know I sound like a broken record, but that's the job of the police. Stay out of it, Shannon."

Shannon pursed her lips. "I'm just asking a few questions. Nothing more." She paused and then carried on. "And then there's this former business partner of Malcolm Walker's. At the funeral, he mentioned to Piet that he had hoped to take over Malcolm's Rice Lake collection. I wonder if that ever happened. Maybe Mal said he wouldn't do it."

Emma topped up her wine glass. "You have lots of theories, but they seem pretty weak to me. I can see why they think Violet Walker is guilty. She makes the most sense, in my opinion."

"Let's keep an open mind. You're right. I need a photo of Jennifer. What else do I need to find evidence that someone else did this?"

"When you told me about the day of Mr. Walker's death, you mentioned that Mrs. Walker called her daughter and some nephew. Who's that?"

Shannon widened her eyes. "You're right. I don't know anything about him at all." She made a note. "I wonder if Piet remembers him from the funeral, and to that end, are there other relatives? If there's a nephew, there are probably sisters or brothers of either Mal or Violet. Oh, well done, Emma."

Emma smiled and tipped her glass in Shannon's direction. "I've earned my wine, then."

"Yes, you have, my friend."

"Can we move on to talk about something other than death, then? The whole idea of someone murdering a poor old man like that is too awful. Maybe it was someone from up there, around Rice Lake? Not from here in Port Hope at all."

Shannon closed her portfolio. "Anything's possible, I guess. You've given me things to think about. Thank you."

They spent the rest of the evening sharing stories of family, work, and Shannon's adventures on her motorcycle ride and with Dusty before Emma rose to leave. She leaned down to cuddle the small dog. "You're a bad little girl. You shouldn't scare your mum like that. Wait until you have that GPS on you. No more great escapes then."

Shannon nodded. "You got that right. In fact, I'm going to research that tonight and order something. She gave me such a scare. Thanks for coming, Em. You always bring such sensible ideas to a problem."

When she was alone, Shannon researched and ordered a pet tracking system. She then ran several searches, hoping to find photos of Jennifer Walker-Jones, but without success.

I wonder if I can meet Violet Walker before the police swoop in and arrest her. Will Kal be furious? Will Uncle Bob be angry?

Chapter Ten

ON THURSDAY MORNING, SHANNON made some calls and an appointment to look at one of the listings she had sent to the Sullivans. They were interested enough to want a comparison to the Walker house. Still, Nick told her gleefully that he thought Jessie was coming around to his way of thinking about the possibilities of that older home. He sent over the list of updates they wanted to make, and Shannon promised to get a ballpark estimate from the contractor she knew.

At 10:30, she drove over to the Manse carrying a bunch of flowers. It had been several years since she had been in the seniors' home when a former teacher had lived there. She remembered the suites were quite spacious and bright. Shannon stopped at the reception desk and asked how to find Violet Walker. "I'm an old friend. I only recently found out that her husband, Malcolm, passed away, and I wanted to drop by in person to offer my condolences. Do you know if she's in?"

"Let me phone upstairs to see if she's accepting visitors. Your name?"

"Shannon Coyne. We volunteered together a few years ago at

the Seniors' Day Centre. She and Malcolm ran a music and dance program with which I helped."

The woman nodded and turned her back to Shannon to make the call. She spoke for a few minutes and then hung up, smiling."

"Mrs. Walker remembers you very well and will be pleased to see you. She's on the third floor. Suite 301."

"Thank you." In the elevator, she considered what she should say. *Nothing about the coat. Of course! I'm showing her house to clients. It's perfectly natural I should look her up once I realized who the sellers are.*

She stepped off the elevator and saw Violet standing in the open doorway of the apartment at the end of the hall. Shannon smiled and waved.

Violet shook her head and reached for Shannon's hand when she arrived. "I didn't believe my ears when Judy called from downstairs to tell me you were here. How marvellous to see you. Come in and sit down."

Shannon handed her the flowers. "I was so sorry to hear about Mal."

The elderly woman nodded. "Thank you. I'll just put these in water."

Shannon sat on a loveseat studying Violet. She wore a bright, teal-coloured velveteen cardigan that brought out the blue of her eyes, but her snowy hair had thinned since Shannon had last seen her old friend. Creases and dark spots covered her face. Some were laugh lines around the eyes and mouth, but her forehead was heavily furrowed with worry wrinkles.

Shannon turned away so she wouldn't get caught staring. "This is a lovely apartment. I once had a teacher who lived in this complex. Hers was a nice spot, too."

Violet came back and set the vase of flowers on the coffee table. "Thank you for this. Your visit has really brightened my day."

Shannon smiled. "I wasn't sure you'd remember me. It was so long ago that we volunteered in the music and dance program together."

The older woman frowned, causing the furrows on her forehead to deepen. "It feels like no time at all in some ways. I remember how Mal grumbled when I first suggested that program, but once we started, he enjoyed it."

"I remember. He was such a favourite with the ladies. He danced like a dream with you playing the piano."

Violet smiled. "Yes, he was always a ladies' man. He could be quite charming when he wanted to be. I didn't mind. It was good for us that one afternoon a week. After a year, we gave it up because we moved up north full-time, and it was too far to come."

Shannon nodded. "That's how I discovered Mal had passed. I'm a realtor now, and I have shown your house to some clients. When the agent who has the listing, Rod, told me your name, I couldn't believe it. What a small world."

Violet put her hand to her mouth. "Oh, my. You've seen my house. I want it to sell, but I hope it goes to people who will love it as I did."

"I have a good feeling about these people. A young couple with a toddler and a new baby due in three months."

Violet smiled. "That's nice. I suppose there are things I need to get out of there." She looked around. "I don't have room here, though."

Shannon took a deep breath. "Violet, I also heard that Mal's death is being treated as suspicious. Your name came up."

Violet stepped back as though Shannon had threatened her. "Do you moonlight as a newspaper reporter now or something? Are you looking for gossip?"

"No, no. Absolutely not. Quite the opposite. I came to see how I can help because I know there is no way you had anything to do with your husband's death."

The older woman's shoulders slumped. "Thank you. It's been a nightmare." Again, her forehead creased. "How did you hear that the police think I did something? That's not in the papers, surely?"

Shannon felt her heart race. *Sorry Kal.* "No. My uncle is with the police department, so I know some people there, and your name came up when I mentioned your house."

"I see." Violet was still cool.

"Will you let me help you?"

The elderly woman blinked back tears. "I don't know what you can do."

"Can we sit down and talk everything through? Something may jump out at me."

Violet stood. "Will you have some tea?"

"I don't want to put you to any trouble."

"Not at all. It's been such a trying time; I'm glad for the distraction. Milk and sugar?"

"Just milk, please."

When her hostess went to make the tea, Shannon wandered around the room looking at family photos. Glancing over to ensure her hostess was busy, Shannon took pictures of the framed images with her phone. When Violet carried in the tea, Shannon returned to her seat and took the fine porcelain cup. "Thank you." She took a sip and then pulled a small notebook from her purse. "OK. Take me through the day that Mal died."

The events were told from Violet's perspective but were essentially the same as what Shannon already knew.

When Violet wound down, dabbing at her eyes and nose with a crumpled tissue, Shannon gave her a moment and then moved on to dig deeper.

"You mentioned your daughter. Tell me a bit more about her. Maybe she can store some of your things for you."

The elderly woman sniffed. "Unlikely. She lives in an apartment no bigger than this. And what's the point of storing stuff? I need to decide about it. Once this mess is behind me, when the police figure out what really happened, I'll move to Florida. I suppose maybe I can rent a storage unit until then."

Shannon stood to walk over to the shelving unit. "I met your daughter once, but I don't recall what she looks like. Do you have a photo?"

Violet rose and joined her. She pointed to a photo with four people: Violet herself, Malcolm, a woman in her early thirties, and a man about the same age. "Here. This is her."

Confirming her assumption, Shannon nodded. "Yes. Now I remember her. Who is this young man?"

She smiled. That's my nephew, Chris. Technically, he is Mal's nephew, but we never made that distinction."

Shannon picked up the photo. "You all look very close, although I admit, Mal doesn't look best pleased."

Violet sighed. "Sometimes, he was a grouch, but he didn't mean anything by it. We raised Chris from the time he was eight when his parents, Mal's brother and his wife, were killed in a car accident. Her eyes filled as she thought about her loss. "It's still sad to think of it, but it was never a hardship for us. Chris was such a lovely boy."

"Oh, my. That was a big undertaking. How good you were to take him in."

She shrugged. "There was no one else. Mal's parents were elderly so that they couldn't care for their grandson. The boy's mother was an only child, and her parents lived in England. It just wasn't an option for him to go there. No. We were it, but he knew us, and we knew him already, so it was the obvious answer. He came to look upon us as his parents. He and Mal were very close. Poor Chris is still broken up over his death."

"I suppose your daughter and Chris were about the same age, were they?"

"Jennifer was two years older, so she was ten when Chris moved in with us. We hoped they would come to be like a sister and brother. They always got along before that."

Shannon raised her eyebrows. "But they didn't?"

"Not really. I think Jenn liked being the only child. We had to give Chris a lot of attention at first. He was so lost."

"Jennifer was jealous."

"I suppose she was. We all managed, though, and it was years ago now."

They sat back down. "After they found Mal, did you talk to your neighbours? Did anyone see anything that afternoon?"

She shook her head. "No one saw a thing. We have a boat, but Mal hasn't used it for a couple of years. It was still in the boathouse, covered in its winter tarp."

"Your daughter didn't drop by that afternoon?"

"Oh no. Jenn didn't do that sort of thing. She and her father haven't seen eye-to-eye for years now. Our daughter didn't visit us up there. I meet her for lunch occasionally, but down here in Port Hope. Never up in Pengelly Landing."

"And Chris? He didn't go by?"

"No. He was working at home in Peterborough. Chris is a designer and project manager for an architect firm and works all the time." She smiled. "That boy is so clever. He started as a contractor and then went to night school to get his degree as an architect."

Shannon smiled, hearing the pride in her voice. "OK, switching topics, I believe Mal was a collector. I think he had a Rice Lake collection. Tell me about it."

"Oh, there's nothing to tell." Violet waved her hand dismissively. "Mal liked to putter with things like that. He'd buy an old picture here and sell the same thing a few years later. After his partner bought him out of the antique business, the collections allowed him to keep his hand in."

"Is it here? The collection? I'd love to see it."

"Oh, no. That's still at the house."

Shannon bit her lip. *I can't ask specifically about the autopsy report without betraying Kal's trust.*

"Violet, why do the police imagine you had anything to do with Mal's death? It sounds like a terrible accident. You weren't even there, right?"

"That's right. I was away at lunch when Mal left the house. The problem is that he had some diazepam in his system." She hesitated. "My diazepam. I have a prescription to help me sleep. I don't take them often. Well, I didn't take them often, but now I need one every night," she amended.

"I see. Why might he have taken one of your tranquillizers? Did he sometimes do that?"

Violet shook her head. "Not that I know of, but I didn't count them. For all I know, he did take them sometimes, but if he did, he never let on to me."

"Was he worried about anything?"

"Nothing specific. He was frustrated with his deteriorating health. I told him he just had to put up with it, like the rest of us, but he wasn't a man to put up with things."

Shannon nodded. "I remember he was so active. When we were at the centre, he'd set up the chairs before I arrived, and I told him not to. That was my job. He didn't need to do all that physical work, but he said he didn't mind."

"And he didn't. Lately, though, his vision has caused him problems, and that upset him so much. It slowed him right down."

"I know it's hard to imagine, but is it possible he took the diazepam and then went into the lake himself?"

Violet clenched her jaw. "Suicide. That's what you're suggesting."

"Yes. Is it possible?"

"No. We didn't attend church every Sunday, but he was very religious. He was spiritual and believed his life was in God's hands, and deciding such a thing wasn't up to him. I know he would *not* do that." The older woman pushed herself off the couch. "I think it's time you left. I appreciate your offer to help me, but I'm tired now and want to lie down."

Chapter Eleven

THE SKY HAD CLOUDED over, matching Shannon's mood for her drive home. *What have I done? That poor woman. All I want to do is help her, but I don't know how. She looked exhausted by all my questions.*

Her phone beeped to let her know she had a text message from her contractor requesting Shannon call her. *That'll give me something else to think about, at least. Shannon Dierdre Coyne, you need to let this drop. Just like Emma said. Just like Kal insisted.*

Her cheerful contractor's voice had a hint of a German accent. Shannon first met the woman builder at a house she was flipping. The finishes and workmanship impressed Shannon, and the two hit it off immediately. Since then, they had worked together on several projects.

"Hello, Shannon. I have that estimate for you. Now, you know this is only very rough until I see the house, but it will give your clients a ballpark idea of what they're looking at."

They spoke for half an hour, and then Shannon let her friend return to work. "OK, Anja, thanks for this. I'll let you know if anything comes of it."

Nick Sullivan was enthusiastic when Shannon went over the information with him. "I know we're going to look at the other place this afternoon, but I think these numbers make the Pengelly Landing house pretty attractive."

They confirmed their appointment to view a cottage on Tait's Beach Road later that afternoon.

Shannon reminded Nick, "You remember it isn't waterfront, right?"

Nick's voice didn't sound disappointed. "I know, but as long as it's move-in ready, I can feel we've looked at all the options."

"Yes, it is. And it does have deeded lake access just a few minutes away."

"Well, we'll see what Jessie thinks. See you later."

She smiled when they disengaged. *Nick has no intention of buying the move-in-ready home; he wants the Walker house.*

🔥

The sky continued to threaten rain as Shannon drove north on Highway 28, but when she turned east on County Road 9, she saw small patches of blue sky. *Enough blue sky to cut out a pair of sailor's pants.* Her father used to say that when they were children, and he was usually right when he claimed the weather was about to improve.

The grey-sided cottage was tucked in amongst trees and bushes, the front window almost obscured by a large bush Shannon couldn't identify. *I'd clear most of this away. How can they even enjoy the lake view with all that growing in front?* She unlocked the door with the key from the lockbox. The inside looked much different than the outside. The open-concept room had an updated kitchen with white cabinetry, good-quality vinyl plank flooring in a light wood embossed finish, and walls painted a neutral greige colour; the blend of grey and beige was just a bit lighter than the floors.

By the time the Sullivans arrived, Shannon had explored the

house and was able to show them through it, highlighting specific admirable features and pointing out the lack of storage and the windows that would need replacing within the next few years.

Jessie ran her hand along the small island finished with a concrete top. "I love this."

Shannon nodded. "It looks lovely, all right. Concrete is durable, but it does need maintenance to keep it sealed to prevent staining. I'd also say this island is perfect for this space, but you can't all eat here because it's too small. In the Walker house, you could design an island to suit you and make it big enough to accommodate all four of you if that's what you want."

Jessie frowned and then touched her belly. "Yes. All four of us." She smiled to acknowledge Shannon's consideration of their growing family.

Nick had moved to the front window. "This is move-in-ready on the inside, but we'd need to spend money on the outside, and even when we cleared away some of these bushes, we'd still only get a partial view of the lake. Mostly, we'd be looking at the garage across the way."

Shannon glanced around the home. "I think you've seen everything inside. Do you want to walk down to the deeded access where you can get a boat into the water and enjoy the bit of beach?"

Jessie and Nick exchanged a glance, and then she spoke. "No. That's not necessary. I'd like to see that other house one more time. Do you think your friend, the contractor, is willing to meet us there so we can talk specifically about the cost and time to make it our own?"

She nodded. "I'm sure she'd be open to that. Let me find out her schedule, and we can set that up as soon as possible. I heard from Rod someone else was going in today to look at the house."

Nick looked alarmed. "Babe, let's not wait. I don't want to lose it. We can do all that after we know we've got it."

Jessie bit her lip. "OK. I agree. Let's put in an offer."

"We'll go to Bewdley. There's a restaurant called the Lakeview where we can sit and do the paperwork. I think you're doing the right thing. It's a great location, and I'm surprised it hasn't been snapped up yet."

※

Shannon breathed a sigh of relief when she returned home. Rather than waste time, she drove right over with the signed offer to deliver it to the agent by hand. Since the offer was for the full asking price, she had a good feeling about it. *I'm glad they decided that on their own. I would have presented whatever they wanted, but the house is worth what they're offering, and I'll be happy for Violet if it works out.* She no sooner went into the yard with Dusty when her phone rang.

"Rod. I didn't think I'd hear from you so soon. I hope it isn't bad news."

She listened to his response and stopped walking. "Oh, no. Thank you for letting me know. Please phone me when you hear more."

Shannon watched her dog poke under the bushes but saw little while her mind raced. It wasn't until Piet called down to her from upstairs that she blinked and realized Dusty had taken herself back inside while she herself stood in the middle of the yard.

"Are you all right down there?"

Shannon looked up. "Not really. Do you have time for a chat?"

"I'll be right down."

Piet arrived carrying his mug of coffee and settled on the loveseat while Shannon put the kettle on to make herself a cup of green tea. He waved her over to sit across from him on the couch. "Tell Oom Piet all about it."

She smiled to hear him use the Dutch word for *uncle*, grateful for his attempt to lighten her mood. Shannon started by updating him on her visit to Violet and then concluded by telling him about the call she had received from the other agent.

He set the half-full mug down on her coffee table. "I can't believe the police have arrested that poor old woman."

"I know. I'm still in shock. Kal said they planned to arrest her, but I didn't think they'd go through with it. It's just not right. Anyone can see she's not that sort of person."

Piet raised his eyebrows. "It's not always obvious, as you well know."

Shannon sighed as she remembered her brush with death only months ago. "That's true. But in this case, if they just asked around, they'd find out what a good person Violet Walker is and how close she and her husband were."

Piet shook his head. "Don't get involved. I'm sure they are doing their due diligence and must have enough evidence to believe she's guilty."

She pursed her lips. "They don't always get it right."

He nodded. "Maybe not at first, but they'll get there in the end."

"Meanwhile, this elderly woman is under arrest."

"What does this all mean for the sale of the house?"

"Well, I need to deal with the dreadful daughter, Jennifer."

He tilted his head. "You mean your pal Rod needs to deal with the dreadful daughter. You deal with him, right?"

Shannon shrugged. "Technically, yes, but just knowing that she's the client we now need to negotiate with instead of Violet feels more challenging."

"It sounds like she might be easier because if she's that greedy, she'll jump at the chance to sell."

She considered his comments. "Unless she knows I'm the other agent. She didn't like me, remember?"

"Money trumps everything. She'll sell, and the sooner, the better." Piet predicted.

"Let's hope so." She dismissed the real estate challenge and returned to thinking about her old friend. "Would they really put a woman her age in jail?"

"I don't know. But you have an inside track to answer that

question, right? It must be time to take in some of your uncle's favourite pastries from Dreamer's Café."

Shannon nodded. "You're right. First thing tomorrow morning, I'll pick up some Crazy Cookies for the station. I also want to visit the pub where Jennifer Walker supposedly was the day her father died. Feel like coming with me?"

He smiled. "Sure. Tomorrow evening?"

"You're on. Tomorrow will be busy. Hopefully, I'll be able to give the good news to my clients, and I'm going to spend some time figuring out what happened to Malcolm Walker."

Chapter Twelve

THE CONSTABLE BEHIND THE reception desk smiled when she saw Shannon approach. "We haven't seen you in a long time." Her eyes widened when she saw the white box. "Treats for your uncle?"

"Treats for everyone, but if he's available to see me, I'll let him choose first."

After calling her boss, Detective Bob Miller, the constable nodded and pushed the button to allow Shannon entrance. "Go ahead."

The last door on the left was her uncle's office. The polished brass nameplate on the wall read: *Staff Sergeant Robert Miller.* The window blinds were open this morning, brightening the room with early summer sunlight. Her uncle sat behind his large oak desk, a laptop open in front of him. The grey file tray to his right held several manilla folders, and Shannon knew that despite being busy, he once again made time for her. He waved her to come in and sit in one of the two black visitor chairs opposite him. He leaned back in his high-backed leather swivel chair. "How's the world treating you?"

"I won't keep you. I brought a small bribe." She slid the box across the desk. "Whatever you don't want, I'll take back to reception."

He selected a cookie and a muffin and closed the box again. "OK, what's the bribe for?"

"I know Violet Walker, an elderly woman who is now in custody, accused of killing her husband."

He tapped into his computer and read briefly before looking back at her. "And?"

"And the woman I know isn't capable of such a thing. You've been investigating for some time, and something must be compelling to have you move forward with her arrest. I hope you can tell me about it."

Her uncle tilted his head. "Why? There's nothing you can do to change this, Shannon." He held up his hand before she spoke. "I know you believe that any time a friend of yours gets into trouble, you know better than the police, but you need to stay out of it and let us do our job."

When he finished, Shannon lifted her chin. "I'm not always wrong."

"I never said that. We continue to build our case, so if we have this wrong, we'll find out soon enough."

"Meanwhile, this elderly woman sits in jail. That's cruel."

He sighed. "I happen to know the Crown is prepared to recommend a conditional release."

"Oh. But she's in jail now?"

"Mrs. Walker is in custody pending her bail hearing scheduled for later today."

Shannon bit her lip. "OK. That makes me feel better." She changed her tone from defensive to coaxing. "Can't you tell me what made the police decide to arrest her now?"

He clicked a few more times on his computer, reading notes before returning his gaze to her. "This is my last word on it. An eyewitness came forward."

Shannon widened her eyes. "You're saying someone saw Violet Walker shove her husband into the water?"

"I'm saying nothing more other than to reiterate that you need to stay out of it."

Her mind spun, and she stood up in a daze. "All right. Thank you, Uncle Bob. I appreciate your time."

He held out the box of baked treats. "Take these away before I eat more."

As she made her way back down the sun-filled hallway, Kal Khan came towards her. "Hello. I didn't realize you were here. Are you all right? You look pale."

She blinked a few times to control her emotions. "Hi, Kal. I'm not sure I am OK. It looks like I've made a big mistake in my judgment of someone."

He nodded. "It can be disappointing to realize you have misplaced your trust."

Shannon tried to smile and handed over the box. "Will you put these in the lunchroom for folks to enjoy? Uncle Bob already had a couple."

Kal bobbed his head as he took the box. "Thank you. Everyone will enjoy them." He hesitated and then continued. "If you ever want company, please don't hesitate to contact me. I know you have many good friends, but I can be a good listener."

She nodded and touched his arm as he escorted her to the front desk to let her out. "Thanks, Kal. I will."

※

Shannon was busy in the office all day. There was a fax waiting with a sign-back for the offer. The price was accepted, along with most of the conditions, which were standard: water test for potability, pump out the septic tank, provide a property survey and allow the buyers to arrange a house inspection. The only change was to the closing date, requesting a three-week closing. *Wow, that's fast. This girl wants the money as soon as possible. It's a good thing the Sullivans have been pre-approved for financing.*

Nick and Jessie Sullivan were thrilled. They came in to sign off on the change to the closing date and immediately went off to start arranging the financing and contact a house inspector.

When Shannon arrived home, she heaved a sigh of relief and scooped up Dusty to cuddle the cocker spaniel. "What a day, Dusty. I'll get changed, and then we'll go for a walk."

They walked down Thomas Street and entered the green space adjacent to the Legion. Shannon switched from the new leather leash to a 12-foot-long line to give the dog more freedom without letting her go. Dusty now had a fancy GPS monitor clipped to her collar to avoid further dramas, but Shannon still didn't let her roam free. She looked down at her pup. "You're too important to me, little girl."

Shannon revelled in the bright, warm day as they strolled through the late afternoon. Sunset was still a long way off, and if it hadn't been for her troubling thoughts about Violet Walker, Shannon knew she'd be loving this day. Her mind conjured up the image of her sweet elderly friend pushing Mal into the lake to immediately reject the thought. *No. I don't believe it. The eyewitness got it wrong. The person must have seen someone else or just misunderstood what they saw. I need to talk to Violet. I'll call tomorrow when I hope she'll be back at home. I have to ask about clearing out the house anyway.*

"OK, Dusty. I have a plan. Let's go home and figure out what's for supper."

※

Later that evening, Piet called her to ask if she had spoken to her uncle.

"I did. He didn't tell me much, but he did say there's an eyewitness. The report the witness provided prompted them to arrest Violet."

"Oh, no. That doesn't look good for her. Is it possible you're wrong about her?"

Shannon sighed. "Anything's possible."

"But not likely?"

"No. I know I'm wrong about many things, but I have a good sense about people. You need to have it in this job."

"So, now what?"

"As soon as Violet is home and willing to see me, I'll visit and find out more."

"Are we still on for a drink later?"

"Absolutely. Eight o'clock down here? A few people should be there by then on a Friday night."

"Sounds good. I'm curious how you plan to ask total strangers about Jennifer Walker."

Shannon laughed. "I was going to ask you to do it."

"Good luck with that, sweetie. I'll be sitting in the corner, observing."

༄

By 8:30 that evening, Piet and Shannon had settled on high leather stools at the bar.

Piet pushed his dark-framed glasses further up his nose. "I thought we were going to sit somewhere out of the way."

She spoke under her breath. "I'll never get to quiz anyone if I do that. This is the best place."

When the bartender, a young man in his late twenties with a shock of flaming red curls and a trim beard to match, brought Piet's half-pint of Guinness and Shannon's glass of merlot, Shannon smiled. "You look like you have Celtic heritage."

He grinned and ran his hand through his hair. He asked in a thick Irish accent: "What gave me away?"

"We come from the same stock, then. My name's Shannon Coyne. My folks are from Northern Ireland."

The man smiled, showing off his dimples. "Connor Doyle. Dublin through and through."

Shannon introduced Piet. "This is Piet Van Loo," making sure to pronounce his surname correctly as 'Van Low.' Connor reached across the bar to shake Piet's hand. "Not Celtic, then?"

Piet smiled. "Dutch."

"Ah. King Billy's mob. I won't hold it against you."

Piet laughed. "Only the Irish can refer to history that took place in the 1600s in everyday conversation."

Connor was called away to fill an order but returned to chat with them a few moments later. "I don't remember seeing you here before. Are you a couple on vacation, then?"

Shannon grinned. "No, and no. We are great friends, but not a couple, and we live here in town."

"Each in our own flat," Piet added.

Connor glanced at Piet. "Right, so. What brings you here tonight? Celebrating something?"

Shannon pulled out her phone. "Not exactly, and honestly, I don't know why we never come here. It's a lovely spot."

Connor nodded. "'Tis. The patio's popular on a night like this."

Shannon opened her phone. "Someone I know comes here sometimes. Recognize her?" She showed Connor the photo of Jennifer Walker.

He nodded. "Ah, yeh. I remember her. I only saw her the once."

"Do you remember when that was?"

He frowned. "Weeks ago now. She was part of a group celebrating something. I only remember it because I came in for the afternoon shift to help out and stayed right to closing. A double shift. It was a long ould day."

Shannon felt her shoulders slump. "And she was here most of that time?"

His curls bounced as Connor shook his head. "Oh, I don't think so. She left quite early, and when they arrived, someone said to put it all on one bill because they'd divide it amongst themselves, and then this one wanted hers split out after an hour." He raised an eyebrow. "She's a friend of yours, is she?"

Shannon flushed. "No. I can't say that. I'm trying to confirm something she's said."

"Well, she was a pain in the butt, and for all that aggro, she tipped me like five percent."

She shook her head. "I'm not surprised. If she left after an hour, would that have been around one or two o'clock? I know it's weeks ago, but do you recall?"

He held up a finger, poured some drinks for the waitress, and then returned. "The group started arriving when we opened at eleven. They all ordered food, including your one there." He nodded at Shannon's phone. "I'd say she was done eating around twelve thirty and then had tea or coffee, don't remember which, and then came the argy-bargy about the bill. The rest were getting into pints and Caesars by then, and I'm not sure they even noticed she had left."

Shannon nodded. "So maybe around one o'clock?"

"Sounds right."

"That's magic, Connor. Thanks for this."

He nodded. "Another round?"

Piet spoke up. "Definitely. We're not driving. It's a short walk home."

Connor grinned at Piet. "This should be your local, then."

"I believe you're right."

When Connor left to get the drinks, Shannon looked at Piet and raised her eyebrows.

Piet shrugged. "What?"

"Nothing. Nothing at all. You look like you're settling in for the evening."

"Maybe I am."

Chapter Thirteen

ON THE WALK HOME, they discussed what she should do with the information about Jennifer's early departure from the group event on the day her father died. Piet strongly suggested she pass it along to Kal or her uncle, but Shannon wasn't sure.

"If they were interested in finding other suspects, they would have checked Jennifer's alibi more closely, wouldn't they?"

Piet shrugged. "You don't believe they want to railroad an innocent woman, do you?"

"No," she acknowledged. "I just think I need to get more information before taking it to them."

He narrowed his eyes at her as they reached their front door, and Shannon unlocked it. "You plan to talk to her, don't you?"

"I might."

"Oh, Shannon. Didn't you learn anything about taking chances like that?"

They stood in the front foyer. "I won't do anything rash. Don't worry. First, I'll talk to Violet. I may throw it out there to see her reaction to the news that Jenn wasn't at the event all afternoon."

"What if she's shocked or angry? What then? It still isn't evidence. You may just upset her for no reason."

She tilted her chin up. "I don't know exactly, but talking to Violet is my first step."

Piet yawned. "I know that determined look, so I won't say anything else about it. Thanks for taking me along. I haven't been to the Beamish in years. I don't know why. It's a great place."

Shannon smiled. "Especially with a cute bartender named Connor?"

He gave an enigmatic smile in return. "Goodnight, Shannon."

※

On Saturday morning, Shannon arranged to meet the Sullivans in Pengelly Landing for the house inspection later that afternoon. She did some errands and then, by eleven o'clock, felt it was a reasonable hour to call Violet Walker. Crossing her fingers that the woman was home again and not still in custody, she was startled when the phone was answered on the second ring.

"Violet? This is Shannon Coyne."

The woman's voice was tired and strained. "Shannon. Yes. What can I do for you?"

"I heard what happened and wanted to check how you are."

The audible sigh was long. "I suppose I'm as well as can be. I have an ankle bracelet on to ensure I don't leave home. It's not very pretty." She made a brave attempt to joke about her house arrest.

"How can I help? I'd love to see you, and I can bring groceries or baked goods. Maybe a bottle of wine?"

"I've left a message for my daughter to pick up some groceries. I haven't heard back, but I'm sure she'll be by later. I heard she accepted an offer on the house, so I suppose she'll want to talk about that."

Shannon bit her lip. "Violet, I'd like to talk to you. About the house, yes, but I'm sure Rod has given you all the information you need there. What I really want to talk to you about is Mal's death. I've found something out I think you should know."

The woman's voice perked up. "All right. Do you want to come when Jenn is here? I can call you when or if she shows up."

"Honestly? I'd prefer to see you on your own. I could come now if you feel up to it?"

"Yes, all right. Maybe it will take my mind off everything that's happened."

❦

Shannon stopped at the Your Independent Grocer's store to pick up a loaf of freshly baked multigrain bread, a jar of tomato soup and a small platter of cut fruit and vegetables. Once again, she was vetted before being admitted into the residence. When Violet opened her apartment door, Shannon held out the bag with food. "I felt this was more practical than more flowers."

Violet swallowed, and tears slid down her cheeks. "Thank you. That's very thoughtful."

The older woman led her into the tiny kitchen and watched Shannon unpack her gifts. As the young woman put the jar of soup in the fridge, Violet filled the kettle with water for tea.

They sat in the living room, and Violet slumped into the corner of the sofa. "What do you want to talk to me about?"

Shannon took a deep breath. "I visited the pub last night where Jennifer said she spent the afternoon on the day Mal died. Violet, did Jennifer tell you she had been there when you called her with the news that Mal was missing?"

Violet frowned. "I think so. I hardly remember. It seems so long ago now."

Shannon nudged her. "Think back. You were at the house, and everyone was searching for Mal. You called your daughter and your nephew Chris. That's what I recall you saying to me."

The elderly woman nodded. "That's right."

"Can you remember roughly what time that was?"

"It was late afternoon or early evening. Why? Is it important?"

"When you spoke with Jenn, did she say she was at home or somewhere else? Maybe she didn't even say where she was?"

"She said she was out with friends to celebrate someone's birthday. She was short with me because I interrupted her enjoyable afternoon. She doesn't go out that often, so I understood why she was irritated, but I had to let her know, didn't I?"

"Yes, of course you did. Did it sound noisy? Like she was in a pub with lots of people?"

Violet considered the question, the deep wrinkles forming grooves on her forehead. "It's hard to say. I didn't hear people talking. It sounded a bit…echoey."

Shannon thought about that. "Like she was on the speaker phone in her car?"

"Yes. That's exactly it. Maybe she was sitting in the car having a cigarette."

"Does she smoke?"

"Sometimes. She thinks I don't know, but I smell it on her. Why does all this matter? It's me the police are interested in. They think I killed my husband for the insurance money. It's so crazy."

"The reason it's important is because when I was at the pub last night, I got chatting with the bartender, and he remembered your daughter. He's clear that she left by one o'clock, which surprised me."

Violet stared at Shannon. "Are you saying she lied about where she was when we were searching for Mal?"

Shannon pursed her lips. "I can't say that definitively, but I think it's worth asking her to take you through that afternoon again."

"My daughter and I have our differences, but she wouldn't let me be charged with the death of her father. She may have been on the way home or somewhere else than that pub, but nothing more…" she searched for the right word… "sinister."

Shannon nodded. "I'm sure you're right, but I still think it's worth the conversation."

Just then, the two women heard a key in the door. Violet nodded. "Well, here she is. You can ask her yourself."

Chapter Fourteen

SHANNON RECALLED THE WOMAN from years ago standing in front of the open door, staring at her. Wordlessly, she came inside, closed the door, and moved to the kitchen, thumping a litre of milk on the counter.

She had the same round face as her mother, but Jennifer Walker's shoulder-length hair was dyed black, making her skin appear sallow. She wore it pulled back in a ponytail, held in place by a purple scrunchie. She shifted into the living room and stopped in front of the sofa. Her mouth was in a tight, straight line as she glared at Shannon. "I remember you. You worked at the seniors' centre. Do you work here now?"

Shannon stood and stepped over to Jennifer, holding out her hand to shake. "No, I'm a realtor. I represent the clients buying your parents' house in Pengelly Landing."

Jennifer Walker furrowed her brow. "So, why are you here? We have our own real estate agent."

"Yes, I know."

Shannon's throat was dry.

Jennifer continued to frown. "Well?"

Violet spoke up. "She brought me some things from the grocery store, which is good, because when I see what you brought me, I suppose I'd have to live on cereal and hot drinks."

Jennifer folded her arms across her chest. "I was going to run out later. I just brought the milk to start with."

Her mother nodded. "If you were at the store, why didn't you get everything I asked for?"

"Never mind all that. It's bizarre that the real estate agent is bringing you food."

Shannon finally found her voice. "We were talking about the day your father passed. You'll remember that I also knew him, and your mum's been telling me about what happened. It sounds like she's been through the wringer over your father's death."

Jennifer seemed to recollect that her mother had just been released from custody. "She has been, so you should move on rather than bother her."

Violet shook her head. "We were talking about my call to you that afternoon. You were at a party, right?"

Jennifer's eyes narrowed. "What of it? I couldn't know he was drowning. He shouldn't have been out alone with the way his eyesight was. I came as soon as I could when you called me."

"Yes, you did. Did you come straight from that party?"

Jennifer ignored her mother's question and turned to Shannon. "I don't know why you're still here. I'd like you to leave."

Shannon nodded to Violet. "I'm going up to the house now to meet the clients for a house inspection. I'm sure it will go well. We'll let Rod, your agent, know when it's done. Goodbye, Violet." She turned to the frowning Walker daughter. "Goodbye, Jennifer."

Violet walked with Shannon to the door and spoke under her breath. "I'm going to talk to her further. I have your phone number, and I'll call you later."

Jennifer called her mother. "I'm putting the kettle on, Mum. Are you coming?"

Shannon squeezed the fragile hand of her elderly friend and left.

In the elevator, Shannon felt her shoulders drop. *I thought Violet was going to say I was accusing Jennifer of killing her father. I'm not ready for that woman's wrath yet. I need more evidence, but I don't know what or how. I hope Jennifer doesn't get aggressive with her mother. If I'm right, she might be a danger to her just like she was to her father.*

※

Shannon scrolled through her social media as she ate a banana and mayo sandwich and sipped on green tea. She widened her eyes when she received a link from Emma to a new review of her as a realtor.

She phoned her friend, too impatient to send her an email. "Emma. I can't believe this. I've *never* shown an inappropriate home to a client. I may mention something to offer up a different perspective or something they may not have considered, but this review claims I took them to a bunch of houses that didn't match their wish list."

Emma's voice was calm. "It's nonsense. Of course it is, and that's why they posted anonymously."

Shannon protested. "But people won't know that. It sounds like I wasted time driving them to places I knew they'd never want. That's not fair. Every buyer I've had has ended up with a place they've loved."

"It's a troll. Look, they say that you pressured them into making several offers for homes they didn't want. Classic troll behaviour. Telling lies. How would that even be possible?"

"I know, right? Imagine all the paperwork and waste of my time if I did anything like that. It's crazy."

"Anyone who reads this review, and I'm not saying anyone does read them, will know it sounds fishy. You've got half a dozen great reviews where your clients can't say enough nice things about you. I only sent it so you'd know about it, but don't let it stress you out."

Shannon glanced at her watch. "Speaking of clients, I have to run. I'm meeting the Sullivans for their home inspection."

"Good luck. Let that good country air wash away this nonsense."

"Thanks, Em. I'll talk to you later."

※

As Shannon drove north on Highway 28, she tried deliberately to put the bad review out of her mind and thought instead about Violet Walker. *I would love to know if she got any further probing Jennifer about the day Malcolm died.* As soon as the vision of Violet's daughter came into her mind, Shannon was sure who had written the negative review. *Of course. Jennifer did. Just like she complained to my boss back at the seniors' centre, now she's found an even more public way of complaining about me.*

While the thought of Jennifer trolling her upset her, she also felt better. *At least I know it isn't an actual client. How do I stop her, though? Maybe Piet has some ideas.*

She arrived at the house a few moments before the inspector, followed by Nick Sullivan. The three of them chatted for a few moments as Shannon described the house layout. The inspector reviewed what he intended to examine and welcomed Shannon and Nick to follow him through the inspection. Nick was enthusiastic and asked questions as they went through room by room, running water, checking for signs of leakage and blockages, flipping switches, checking electrical outlets and the myriad of other potential sources of issues. When they went upstairs, the inspector pulled down the attic stairs leading up through the hatch into the attic.

Nick blinked as dust fell to the floor and brushed his black shirt free of bits of fallen insulation and dust. "I think I'll just stay here unless there's something you really think I need to see."

The inspector nodded. "Fair enough. I'll take some video up there. Just checking to make sure there haven't been any signs of the roof leaking, rodent activity, or black mould."

As Shannon and Nick waited in the comfort of the room that

had served Malcolm Walker as an office, Nick wandered around to look at photos on the wall while she noted what they had seen so far. *All minor issues, anyway.*

"This is interesting."

Shannon went over to see what Nick was looking at. Although she had walked through the house twice, the photos on the walls hadn't been her focus.

The centrepiece of the grouping of framed photos was a newspaper article dated from 1877 titled "Another Sea Serpent."

"Oh! This must be part of the collection I heard about." Shannon took a photo of the framed pieces. There were photos of two women and a man who claimed to have seen the sea monster in Rice Lake and reported it to the police as they stood grouped in front of the Rice Lake Inn. There was also a page from a notebook that appeared to be an original police report and another framed news article about a sea monster in Massachusetts dated 1920.

Nick said. "This is cool. All this stuff about a sea monster. This is probably worth money. I wonder if it comes with the house."

"Oh no, I'm afraid it doesn't. Of course, if you put it explicitly in the offer and are willing to pay for it, perhaps you can have it, but I have a feeling Jessie might prefer the money to be spent on renovations."

Nick smiled. "Yeah. I'm sure you're right." He moved on around the room. "I wonder what was here." He pointed to a nail and a bare spot on the wall surrounded by various frames.

Shannon joined him to study the remaining display. Frowning, she peered at a grainy black-and-white photo of a man sporting a heavy black mustache in the fashion of the late 1800s. Beside him was a photo of a stern-looking woman with her hair pulled back in a severe bun and dressed in a dark dress adorned with the smallest possible lace collar.

She read the inscriptions aloud. "Eliza Catherine Roche and Joseph Medlicott Scriven. I've never heard of her, but I know his name."

Nick shrugged and moved back to the ladder's base leading to the attic. "How's it going up there? Anything I should worry about?"

The inspector's voice floated down. "Nope. It all looks good other than signs of rodent activity. I'll be down in a minute and show you the pictures."

Shannon frowned, and then it came to her. "I know why that name is familiar. There is a monument to this man in Port Hope. Good Lord, I walk past it several times a week but can't say I ever really stopped to look at it. I wonder who he was."

The inspector descended, and Shannon put the thought of Scriven to the back of her mind to focus on the report.

Half an hour later, she waved off the inspector and Nick Sullivan. Before she locked up, she returned to the office and studied the framed pieces. Along with the portraits was a glass-fronted box frame enclosing a small booklet written by someone named James Cleland. Directly beside the blank space was a music score with a hand-written title, 'Pray Without Ceasing.' She took photos of the collection, including the blank space. *Violet will know what was here.*

Chapter Fifteen

AS SHE DROVE SOUTH from Pengelly Landing, Shannon called Rod and told him the inspection went well. "We know it needs new windows, but there were no surprises structurally or with the wiring and plumbing. I took a sample of water and will get that tested. By the time I get the water test results, they should have confirmation of financing, and we can do the final sign-off. I don't see any major issues moving forward."

When she reached home, she had turned her mind back to the Rice Lake sea monster collection. *Surely, that isn't worth killing someone over. It's another question for Violet. Piet thought Malcolm's partner was interested in it. Enough to endanger Malcolm's life? I'll make a list of things to talk to Violet about, starting with what Jennifer had to say.*

Dusty was anxious to go for a walk. Shannon smiled at her dog as she clipped the new leash onto her collar. "Between the new leash and your GPS, I can take you anywhere now, little lady. Let's go check out that monument."

They wandered along Walton Street and turned right on Queen Street. Shannon allowed Dusty time at the memorial to sniff around the semi-circular stone structure as she read the three plaques. It wasn't until she read the last one with its words from a hymn that she finally realized who Joseph Scriven had been. *He wrote the words for that hymn. What a Friend We Have in Jesus. And he lived in Port Hope. Imagine.* When her dog tugged at the leash, nudging her on, Shannon walked on past the bandshell. The patio at Beamish House was busy on this mild June evening, and she intended to walk past the sea of faces when Dusty surprised her by yanking hard at the leash, dragging her forward.

"No! Dusty!" Shannon gripped the leash firmly while the small dog whined in protest.

"Shannon!"

She looked up at the patio and realized why Dusty was so anxious to join the crowd. Piet sat in the early evening sun, waving a beverage at her. Giving in to their combined efforts, she climbed the stairs up to the deck to join her friend.

Sitting down, she looked around. "Are you on your own?"

Piet smiled. "For the moment. Connor finishes work in a bit."

"Ah. Shall we keep you company until then?"

After giving Dusty some attention, Piet rose. "Definitely. What can I get you? A glass of red wine?"

"Sounds good. Thank you."

When he returned with a glass of Merlot, Piet settled down and smiled, with one hand lazily stroking Dusty's ears. "OK, tell me what's been going on with you."

Shannon took a deep breath and told him about the bad review. "I know it's her. It's Jennifer Jones."

"But what does she have to gain?"

"She wants to warn me off."

"Warn you off talking to her mother?"

"That, and she knows I suspect she's involved with her father's death."

Piet sighed. "She can't feel threatened by you. You have no

evidence. If there were anything, the police would have found it by now." He held up his hand to stop her protest. "Let's say you're right. She wasn't where she claimed to be when her father died." He waved at the pub. "Here. She wasn't here. What does that prove? No one saw her at the lake, right? And what's her motive to kill him?"

Shannon glowered. "I don't know that yet, but dollars to doughnuts it's about money. She wants that house sold, and I have no doubt she expects to get a chunk of money from the sale."

"Did Violet tell you that?"

"No. But once the money is sitting in Violet's account, Jennifer will find a way to get her hands on it." She widened her eyes. "And, if her mother's in jail, she'd certainly be put in charge of the money."

"Maybe. I'm not a lawyer, but wouldn't the money be frozen because you can't gain through committing a crime, right? Isn't there something about forfeiture of proceeds from a crime?"

Shannon nodded. "I think you're right. But it's not a crime to sell your house. If it was just about a life insurance policy, I can see a problem, but this? I'm not sure, but it could mean the money would be tied up for a long time. Jennifer isn't the sharpest knife in the block. She may not have thought that through."

Piet took another sip of his Guinness. "That takes us back to where we started. Maybe it wasn't Jennifer who posted the bad review. I wouldn't waste too much energy on it. It could just as well be someone you don't even know. Emma's probably right. Just a troll."

Shannon sighed. "I still think I'm right, but if it's just one review, you're right. I'll try to put it out of my mind."

"Good girl. Enjoy this gorgeous evening and think of something else."

"OK. Let me tell you about the sea monster collection."

They chatted about the collection of artifacts of the Rice Lake sea monster until Connor joined them.

The young man's red curls flamed in the setting sun's light. He set down three drinks. "I took the liberty."

Shannon lifted her glass. "Thank you. Sláinte."

They clinked glasses to the Irish toast to wish each other good health.

Piet nodded to Shannon. "I'm just hearing about the curious collection of sea monster memorabilia Shannon saw today."

She shrugged. "It was interesting, but not enough to cause murderous envy in anyone, I don't think. There was another collection, too, and that was more interesting." Talking about the photos of Scriven and his fiancée somehow made it seem less exciting than Shannon had first thought. "So there's a missing frame, and I'm curious what it might have been."

Piet shook his head. "If you're looking for motive, I can't see it. And maybe it was removed ages ago."

Shannon nodded. "I know. I'm going to ask Violet about it."

Connor set his pint of Guinness down. "This all feels oddly familiar."

Piet raised his eyebrows. "What does? Sitting out here having a pint?"

"Ah, no. I mean, hearing someone talk about some Scriven thing. I had to ask later who Scriven was."

Shannon bit her bottom lip. "Who was it? Do you remember? Who was talking about it?"

Piet chimed in. "And was it recent or a long while ago?"

Connor shrugged. "I've only been working here six months, so not that long ago, but no. I'd say in the past couple of months." He frowned with an effort to remember the conversation. "It was quiet, so it might have been a Sunday. I wouldn't have heard two people talking otherwise." He nodded. "Right. It *was* a Sunday a few weeks ago. A woman and a man." He turned to nod to Shannon. "I remember now. It was yer woman you asked about the first time you were here." He ignored her gasp and went on. "I was behind the bar, and they sat at the table just in front. I don't think she liked it, but the fella got there first and sat there because there was a newspaper on the table." Connor nodded and continued. "She had some photos on her phone she showed him, and that's when I heard her say something like, 'That's Scriven.' After that, she looked around the room, saw me there, and lowered her voice, forcing him to lean in close. I thought they were talking about some big scandal the way they acted, so I asked someone I work with if they ever heard tell of this Scriven one, and she laughed and said he was some local hero, long dead, and I lost interest. That's why I totally forgot I'd seen her another time."

Shannon picked Dusty up, settled the dog on her lap, and turned to Connor. "Do you remember what the man looked like?"

He closed his eyes for an instant. "Lots of white hair." He shrugged. "Sorry. I don't remember anything else."

Then she nodded and turned to Piet. "Now, do you believe me? I'll bet it was his business partner. You said yourself he was interested in the Rice Lake collection. Maybe he also felt the Scriven collection should be his. Does that description sound like him?"

"It could be. That describes any number of senior men. I agree it looks suspicious, all right. I don't think it adds up to murder, but Jennifer may have taken advantage of the situation and started selling pieces off."

Connor drained his drink and turned to Piet. "I've seen enough of this place for one day. Shall we go get something to eat?"

Shannon held up her half glass of wine. "You two go. I'll finish this, and then Dusty and I will go home. I need to think this through."

After they left, Shannon considered if Piet was right. *Jennifer may have behaved in suspicious ways, but does that mean she killed her father?*

Chapter Sixteen

WHEN SHANNON ARRIVED HOME, it was time to get supper for Dusty and herself. She heated some homemade pasta with shrimp and cherry tomatoes, and as she ate, she thought about calling Violet. *I can't just ask her if she thinks her daughter killed Mal. That would be too awful for her to imagine, but I will ask her what happened after I left. And then I'll tell her I saw the Rice Lake collection and the Scriven photos. See what she says.*

Violet answered on the first ring. "Yes, Shannon. Hello. I wondered if you'd call again. I meant to call you; sorry."

Shannon hoped Jennifer wasn't there now. "Violet, I know Jennifer was irritated that I was with you this morning. I hope my presence didn't cause problems between you."

"No, you weren't to blame. We have problems whenever we're together. You're right, though. She was annoyed to see you here. She remembered you from the seniors' club. I have to warn you, she may complain about you again."

"Don't worry about me. Did she have anything further to say about the day her father died?"

"Jenn has always been casual with the truth, I'm afraid. She was very offhand when I asked her where she was when I spoke on the phone to her that afternoon. She said she was driving somewhere, and when I pressed her, she became angry and asked why I was grilling her about her whereabouts. I was too tired to fight with her. I need her right now and can't afford to have her go off in a huff."

Shannon spoke soothingly, "Of course not. I'm sure it doesn't matter. I was at the house this afternoon and was so interested to see the collection of Rice Lake memorabilia hanging on the wall of Mal's office."

"Oh, that's right. That's where that stuff is. I'd forgotten. I so rarely went into Mal's office."

"There were some things about sea monsters, or I suppose we should say, lake monsters, and some articles about Scriven. It was quite intriguing."

Violet sighed. "It's all just old tat. Things I have to get rid of."

"Is it, though? I mentioned it to a friend, and he thought a collector might be interested. Didn't Mal have a business partner?"

Violet's voice hardened. "Nate Stevens. I wouldn't sell anything to him if he were the last person on earth. He took advantage of Mal when they closed the business. Mal still saw him occasionally and said, 'Let bygones be bygones', but I refused to see him."

"Oh dear. I'm sorry. I didn't mean to upset you."

"They met for lunch a couple of weeks before he died, and I know Mal was upset when he came home. He didn't tell me what happened but said, 'You're right about him, Violet. I won't be seeing him again.' "

"Good heavens. Does he live in Port Hope?"

"No, he's on the lake somewhere. He used to live in Cobourg but moved up to Rice Lake a couple of years ago, but I don't know the exact location."

Before Shannon could ask further questions, Violet said she had another call coming in. "It's Rod. I have to go."

"Bye, Violet."

Shannon saw her pup was curled up and sound asleep on the sofa, so she sat at the table with her laptop. Keying in 'Nate Stevens, Rice Lake,' her search returned a list of results for a hockey player who had no connection to Rice Lake. She took out Rice Lake and put in Cobourg. *Bingo.* She studied the photo accompanying an online article about the former antique broker. 'Lots of white hair' was the description Connor had given. This man had a long pale face and high forehead topped by a full head of fluffy white hair. Shannon imagined him sporting a blond afro as a folk music follower of the Woodstock era. The article talked about his love of unique pieces, and he travelled extensively, sourcing pieces from the late 1800s to mid-century modern. Nate admitted he was drawn to items from the sixties. "I suppose they take me back to a happy time in my life."

Shannon stared at the photo. *Are you the one who met with Jennifer?*

She took a screenshot of the image and texted it to Piet with a short message: "When u can, plse show this to Connor and ask if that's the man he saw with Jenn."

She received a thumbs-up from Piet in seconds to acknowledge her message.

After exhausting her interest in Nate Stevens, Shannon decided to research Scriven. She discovered that, like her own family, he was originally from Northern Ireland, but his family moved to Dublin, where he was educated. He came to live in Canada in 1847. By then, he was a member of a fundamentalist sect called the Plymouth Brethren. Before starting his life in Port Hope, Ontario, he wrote a poem called *Pray Without Ceasing*, the first line of which was *What A Friend We Have In Jesus*.

"Hunh," Shannon said aloud, and smiled when Dusty lifted her head. "Go back to sleep, sweetie. I'm talking to myself."

She shook her head when she read that Joseph Scriven had spent time as a tutor with the Pengelley family near Bailiboro. *Wow. Small world*. She read that Scriven moved between Port Hope and Bewdley, working both as a handyman and as a preacher in a small church in Bewdley built on the former property of James Sackville, and was intrigued. *No wonder someone might be interested in Scriven artifacts. Who knew there was so much history up there? I know there's an old bridge called Sackville Bridge. The church must be near there.*

She concluded her reading about Scriven and tucked herself on the sofa beside her dog. Flipping through the television channels, Shannon was restless and glad when her phone rang. "Hi, Mammy."

"Am I disturbing you?"

Shannon smiled. Her mother thought she was always frantically busy. "Not at all. What's the craic?" She always fell into the Irish way of speaking immediately when she talked to a family member. This question let her mother know they could have a good catch-up.

"Ah, well, I just wondered if you'd talked to Meghan lately?"

"Not since we were all together for supper. Why? Is she all right?"

Shannon heard her father in the background talking to her mother. Something they often did. One of her parents would be on the phone while the other chipped in with comments, usually making for a confusing conversation, as she didn't always know if the parent on the phone was talking to her or the other parent.

"Why is Daddy saying don't make a big thing of it? Of what?"

"I don't like to upset you."

"Mammy, whatever it is, best just spit it out."

"Right, so. Meghan is out for a date tonight. She's had several now with the same boy."

Shannon laughed. "Why would that upset me? I'm delighted. Who is it? Anyone I know?"

"It's Declan."

Shannon raised her eyebrows. "Declan Moore? The nephew from Gilligan's pub?"

"None other."

She knew her mother harboured hopes for Shannon herself

to have developed a relationship with the Irish electrician. "Oh, Mammy, you don't need to worry about me. He's a lovely man, and you know we went out a couple of times, but we were never going to do a serious line together."

"Why not? He's nice-looking and has a good job, and some day he might inherit the pub from his uncle."

Shannon considered the image of the man with his rugged Celtic appearance. "You're right, Mammy. He's all of that, which makes him perfect for Meghan."

Her mother sighed, probably realizing she wouldn't get an answer about why he didn't suit Shannon. "You're not upset, so?"

"Not at all. And to show you, how about I come out for a visit tomorrow, and we can have a proper catch-up?"

"And if Declan was here for supper, would you be bothered?"

"No, Mammy. It'll be good to see him. As long as Meghan wouldn't think I'm trying to push in."

"I'm sure she wouldn't think that. Well, then. I'll make a proper supper for the family and invite Bernadette and Danny, as well."

"That sounds perfect."

They chatted, and then her mother signed off to plan the family gathering.

Dusty had crept up, and now Shannon stroked her dog's long ears. "Well, Dusty. One of these days, I'll connect with someone, but right now, I'm having too much fun alone. We're good here together, aren't we? Who needs romance? Declan and Meghan are much more suited for each other."

Before going to bed, Shannon sent her sister Meghan a text: "So happy to hear u and Declan are dating! I'll see you tomorrow at supper. Big hugs, S"

Meghan sent her a heart in return, and Shannon knew all was well between them.

As she drifted off to sleep, Shannon was glad her mother had called. *I needed a distraction from Malcolm's murder. I can't get obsessed about it. Whatever I feel about the wrongness of Violet being accused of her husband's death, I need to step back.*

With those thoughts, she remembered she had intended to get some butter tarts to take to her parents and decided to drive back up north tomorrow to pick some up before her visit home to Colborne.

Chapter Seventeen

OVERNIGHT CLOUDS HAD MOVED in, and although the temperature at eight o'clock was in the low teens, Shannon shivered as she walked with Dusty around the yard. She glanced up to Piet's flat on the second floor to check for any sign of movement, but either he wasn't home or still sleeping. He hadn't responded to her text from the previous evening. Shannon returned through the French doors into the warmth of her living room, leaving Dusty to wander on her own.

She poured herself a second cup of tea and sipped it as she scrolled through emails and social media. Tea spilled when she plunked her cup down on the table. "No!"

She studied the new one-star review. Muttering aloud, she read it. "Anonymous, of course. What can I do about this? It's so unfair. There must be a law against it." Shannon blinked. "Maybe there is. I'll ask Kal."

Without pausing further, she took a screenshot and emailed it to Kal Khan: 'Hi Kal, is this allowed? These are fake reviews, and they're tarnishing my reputation.'

Despite the early hour, he responded almost immediately: Good morning, Shannon. I'm sure this must be very upsetting for you. The short answer is no; civil and criminal provisions prohibit making false or misleading representations to the public. I'm afraid it is rather a process though to prove it, especially against anonymous reviewers, but with time and money, I'm sure a lawyer might help you here.'

Shannon sighed and then smiled. *He's so sincere. He could have just said good luck with that, but he always takes me seriously.*

'Thank you, Kal. I have a feeling I know who's posting these reviews, but I don't know how to prove it.'

'Perhaps you can approach Google to plead your case for removal?'

Shannon nodded. 'Great thought. I'll check into that.'

'How is everything else going for you?'

"Pretty good. I'm off for a family dinner today, so that's always nice.'

'Yes. Please give my regards to your parents.'

'Do you go home for family get-togethers on Sundays too?'

'Not this week. I am catching up on work.'

'Ah. Well, I better let you get on with it then. Take care.'

'Have a lovely day.'

Dusty stared through the glass at her, and Shannon got up to let her in. "Come in, baby. We'll get organized to go up and get some butter tarts."

Before leaving, Shannon called Rod. "Hi, there. I will be up near the house and have a blank wall plate to put over a receptacle that isn't functioning. The house inspector discovered it, but rather than make a big deal, the buyers agreed to cover it and not use it. There are plenty of working plug receptacles in the room. I remembered I had one and said they could have it. Do you think anyone would mind if I popped in to do that? Is Jennifer there packing up the house?"

Shannon heard the irritation in Rod's voice. "I'm sure that will be fine. Jennifer will *not* be packing up the house for her mother. Apparently, she's far too busy. It sounds like she hasn't gone near the house for weeks. Violet tried to get her nephew Chris to help, but that didn't work out either, so I've arranged for movers to go in and pack next week. Violet has rented a POD, and the movers will put everything in that, and then the POD will go into storage until all this misery is behind poor Violet. She might have the whole thing moved down to Florida, but at least for now, it will be out of the way, and the house will be ready for closing in two weeks."

"Violet's lucky to have you, Rod. All right. I'll take my tool kit and cover over that receptacle. I won't be there long."

❦

To Shannon's dismay, she discovered the bakery was closed on Sundays. "Oh, Dusty. I should have checked. What a careless thing to do. We could just have gone over to pick up tarts at Betty's, which are also delicious. I guess that's what we'll still do."

Dusty wagged her tail in agreement.

"We'll go to the Walker house and do this cover anyway, so it isn't a wasted journey. I'll let you have a little run-about, but don't find anything strange. You found Malcolm's overcoat the last time I let you out there."

Shannon pulled into the familiar driveway. Despite the overcast day, the view looking south over the lake was beautiful. The choppy, small waves rippled grey and white against the backdrop of the dark green foliage across the lake on the south shore. She carried Dusty so her small paws wouldn't track dirt inside. Setting the spaniel down, Shannon pulled the receptacle plate and screwdriver set from her coat pocket. She knelt behind the sofa and examined the screws holding the current faceplate on. "Wouldn't you know it? One flathead and one Robertson." Engaged in her task of replacing the faceplate, it wasn't until she heard a sharp yip of excitement from Dusty that Shannon realized her dog had gone upstairs. Leaving the old faceplate and screwdrivers on the floor, she hurried up the steps.

"What is it? What are you doing?" With visions of Dusty chasing a mouse, she followed the sound of her dog's whines.

"Oh!" Shannon stood in the doorway of Malcolm's office and gaped at the mess. Only yesterday this office was tidy. Now, papers were pulled from the desk drawer and scattered on the floor. Books neatly shelved yesterday now sat stacked on the desk; two had toppled off to the floor below.

Dusty scurried around the room, her nose to the ground, following a scent that seemed especially intense along the bookshelves. Gazing around the room, Shannon gasped. "Oh, Dusty, they're all gone." She pulled out her phone and took photos of the walls, which, only yesterday, had been adorned with framed artifacts of the Rice Lake monster and the Scriven collection.

Triumphant, the small dog finally managed to root out the prize she had discovered in the corner beside the bookcase and delivered it to Shannon.

"A hair scrunchie." Shannon recalled the sight of Jennifer Walker wearing her hair in a ponytail held by a purple version of the green and yellow one she now held in her hand. "Let's get out of here, puppy. I need to call Rod."

After a quick check around the house to ensure nothing else had been disturbed and that all doors and windows were securely locked, Shannon picked up her screwdrivers, the old faceplate, and her dog and returned to her car. First, she texted the photos from yesterday showing the collections, and those from today showing the bare walls, and then she followed up with a phone call.

"Rod, I've just sent you some photos. The house has been disturbed since yesterday. It doesn't look like a break-in since the doors and windows are secured, but someone's gone through Mal's office and taken some things. I don't know what, if anything, you want to do about it."

"I'm looking at your images. If there's no sign of a break-in, I don't see anything I need to do. Perhaps Violet asked someone to fetch some things before it gets packed up. Sure, they made a mess, but it'll be a mess once the movers pack, anyway."

"All right. I just thought someone should know."

"Don't worry about it. The sale is going through, and I promise the house will be ready in two weeks when your clients take possession."

"OK. Thank you. I'm just being alarmist, I guess."

"Go enjoy your Sunday."

"Thanks, Rod. You too."

※

Piet answered her call on the first ring. "Good morning, or is it afternoon by now?"

"It's afternoon, but not by much. How are you today?"

"I'm feeling quite languid. You, on the other hand, sound like you're driving somewhere."

"I am. I've been up to the Walker house."

"Oh, yes? I thought you were all done there until whatever paperwork gets done for the closing?"

"I am, really, but I just popped in to replace a receptacle faceplate."

Piet laughed. "Shannon, the Tool Girl."

Shannon frowned. "That's a reference to some old TV show, isn't it?"

"Don't tell me you don't know *Home Improvement*?"

She dismissed her friend's love of old shows. "Listen, did you get a chance to ask Connor about the picture I sent you?"

"I did, but no joy, I'm afraid. He didn't get a good look at him. He doesn't think the fella's hair was quite so fluffy."

Shannon sighed. "OK, thanks anyway. I'm pretty sure Jennifer went and took the rest of the collections from the house and will probably sell it." She told Piet about the state of Malcolm's office, concluding with: "And Dusty found a hair scrunchie similar to the one I saw Jenn wearing."

"It's not illegal for the owners of the house to take stuff out of it, and as for the hair tie, it may be evidence that Jennifer is the one who was there, but it may just as easily have been there for months. There's no way to tell."

"I know. Should I check with Violet to see if she asked Jennifer to go and clear out Mal's office?"

"No. If she says 'yes', you'll look like a Nosy Parker. If she says no, you'll get her even more upset. Doesn't she have enough to think about right now?"

"True. OK, thanks, Piet. I better go. I'm picking up some butter tarts, and then Dusty and I will go to Colborne for supper. Do you want anything from the bakery?"

"No, thanks. I'm having a lazy day at home and will probably run out to get myself a schnitzel later from the Schnitzel Shack."

"Mmm. That sounds good. I haven't been there in ages. Enjoy."

※

It was close to five o'clock when Shannon let Dusty out of the car at her childhood home outside Colborne. The old two-storey brick farmhouse with its wrap-around veranda welcomed her. Surrounding the house, the apple blossoms of three weeks ago had given way to glossy green leaves and tiny buds of future apples. As she approached the front steps, her sister Meghan stepped out to meet her. Eighteen months older than Shannon, they were often mistaken for twins. Although both had long red hair, they were very different in personality. While Shannon loved independence, her sister enjoyed being home and still lived with their parents. On the other hand, while Shannon could be overcome with doubts and often second-guessed herself, Meghan was confident about her choices.

Now, her sister linked arms with Shannon. "I knew Mammy would tell you about Declan. You don't mind, sure?"

"Not at all. I want you to be happy, and if Declan is the one, that's a great thing."

Meghan nodded. "Mammy worried. I didn't. You had your chance." She squeezed Shannon's arm before slipping away to lead the way inside.

Shannon followed and laughed to see Dusty spinning circles around her father. "She knows you have treats for her, Da."

Her father ignored Dusty's antics, pulled Shannon in a bear hug, and then leaned over to give the dog a cookie from his pocket. "I have to spoil all my girls a little bit," he said.

Mary Coyne joined them in the foyer, and Shannon leaned down to embrace her mother and hand over the box of butter tarts. "Hi, Mammy. How's everything?"

"Lovely. It's always nice to have everyone together for Sunday dinner."

Her mother hustled back to the kitchen, and Shannon followed her father into the living room. The handsome Irish electrician-cum-bartender sat on the loveseat with his arm resting across the top of the couch, almost touching Meghan. He watched Shannon's face as if to gauge her reaction since he had dated her first, and Shannon grinned broadly. "Hey, Declan. Great to see you again."

He flashed a smile and visibly relaxed. He shifted his arm, which slipped off the loveseat's top and lay across Meghan's shoulders. "Nice to see you, too."

Dusty sniffed Declan, recognizing him and Meghan, and jumped up to stretch across their two laps.

The awkward moment passed, and the room filled with chat; tongues loosened by the Jameson's whiskey her father passed around. Shannon held up her hand when he came to top up her glass. "Ah, no, Daddy. I'm driving home later. I'll save myself for a glass of wine with supper."

It wasn't long before they crowded around the long farmhouse dining table with the seven of them. The three sisters sat around one end of the table with Shannon's brother-in-law, Danny, seated beside his wife, Bernadette and Declan beside Meghan. Her parents took up the other end of the table. They passed platters of homemade soda bread down to accompany the Dublin Coddle.

Declan commented on the dinner. "I haven't had this for donkey's years. It's gorgeous, Mary."

Shannon smiled to hear him say that, knowing he meant he hadn't had it in a very long time.

James Coyne smiled at his wife. "Not everyone from the North can make a Dublin Coddle, but Mary's is one of the best I've ever had." The conversation died down as everyone tucked into the dish packed with sausages, bacon, vegetables, a golden-brown potato crust, and bubbling Guinness-laden gravy.

Shannon was among the first to set her fork and knife on her empty plate.

Her mother raised her eyebrows and waved to the platter of Coddle. "More?"

"Ah, no, Mammy. Thank you. I'm not used to these hearty dinners anymore."

Her mother nodded. "It's why you look so thin."

Shannon laughed. "You'd say that no matter what I looked like, Mammy."

Bernadette finished eating and pushed aside her plate. "So, Sis, tell us what's going on in the glamorous life of a realtor."

"Not so very glamorous, I'm afraid, but I am on the cusp of closing a house sale in two weeks. Remember when I went to take a look at that house, and I found the overcoat?"

Her father corrected her. "You mean when Dusty found the overcoat."

"Yes, all right. Anyway, the wife of the deceased owner of that coat is charged with his murder."

Meghan widened her eyes. "No! Are you in the middle of another murder?"

Shannon saw her mother make the sign of the cross and answered quickly, "No, I'm not in the middle of anything. I'm just saying."

Bernadette shook her head. "Good Lord. Is the coat evidence? Is that why it was in the lake?"

Shannon shrugged. "I don't know."

Her mother frowned. "You've given it over to your Uncle Bob, I hope."

"I have, Mammy."

"Well, I'm glad of that, at least. That's an end to your involvement, then."

"I suppose it is, but I don't believe she's guilty. I knew these people when I worked at the seniors' centre. She couldn't have done it, but I've tried to find the evidence to prove it, and I've been frustrated."

Her father shook his head. "Shanny, we've been through this before. Let the police do their job. They know what they're doing, and if you get in the middle of things, you might just make a mess of their case."

"I know, I know. There's nothing more I can do, anyway. I've spoken to Kal Khan and still want to pass along some ideas to him. Then I'll have to be patient and hope they figure out what really happened."

Shannon saw the glance her mother gave her father at the mention of Kal and flushed.

Her sister also caught the glance. "That's the charming detective that works for Uncle Bob, right?"

"Yes. At least, he's the detective. Is he charming? I don't know." She tailed off, knowing she was digging a hole for herself.

Bernadette smirked. "Well, if he isn't charming, why don't you talk to Uncle Bob instead about these ideas?"

Shannon lifted her chin. "I don't want to abuse my relationship with the head of detectives. I know he's a busy man."

Her mother nodded and frowned at her oldest daughter. "Very right. I'm sure he *is* busy. Don't torment your sister."

Bernadette threw one last smile at Shannon before turning the subject to a discussion about the annual spring fungicide applications in the orchard.

Shannon helped clear the table, put dishes into the dishwasher, and then took her leave of her family.

On the forty-minute drive home, she thought about the evening. *Why* do *I always want to talk to Kal instead of Uncle Bob? Of course, he is charming, and I didn't lie when I said Uncle Bob was busy, but maybe I'm just a bit afraid of making a fool of myself with Uncle. Kal never makes me feel foolish, even though I know at this point I have nothing to go on when I keep saying Violet is innocent. If I were smart, I'd just put it all out of my mind. Get this house deal closed and walk away. That's the sensible thing.*

Chapter Eighteen

SHE SPENT MONDAY WORKING. When Shannon talked to her boss, Amanda or her friend Emma about new properties and clients, she pushed all thoughts of Malcolm Walker's death to the back of her mind. It wasn't until she walked home enjoying the mild June afternoon , despite her best intentions, that her thoughts returned to the Walkers. *Stop. You aren't doing anyone any good by getting in the middle of the investigation. Trust that everything will be all right, and they will exonerate Violet.* Pulling her trench coat tight as dark clouds scudded across the sky, Shannon sighed. She turned up Julia Street. Home was in sight when her phone rang.

"Piet, hi."

"You sound like you've lost your best friend."

She managed a smile. "I hope not. How are you?"

"I'm good. Where are you?"

"Almost home. Why?"

"OK, I'll come down in a few minutes. I have to go to work soon. We have a viewing at seven, but I want to show you something."

"OK. See you soon."

Shannon straightened her back and walked the last few minutes briskly. *It must have something to do with the case. Or maybe not. Whatever it is, Piet always perks me up.*

When her friend knocked, the kettle was on, and Shannon changed into sweatpants and a T-shirt.

Shannon called out. "Come in. It's open."

Dusty was wandering out in the yard, but Shannon left the French door open so she could come in when she chose.

The kettle whistled. "Time for a cuppa?"

Piet looked at his watch. "OK. A quick one."

"Earl Grey?"

"Perfect."

He followed her to the kitchen, where she filled the tea ball with loose tea leaves and poured boiling water over it. The bergamot oil filled the kitchen with its light citrus and floral scent. Carrying the tray with teapot and two cups, Shannon led the way into the living room. "OK. I'm busting to know what you have to show me. It's not another cat video, is it?"

He smiled. "No. I save those to share with my Toe Beans pals", referring to the local café where cats roamed the café which served as their foster home.

She poured tea into a cup. "I'm not against the odd cat video, but I need something more today."

Piet scrolled through his phone and handed it to her when she finished filling both cups with tea.

Shannon studied the image and frowned. "Who's this?"

"It's the man that Jennifer Walker met."

She widened her eyes. "This is the same man as before?"

"Connor is pretty sure. The two of them were in there again last night. He had to do some real contortions to get that shot with no one seeing him. That's why you don't see Jennifer. He waited until she went to the washroom because every time he thought he could take a photo, she'd be peering around the room like she didn't want anyone she knew to see her."

Shannon enlarged the image. "Who are you?" She looked at Piet. "This doesn't look like the picture I have of Malcolm's old business partner. What do you think? You met him."

"I'm not sure. It might be, but it's hard to tell. This guy seems to have more hair."

Can you send it to me?"

Piet took his phone back and tapped into it. Seconds later, the image showed up in her text messages.

Her friend sat back and sipped his tea. "This is lovely. You have the best teas. So, now, what are you going to do?"

Shannon chewed on her bottom lip while she considered the question. "I don't know. I had decided to do nothing, but now I want to know who this guy is. Why is Jennifer being so cagey if he was just some friend?"

"Why, indeed?"

Shannon drained her cup. "No. I can't sit around doing nothing. I'll ask Violet if she knows him."

Piet creased his forehead. "Can you clip it, so it isn't so obvious it's taken in the Beamish? I don't want Connor getting into trouble."

"No worries. I've got an app for that. I'll take the background right out."

"Just be careful. Don't visit this man at his home alone or anything foolish like that. We don't want a repeat of last year."

She held up her hand. "I promise. Public places only."

Piet rose and carried his cup to the kitchen. By this time, Dusty had come inside and was dancing around his feet. He set the cup in the sink and lifted the thirty-pound spaniel into his arms. He let her nuzzle his neck for a moment. "That's enough snuggles. I have to get ready for work."

Shannon walked him to the door. "Thanks for this, Piet, and please thank Connor for me. I appreciate the trouble he took."

After her friend left, she tidied up the kitchen, humming a tune as she did. *Even if I can't find anything useful, I feel better about trying, anyway.*

🔥

Shannon inhaled the fragrance of the Irish stew heating in her microwave, happy now that her mother had ignored her protests when she pulled the container out of the freezer with the comment, "I made far too much stew last week. You need to take some home."

When supper was ready, she sat at the table to eat with the laptop open in front of her. *OK, buddy. Who are you?*

She searched various terms, from 'antique dealers' to 'local collectors,' without success.

Drumming her fingers on the table, she sighed. *You knew it was a long shot. Nope. I'll need to visit Violet again. There's no other answer. And, after identifying buddy, I'll talk to Kal.*

🔥

After a night of tossing and turning, Shannon rose, feeling groggy and uncertain. A hot shower helped to convince her she was on the right track with her plan to check in with Violet and ask her about the man. She first spent time submitting the paperwork to show that both sides had met all the conditions for the Walker house sale. From the buyers' side, the inspection was done, the financing was arranged, and the water tests returned clear. The seller had the septic tank pumped. And this week, the sellers would finish emptying the house, making it ready for the Sullivan family's renovations to begin the following Monday. It was now in the hands of the lawyers, so Shannon turned her focus on other files her boss had asked her to review. Queries came through the website or via phone messages; each one needed follow-up, and some were assigned to her. Meanwhile, Shannon had the flexibility to visit Violet. *Call or just drop in? I better call. I don't want to run into Jennifer.*

"Hello, Violet. It's Shannon Coyne. As I'm sure you know, the house sale is moving along without a hitch. I'll be in your area later today, and I wondered if I might drop by to say hello?"

"That would be nice. Thank you. What time are you thinking?"

"What suits you? Two o'clock?"

"That's fine. My nephew might come by as well. He said he'd bring me a few things."

"I don't want to intrude, but I'd love to meet him. Chris, isn't it?"

"Yes, Chris. You won't be intruding, and I'm not sure what time he's coming, so two o'clock is fine."

"Can I bring you anything?"

"Oh, no. I've already given Chris my list."

"I'll see you later, then."

※

At two o'clock, Shannon knocked on Violet Walker's door. She heard a man's voice rumble, so she wasn't surprised when a man in his thirties opened the door. His short, cropped dark hair revealed a high forehead and neat ears close to his head. His grey eyes and full-lipped smile looked so much like Malcolm Walker's features that, for a moment, Shannon blinked in surprise.

He held out his hand. "Hi. I'm Chris Walker. You must be Shannon."

She shook his warm, dry hand. "Yes, hello. Violet's spoken of you."

Violet held up a bag of cookies and waved them in Shannon's direction. "Look at everything Chris brought. He spoiled me. Oatmeal cookies or chocolate chip. What will you have with your tea?"

Shannon went to her to look at the groceries spread out on the counter. "How wonderful. You deserve a bit of spoiling. I love both sorts of cookies, so whatever you want to open is good with me."

Violet filled the teapot with boiling water. "He even brought me Yorkshire Tea. Can you imagine?"

"I've never had it. Is it good?"

"Oh my, yes. It's a real cup of tea. None of this brown water with no flavour." Violet turned to her nephew. "You'll stay for a cup of tea, won't you?"

He smiled. "I can't stay long, but yes. Time enough for a cup of tea."

When the three of them were settled in the living room with their drinks and oatmeal cookies, Shannon talked about the house in Pengelly Landing for a few moments. "It's such a beautiful spot, and while I know it holds sad thoughts for you now, Violet, I'm sure you had years of pleasure there."

"Oh yes, we all loved it so much, didn't we, Chris?"

"Yes." He turned his sea-green gaze to Shannon. "I grew up at the family home, but the lake house was my favourite place in many ways. It's where Uncle Mal and I had our best times together." He sighed. "Everything changes." Chris closed his eyes for an instant and then seemed to shake off his solemn mood. "Never mind. Time for another family to make happy memories there."

Shannon nodded. "The family that bought it loves it already."

Chris glanced at his aunt. "I don't think I could ever look at the water the same way again, knowing about Uncle Mal."

Violet reached for his hand and squeezed it. "You can't think like that, Chris. Just remember the good times."

"Easier said than done."

Shannon took a breath. "Did you go out to help search for your uncle, Chris?"

He frowned. "Of course. I got there as soon as possible but was home in Peterborough, so it took a while to get there. It was too late. I don't think I can ever forgive myself."

Violet patted his arm. "There was nothing anyone could have done, Chris."

Shannon saw the man's eyes fill with tears and pulled out her phone to change the subject. "While I have you both here, do either of you know this man?" She rose and took the phone to show them the image of the man Connor had sent her.

Violet peered at the photo, so Shannon enlarged it to make it easier to see.

Chris shook his head. "Not me. Aunt Violet?"

"No. I've never seen him. Why? Who is he?"

Shannon closed the image and slipped the phone back into her purse. "I'm not sure. It's not important. I thought he might have been a friend of Mal's, but I must be mistaken."

Violet wasn't put off so easily. "You think he knows something about Mal's death?"

"No, honestly, I don't. I thought he looked familiar, but I'm wrong."

Chris stood. "I have to get going. Let me know if there's anything I can do for you, Auntie. Anything at all. Just call me. Promise?"

Violet stood on her toes to kiss her nephew's cheek. "I promise. Thank you for coming and bringing me the groceries. I'll let Jennifer know she doesn't have to come now."

Shannon caught Chris giving a slight shake of his head, unseen by Violet. *He knows Jennifer wasn't likely coming with groceries anyway.*

Picking up her purse, Shannon smiled at Violet. "It's time for me to go, so I'll walk out with Chris. I just wanted to check on you, and it's clear now that you're being well cared for."

As they waited for the elevator, Shannon waved back at Violet, who stood in the hall on the threshold of her apartment. "You're good to your aunt. That makes me feel better. I was worried she only had her daughter looking after her right now, and I wasn't convinced that was enough."

Chris spoke quietly. "You may know my aunt and uncle took me in after my parents died. I owe them everything."

Shannon nodded. "Violet told me. But one would think their daughter owes her mother everything, too."

The elevator came, and they stepped in before Chris responded. "You would think so, but Jenn never appreciated what she had as far as I could see."

"You don't get along?"

"You could say that." He smiled. "My aunt and uncle more than made up for any animosity Jennifer showed me." Chris furrowed his brow. "It upsets me to know Aunt Violet is going through all this now. Anyone with a brain knows she didn't hurt my uncle."

"I agree. That's why I'm determined to figure out what happened."

He turned to study her. "What do you mean? What can you do that the police aren't doing?"

The elevator door slid open, and they stepped into the lobby before Shannon responded.

"I'm not sure I can do anything more. I know they're working on it, but the difference is that I know she's not guilty. It's a different perspective."

He nodded. "I suppose. Are you interviewing people or what? You're a real estate agent, aren't you? Not a private investigator."

Shannon laughed. "That's true. But I'm prepared to keep prodding. Obviously, I can't do any real interviews, but sometimes I think people are more prepared to open up to an ordinary person like me rather than talk to the police."

"Right. So, have you discovered anything useful yet?"

She bit her lip. "I'm not sure."

"Go on. Maybe I can help. Aunt Violet told me Jenn was irritated to find you asking questions. Do you think she had something to do with Uncle Mal's death?"

Deciding to trust him, she took a breath. "Let's put it this way: I'm not convinced she *didn't* have anything to do with it."

Chris narrowed his eyes. "That man. The picture you showed us. How is he involved?"

"He's someone Jennifer met with. I believe she's been selling off some of your uncle's collectibles, unbeknownst to your aunt."

He nodded. "And this man is a buyer?"

"I think so, although I can't prove it yet. Trust me; I'll find out. I can be very persistent."

His face flushed, and his voice deepened with anger. "I wouldn't put it past her. She's always been out for herself. She hardly ever saw my uncle. Christmas and birthdays. That was it unless, of course, she needed something. She's so manipulative. My uncle saw through her, though. He wanted nothing to do with her the past few years."

"That's sad. For both of them."

Chris shrugged. "He had me. And she made her choice." He glanced at his watch. "I better go. It was nice meeting you. Goodbye."

He strode off before Shannon could get in step with him.

Darn. I would have liked to ask him if he thinks Jennifer is capable of killing her father. I suspect I know what he would have said.

Chapter Nineteen

ON HER WAY HOME, Shannon considered her next step. *I did think I'd talk to Kal, but what's the point? I don't know who this man is, so no further ahead.*

There's only one way to tackle this. She thought about the day of her motorcycle ride. *I was so afraid, but Piet convinced me to face my fears, so get on with it, Shannon Coyne. As long as I remember to be sensible and not take foolish risks.* She made up her mind. *That's it. I have to talk to Jennifer Walker directly.*

When she got home, she found Jennifer's phone number in the file for the Pengelly Landing house. She took a deep breath. *All right, then. Here we go.*

The call went straight to voicemail, so Shannon left a message. "Hi, Jennifer. This is Shannon Coyne. Can you please call me back when you get a chance?"

Leaving her phone number, she wondered whether she'd hear from Jenn. *She might think it's about the house sale and won't want anything to go awry with that, so she'll call.*

❖

Shannon had all but given up any expectations of hearing from Jennifer when her phone rang at eight-thirty that evening. It was an unknown number, and she knew it might simply be a spam call, but she answered.

"Hello? Shannon speaking."

"This is Jennifer Jones. You left a message for me."

Her heart thudded, and Shannon took a deep breath to steady her voice. "Thank you for returning my call."

"I can't imagine what it's about. The house sale is a done deal, right?"

"That's right. It's about your mother."

She heard the chill in Jennifer's voice. "What about her?"

"Jennifer, I know you care about your mother, and I'd appreciate meeting with you to discuss what she's going through right now."

"What's it to you?"

"I have such fond memories of both your parents, and if there's anything I can do for your mum, I'd like to help."

"I don't know what you think you can do."

"Please. Let me buy you a coffee. Just give me half an hour of your time to feel I've done something."

Jennifer sighed loudly. "Oh, for God's sake. Fine. Now?"

Shannon raised her eyebrows and glanced at the French doors with its reflection of herself dressed in her pink and green pyjamas. "If that works for you, sure. Do you want to meet at a coffee shop? There's a Tim Hortons on Peter Street."

"All right. I'll see you there at nine o'clock."

After she hung up, Shannon considered letting Piet know what she was up to, but knew he was at work. *It'll be fine. He'll be proud of me.*

❖

The popular coffee shop was busy between the takeout customers and the dine-in patrons. Shannon had to settle for a parking spot beside the drive-through lane. Several cars waited to pick up their orders at the window. Just as she locked her car and began navigating through the busy lot to the front door, her phone rang. She pulled it from her pocket and paused as she squinted in the last sunlight to identify the caller. Those few seconds of distraction were enough. She looked up when a woman screamed: "Look out!"

A small, dark car hurtled toward her, and Shannon tensed to jump back, but it was too late and the jump too short. She was struck, spun around, and flung to the pavement. Her last thought was for the woman who kept screaming until she realized the sound was coming from her, herself, and then the world went dark.

Chapter Twenty

SHANNON HEARD VOICES AT a distance. *A tunnel. Why am I in a tunnel?* She tried to focus on what the voices were saying, but the effort made her head throb, and she allowed herself to drift away again.

The next time she swam her way to consciousness, she lay for a few moments and inhaled the scent of her mother. Mary Coyne was always surrounded by a faint cloud of her unique blend of Obsession perfume and cooked apples. When she opened her eyes, Shannon met her mother's worried gaze.

"Mammy."

"Ach. Here you are, now. Let me just ring for the nurse." She pressed the button clipped to her daughter's bed.

"What happened?"

"You were hit by a car. Do you not remember?"

Shannon frowned. "I don't know. It's all fuzzy."

A nurse bustled in and checked a monitor by Shannon's bedside. "Welcome back. Don't stress yourself now. You're on painkillers, and you've had a concussion. Let your memories come back to you naturally. You're doing fine, though." She nodded and left them.

Her mother touched Shannon's arm. "I'm just going to run outside to call Daddy. I'm not supposed to use my phone here."

"Tell him I'm fine, Mammy."

Shannon lay there, and the sounds of the hospital faded as she focused on the last thing she remembered. *I was at Tim Hortons. Why? Wait. I was meeting someone. Who?* She sighed, the memories confused.

Instead, she tried to move, doing an inventory of her body. *Legs? Moving. Arms? Moving. Head? Achy.* Hearing her mother's voice in the hall, she turned to watch the door. Following on her mother's heels, Piet came in, his forehead deeply furrowed.

He came close and bent down to kiss the top of her head, but pulled away again as if afraid to hurt her. "You've given us all a scare."

Her mother moved a second chair beside the bed so they could both sit down.

Piet folded his long legs, wrapping one around the other in the position he always adopted when stressed.

Shannon reached out her hand with its taped wires and tubes. "Don't look so worried. I'm OK."

He laid his hand on top of hers. "Are you? You've had a concussion and the scrapes and bruises. You look a mess, I'm afraid."

"Do I? I don't feel too bad."

"What in the world were you doing at that time of night? You always make your own chamomile tea before bed. You don't go and pick up a coffee."

"I don't know. I think I was supposed to meet someone."

"A client? Not Emma. I talked to her."

Shannon bit her lip. "I don't think it was a client. There must be something on my phone. A text? An email? Where is my phone?"

Piet shook his head. "Smashed beyond hope, I'm afraid."

"Oh no. It has everything on it." Suddenly, Shannon had a bigger worry. "Dusty! Is she OK? She must need out by now. How long have I been here?"

"Dusty's fine. You've been here overnight, and your mum called me as soon as she heard from the police last night, so Dusty hasn't been alone since. She and Caesar are keeping each other company, and you know he forgives her for being a dog and happily curls up against her."

"Thank you. What happened to me?"

Piet deferred to Mary Coyne, who brushed the hair from her daughter's forehead. "It sounds like you walked out in front of a car that went too fast, leaving the drive-through at Tim Hortons. A witness said you were looking at your phone and didn't watch where you were going, but another witness said it appeared that the car drove straight at you. This woman screamed, and you tried to jump out of the way. It would have been much worse if you hadn't done that."

Shannon felt her mother shudder. "I'm sorry to make you worry, Mammy. I can't believe I'd be so careless. It's behind us now."

The doctor came in and stopped at the end of Shannon's bed. She tapped on her tablet to look at Shannon's medical records.

Piet raised his eyebrows. "Should I go and wait in the hall?"

"No need. Everything is looking good." The tall woman tilted her chin down to peer over her glasses at Shannon. "How do you feel, young lady?"

"Not too bad. I have a headache, my ribs hurt and I feel groggy. I wish I could remember what happened."

"It will probably come back to you. Some details might not, but considering what you've been through, that's a small price to pay."

Shannon sighed. "I suppose so."

"You have two cracked ribs, and a badly sprained wrist. If we can be sure someone will be with you, we'll keep you in for a few more hours and then release you." She looked at Mary. "Why don't you give her some quiet time and return later? You should be able to take her home after lunch."

Mary squeezed her daughter's hand. "Thank you, Doctor."

After the doctor left, Mary nudged Piet, and they both rose. "I'll be back later, sweetheart. Daddy thinks we should take you to ours."

Shannon's head pounded. "Maybe. With Dusty."

"Of course. I'll go with Piet now to pick up a few things for her and you."

"Thank you, Mammy."

Shannon reached for Piet's hand. "Can you find out where my phone is? Maybe someone can fix it."

"Your mum already has it. You can't fix it, but you might be able to reuse the SIM card."

"Thanks, Piet."

"I'll check on you later. Just rest up and don't worry about anything. I'll call Emma so she can let them know what's happening at work." He glanced at her pale face. "And I'll get a nurse to come in and give you something for the pain."

She closed her eyes, too exhausted to give her friend the smile he deserved.

🔥

Shannon felt surprisingly refreshed when the nurse woke her an hour later. "Shannon. Shannon, wake up. How are you feeling?"

Blinking, Shannon smiled at the nurse. "I don't know what you gave me earlier, but it's helped my headache."

"I'm glad. Everything looks good, so you'll be released when your mother comes back. Meanwhile, you have a friend waiting in the hall. Are you up to seeing her?"

Shannon nodded and immediately regretted it. "Sure." Expecting Emma to walk in, she gasped when she saw who slinked into the room. "Good Lord. Jennifer. You're the last person I expected to see."

Jennifer looped a strand of too-dark hair behind her ear and gazed down at Shannon. Her thin hair against her white skin gave her the appearance of a television vampire. "I'm sorry."

Shannon struggled to sit up in bed. She wondered if she should press the call button. *Am I safe?* "What are you sorry about?"

Jennifer nodded at Shannon as if no further explanation was necessary. "This. You."

Her eyes widened. "Did you hit me with your car?"

Jennifer stepped back as though struck. "God, no! I feel bad that I didn't meet up with you. You wouldn't be here if we hadn't planned to meet."

Shannon relaxed against the cushions, propping her up. "I was meeting you."

Jennifer frowned. "Yes. Don't you remember?"

"No. I knew I was meeting someone but didn't remember who." Shannon added, seeing the shadow cross Jennifer's face as if regretting her decision to visit the hospital, "I don't have my phone with me, so of course, as soon as I check that, I will have been reminded."

Jennifer nodded. "I did text you to let you know, but truthfully, I knew you'd already be on your way. That's why I'm sorry."

"Ahh. So, you didn't go there at all?"

"No. I was with my mother, and I knew I didn't want to go anywhere other than home when I left there."

Shannon's head was throbbing again. "What time were you with your mother?"

"Until nine-thirty."

You can be sure I'll check that. Or maybe the police will. "OK." Shannon frowned as images from last night started to come back to her. "A text. I remember getting a text. I tried to look at it as I walked from my car. That must have been from you. It's why I wasn't paying attention, and a car hit me."

Jennifer pulled a chair towards her and sagged into it. "Oh, God. I really am sorry." She scowled at Shannon. "I don't like you much, and I can see on your face you don't like me either. Still, I would never deliberately want to see you hurt."

Shannon tilted her head. "Why don't you like me?"

Jennifer closed her eyes for an instant before glancing at Shannon and then turning away to gaze out the window. "When I first met you at the seniors' place, it was obvious that my father had bamboozled you." She turned back to pin her gaze on Shannon. "What you didn't know, and I wasn't about to explain to a complete stranger, was that I needed money to pay my rent. My mother said I had to ask my father, and I had. For a week, he kept stalling me. It was a power thing with him, so I was desperate that day I came to find him. And I was angry. The landlord threatened to put my stuff out on the front lawn if I didn't come up with the money."

Shannon felt queasy. "Your father told me you'd have to wait until he was finished."

"Of course he did. I knew that, but I wasn't in any state to be patient."

"Your dad always seemed so kind. The way he looked after your mum was so caring. He made sure she didn't overdo things or didn't get stressed by any of the residents."

Jenn snorted. "My father was a misogynist. It was all about control. He was *not* nice to my mother, and he was worse to me because I didn't stand for it. As a teenager, I'd challenge him on things he'd say or do. So, he was happy when I needed to go to him to beg for money. He said as much to me. I'd lost my job, and yes, in hindsight, no doubt I was partly to blame, but he had the chance to insult and berate me, and because I needed help, I couldn't say anything in my own defence."

"If what you're saying is true, I'm sorry for what you went through."

"Oh, it's all true. When I was around thirteen, I thought my mother would stand up for me, but that never happened. She didn't stand up for herself. How could she defend me?"

"Was he…physical?"

Jenn shook her head. "Not like what you mean. He liked to scare us. He'd break things. I remember a little statue my mum had and loved. One day, he was angry with her for some reason, so he took that thing, dropped it on the kitchen floor, and stepped on it. Just deliberately dropped it, leaving my mother to sweep up the hundred little pieces."

Shannon put her hand to her mouth.

Jennifer shrugged. "Maybe now you can understand why I feel as I do. I know my duty and did my best to arrange the funeral to keep up the façade. I'll do what I can to help my mother through this, but the sooner that house is gone and the money available to start a new life, the happier I'll be."

Shannon licked her dry lips.

"I'm sorry. I made assumptions I had no right to make. I didn't like you and thought the worst of you."

Jenn tilted her head. "I didn't like you either." She smiled sheepishly. "I might as well admit I have anger issues. I did something concerning you I'm now sorry for."

Shannon raised her eyebrows. "Like write bad reviews?"

Her lanky hair fell forward when Jennifer nodded. "Sorry. I'll take them down."

"It sounds like life wasn't all bad. I met your cousin Chris the other day. He seemed genuinely fond of your father."

"Of course. My father was delighted to have a boy in the house. That was far better than a girl. Chris didn't go through any of the stuff my mother and I did."

"He must have witnessed it though?"

"I think Chris saw what he wanted to see. Maybe he was so damaged after losing his parents that he just kept his head down, and if someone showed him kindness, which my father did, he was happy."

Shannon nodded. "I can see that."

Jennifer stood up. "Well, I've said more than I ever meant to. I felt awful when I heard on the radio that a car had hit you when I knew you were only at the coffee shop because you expected to meet me, so I wanted to say sorry." She shook her head. "I don't even know why you wanted to meet me. Do you remember?"

Shannon nodded. "It's all come back to me while you were talking. I wanted to ask if you've been selling off your father's collections."

Jennifer flushed. "I met up with Nate Stevens and sold him the Rice Lake things. At the funeral, he told me my father promised to give it to him, and they met for lunch one day not long before Dad died, but my father raised the price, and they got into an argument over it. Nate said 'stuff it' or words to that effect, but at the funeral, he asked me what would happen to it. When he told me the story, I told him he could have it at the original price." She shrugged again. "I didn't tell Mom. She's already rewriting history and said Nate wasn't fair to my father when it was the other way around."

"What about the other things? The Scriven items?"

Jennifer tilted her head. "You are remarkably informed for a real estate agent. You must have had a great poke around the house."

Now, it was Shannon's turn to flush. "I noticed items were missing from the walls when we went back in after the first viewing."

Jennifer sighed. "Don't worry. I don't care who knows I'm selling off whatever I can. Mom doesn't want it. She's made that clear to me. To answer your question, I tried to sell the Scriven stuff to Nate, but he wasn't interested. He told me that at that last lunch, Dad mentioned some religious guy who was very interested in the stuff. He said it belonged to his group by rights. Nate asked some questions, but Dad made a joke about it and told him if he, Nate, didn't want it, that was fine because he'd get a lot more money out of this religious guy, anyway."

Shannon thought of the mysterious man with the full head of white hair. "Did you find that person?"

"No. I advertised it on Kijiji, and I got a response, but when I showed him the photos of the things, he said no thanks."

"So you took the items from the house and will continue to try to find a buyer for them," Shannon said it as a comment rather than a question until she saw the frown on Jennifer's face.

"I didn't take any of those Scriven things. I've got nowhere to keep it and figured I'd try again later."

Shannon frowned. "Someone's taken them."

Jenn shook her head. "Not me. Going into that house once was enough." She walked away but stopped to turn back when Shannon said her name.

"Jenn?"

"What?"

"Thank you for coming and telling me all this. I just have one last question."

"Go ahead."

"Do you think your mother might be guilty of killing your father?"

Chapter Twenty-One

HER HEAD WAS POUNDING by the time Jennifer Walker-Jones left. *I was so wrong about her. What else am I wrong about?* She had to talk to someone.

"Hi, Piet. Are you OK to talk for a few minutes?"

"Let me just turn the water off. I'm cleaning the preparation room."

Shannon listened to Piet walk, his rubber boots squeaking on the tile floor. The sound of running water stopped.

"OK. How are you? Has the doctor released you?"

"Not yet. My head's throbbing, but never mind that."

His voice was worried. "If it's that bad, you need to tell the nurse. That can't be a good sign. Maybe you should stay another night."

"Piet, listen. Mammy will be here any minute, and I want to talk to you first."

"What is it? Now you're really worrying me."

"Jennifer was here."

"As in Violet's daughter?"

"That's the one."

His voice went up an octave. "What was she doing there? Oh, my God. Did she threaten you?"

"No. Quite the opposite." Shannon summarized the visit and conversation between Jennifer and herself.

Piet was breathless. "You actually asked her if she thought her mother murdered her father? What did she say?"

"She hesitated. For a minute, I thought she'd say she knew her mother was guilty."

"But she didn't?"

"No. She said she believes her mother wanted him gone from her life, but she doesn't believe Violet has it in her to do anything so violent."

"Wow. That's a turn-up for the books."

"It is if it's all true."

"What do you think? Did she seem authentic?"

"She did. But some people are great actors."

"True. Listen to me now. You go and rest. Let your folks take care of you for a day or two. Let it sit and mull it all over; then you'll know what to do."

"Should I tell Mammy? She'll want me to tell Uncle Bob or Kal."

"I think you should sleep on it. Literally. Do nothing. Don't tell anyone else. Nothing's going to change or happen in the next day or so. Trust yourself, Shannon. I do. You have a great sense of people. Just let it stew for a bit."

Shannon heard her mother's footsteps in the hall. "Thanks, Piet. I needed that. Mammy's here. Gotta go."

"I'll call you later, or better yet, you can call me after five o'clock. I don't want to disturb you if you might be sleeping."

"Thanks, Piet. Get back to work."

❦

Shannon's parents came to take her home. Together, they talked enough to mask her silence. When they got to the old farmhouse in Colborne, her mother hustled Shannon to her old bedroom, where the freshly made bed waited. Over her protest that she was perfectly content stretched out on the sofa, her mother firmly steered her into bed with a promise of a cup of hot chocolate. As Shannon settled into her old room with Dusty curled up on the end of the bed, she was glad she had come. *I can think in peace here. I'll have the hot chocolate, and then I'll plan out what comes next.*

The steaming hot chocolate topped with whipped cream made her sleepier than she expected. *I'll just close my eyes for a few minutes.*

Shannon felt disoriented when she woke up an hour later to hear her father climbing the stairs to her room.

She blinked up at him. "Don't look so worried, Da. I'm fine."

"Mammy told me to come wake you."

Shannon sat up. "She did right, and now I'm getting up, and coming downstairs. I smell supper cooking."

"Are you sure? Mammy said she'd bring up a tray for you."

"Good Lord, no. Off you go."

"Shall I take Dusty out?"

"Lovely. Thanks, Da. You're so practical."

Her father smiled, happy to be of some use. He pulled a treat from his pocket and waved it at the dog. "Come on, pup. Let's let your mammy get up."

The three of them sat down to supper in the kitchen. Her mother spooned out thick potato and bacon soup. "Your sisters wanted to come, but Meghan already had something planned, and I told Bernie not to come. I thought you could do with the quiet."

"You're right, Mammy. This is perfect."

She went on then. "But your Uncle Bob is coming over for a short visit later."

"Oh?"

"He promises not to overdo it, but I gather he wants to talk about the accident."

Shannon swallowed. "Of course. I'm grateful he's coming. It

saves me a trip to the station. I knew I'd have to put in some sort of report."

One bowl of the hearty soup was plenty for Shannon. Her stomach fluttered with nerves at the thought of explaining to her uncle what she'd been up to. *What do I tell him? He'll hit the roof if he knows I've been asking questions. Calm and collected is the answer. Don't get too deep into things.*

Curled on the sofa under a soft pink throw, she was relaxed an hour later when Police Detective Sergeant Bob Miller arrived. Her mother made a fresh pot of tea and made to sit down with them until her father shook his head. "Leave them to it, Mary."

Reluctantly, her mother left, but Shannon knew she'd hover in the doorway, following every word.

His Belfast accent sounded like Uncle Bob had just arrived from Andersontown a month ago. Despite the white swath of bandage, he patted the top of her head as if she were a puppy rather than his niece. "Bout ye?'

Shannon smiled to imagine him using the classic Belfast way of saying 'How are you?' to anyone unfamiliar with the slang. "I'm OK. A wee bit sore."

"Aye. Before I forget, Detective Khan asked me to pass on his well wishes for a speedy recovery." He poured tea for each of them without asking, then sat across from her and pierced her with his gaze. His voice took on his usual professional tone. "Tell me, so. What happened?"

"I don't know, really. My attention was on my phone because a text came in, and the next thing I knew, a car came speeding towards me. I tried to get out of the way but wasn't fast enough."

"That doesn't sound like you. You usually pay more attention. What were you doing there? Your mammy tells me you hardly go out to get coffee at that time of night, so why that night?"

She sighed. "I was supposed to meet someone, and they had to cancel. That's why the text."

He nodded. "Ah. A client?"

She glossed over the truth and nodded. "She's selling a house one of my clients is buying."

He narrowed his eyes. "The house up on Rice Lake?"

"The very one."

She heard him inhale and exhale, as if to keep control of his temper.

"Right. Not just any client, then."

Before he asked anything further, Shannon raised her eyebrows. "Have you found the driver who hit me?"

"Not yet, but we have a description of the car. The interesting thing about it is that witnesses say that it appears the car was parked until you started to walk across the lot. Of course, in every case, you have differing points of view from witnesses, but there was more than one person who said it looked like the driver intended to hit you. The fact the person drove off without stopping gives credibility to that version of events."

Shannon bit her bottom lip. "That doesn't make sense. Was I just at the wrong place at the wrong time? Maybe someone on drugs?"

"Anything's possible, but we need to consider you may have been a target. Who knew you'd be there?"

"No one. Other than the woman I was supposed to meet. And she was with her mother."

Uncle Bob's bushy eyebrows went up. "Would that be Violet Walker?"

She felt herself flush. "Yes."

"It's unlikely this is simply about real estate, then. Have you been involving yourself again in matters that don't concern you?"

"Not in a big way. Nothing to warrant someone wanting to run me over," she protested.

"How do you know that? What bears have you been poking, Shanny?"

"OK. I thought Jennifer may have been involved somehow in her father's death, but I don't think that anymore."

"Because the woman sent you a text saying she couldn't meet you? That doesn't make sense."

"No, not because of that." Shannon gave up and decided to tell him all she knew. "She came to see me at the hospital."

The gasp from the kitchen confirmed her suspicion that Mammy was listening in, but she continued anyway. "I suspected Jennifer too, but she told me things that changed my mind."

"Like what?"

"I had the wrong impression of who Malcolm Walker was."

"Oh? How so?"

Shannon told her uncle about what Jennifer had said.

Her uncle drained his cup of tea and set the mug down. He leaned back in his chair and studied his niece, folding his arms across his chest. "You know what this means, I suppose."

"Tell me."

"If Malcolm Walker was cruel to his wife, she had even more reason to want him dead." He ticked off her motives on his fingers. "One. She wanted to move to Florida and now has the money to do that, between his life insurance money and the sale of their house. Two. We have an eyewitness who saw Violet Walker walking with her husband along the shore early in the afternoon. And now, three. He was unkind to her."

Shannon focused on the eyewitness. "Someone saw them together in the afternoon. How is that possible? She was out for lunch, and surely the other women verified that?"

Her uncle frowned. "Kal is still following up on that. Someone is lying. Either the eyewitness or the three women who provided Violet with an alibi. The eyewitness is not a friend, so we feel she had no reason to lie. Whereas the other women are friends."

"Uncle Bob. I can't believe three women would all be prepared to lie to the police about something so serious, no matter how good their friendship is."

"As I said, Detective Khan is pursuing these witness statements."

Her head was throbbing again. "I understand. Is there anything more you need from me about the accident?"

"Not for now. You look done in. I don't like repeating myself, Shannon Coyne, but you need to stay out of the investigation. You're putting yourself in danger."

Right on cue, her parents came into the room. Her father held the bottle of Jameson whiskey and two glasses, and her mother put her arm around Shannon's shoulders. "Come upstairs and into bed."

She bent over to kiss her uncle on the cheek. "Thank you for coming here to see me. Will you let me know if you find anything out about the accident?"

His voice was gruff. "Of course."

Shannon wasn't sure if he was gruff with annoyance that she'd been involving herself in the case or emotion over his concern about her. She didn't ask him.

Chapter Twenty-Two

OVER HER PARENTS' PROTESTATIONS, Shannon insisted on going home again the next day. She didn't say the words aloud, but her first thought upon waking had been, *"One night in this narrow bed of my youth is plenty."* Her ribs ached, although her head was much better. She kept forgetting about her sprained wrist until she used it and tried not to let her mother see her wince.

Her mother drove her and Dusty home and spent most of the trip giving advice. "Don't do too much. I brought a cooler full of frozen leftovers, so you don't need to cook for several days. Don't take Dusty for walks because if she pulls you, you'll aggravate your ribs and wrist. If your headache gets worse, call me, and I'll come to stay with you."

"Yes, Mammy. Thank you; I look forward to having the leftovers. No, Mammy, I'll just let Dusty out in the back garden where I don't need to leash her. Yes, Mammy. If my headache is bad, I'll call you, or maybe Piet."

Shannon was happy to be home, and her mother left after sharing a pot of tea.

Dusty curled up on her favourite wing chair by the door, looking up once to assure herself her mistress was nearby. Shannon stayed where her mother left her, stretched out on the couch, tucked under a soft blue fleece throw. A box containing a new phone on the coffee table nearby waited for her. Piet had called her parents' house yesterday to let her know he'd bought it for her and had the shop extricate the SIM card from her old, smashed phone and insert it into the new one.

As she opened the box to remove the new phone, she admired the updated version of her old ruined one. *God bless you, Piet. Where would I be without you?* She turned it on, saw it had enough charge to make a few calls and set to work.

"Hi, Emma. Yes, I'm fine. Well, OK, not quite fine, but there's nothing seriously wrong. I'll be back at work tomorrow. Meanwhile, I wonder if you feel like coming over later. I'll see if Piet's available, too. That's great. Sevenish? By the way, you know that whiteboard we used before Amanda went all high-tech with her digital screen mirroring technology? Can you bring it with you tonight? No one will miss it, I'm sure. Yes, this means I want to talk about the Walker thing. Thanks, Emma."

Her next call was to Piet. "Hi. Yes, I'm home again. I love the folks like crazy, but enough is enough. I'm obviously calling you from my new, and I admit, improved phone. Thank you so, so much for picking this up. Will you be home tonight, or do you have plans? Lovely. Emma's coming over around seven. I asked her to bring the old office whiteboard. Will you come too? I need to talk to you both."

Shannon plugged in the phone to charge and snuggled under the throw for a nap. Thoughts about Malcolm Walker, Violet, Jennifer, Chris, and mysterious men spun in her mind in a confused parade of images.

By seven o'clock, she had managed a bath in Epsom salts, eaten a reheated meal, wandered outside with Dusty and made a few notes on her computer. She was ready for the arrival of her friends.

Piet came down first, carrying a large bowl of freshly popped popcorn and a bottle of prosecco. "You probably shouldn't drink if you're on painkillers, but Emma and I can toast your safe return."

Shannon smiled. "The two of you are welcome to enjoy. I'll stick with my sparkling water. I will, however, enjoy some of your popcorn."

When Emma arrived a few moments later carrying the whiteboard, Shannon had Piet remove a print from the living room and hang the board up in its place. Piet stood back. "I think your knock on the head has impaired your decorating sense," he teased.

Emma removed four markers and set them on the coffee table beside the bowl of popcorn. She turned to Shannon. "I'm sure you should be resting."

"I've had enough resting. Piet will pour you some prosecco, and then we'll get started."

Emma sat on the couch beside Shannon. "That lump on your head looks sore. Shouldn't it be bandaged?"

"It was. I managed to get the bandage off in the bath and washed the wound, but, as per hospital instructions, put petroleum jelly on it, which is why it looks so gross. I'll put a new bandage on before I go to bed, but figured letting it air for a bit can't hurt."

Piet handed Emma her prosecco, and the three clinked their glasses together. "To friends."

Shannon rose and gestured to Piet to take her place on the sofa. "Here. You sit with Emma so you can both see the whiteboard."

Piet saluted with his left hand, since he held his drink in his right. "Yes, boss."

Before writing anything on the board, she smiled at her two friends. "I'm sure I don't need to tell you we're here to talk about the death of Malcolm Walker."

Piet folded his long legs. "Do you believe his death and your accident are connected?"

"I'm not sure, but I'm not discounting it. I believe the person would have stopped if it had been a simple accident. They had to know they had hit someone. We're Canadians, for goodness' sake. People don't drive away after injuring a person."

Emma nodded. "Especially not here in Port Hope."

Piet shrugged. "People are people everywhere. Maybe it was someone without a driver's licence, or they'd had too much to drink."

Emma bit her lip. "That's true. Maybe."

Shannon nodded. "Let's set the accident aside for the moment. She picked up a marker and began to make notes on the board. *Malcolm Walker. Misogynist?*

Emma frowned. "What? Where did that come from?"

Shannon stopped writing. "Oh. I forgot. You don't know about Jennifer visiting me." She sat down across from Emma and took a few minutes to bring her up to date with what she had been told.

Emma gulped her drink. "Wow. I didn't see that coming."

Piet nodded. "I know. The question I have is, can we trust her? "

Shannon nodded. "I agree. I'm not entirely convinced, either. She sure seemed authentic, though, and it explains a lot about her behaviour, going back to all those years ago when I had the run-in with her at the seniors' centre."

Emma shrugged. "We'll keep an open mind, then."

By the time they finished adding notes and questions, they had written comments beside the names of several people, including Violet. Emma had picked up a pen and added comments beside the widow's name. *Eyewitness? Abused by husband? Life Insurance. Wants to live in Florida.* The other names were Jennifer, Chris, Nate, Religious Man, and Other. Piet argued that if Jennifer was telling the truth, there might have been someone else who disliked Malcolm enough to want to be rid of him. Shannon added the person to humour her friend, but they couldn't develop any specific motive for the 'Other.' Beside each name, they showed motives:

Jennifer: money, hatred

> *Chris: jealousy over Jennifer (inheritance?)*
> *Nate: money/collectibles*
> *Religious Man: collectibles/argument*
> *Other: ? argument?*

Shannon refilled her glass with sparkling water while Piet topped up his glass and gave Emma, who was driving, a half glass more prosecco. They studied the board in silence.

Shannon shook her head. "I say we take out Other. It's impossible to figure out the motive and means. How would someone get Mal out to the lake?"

Emma agreed. "We have enough people to think about without someone completely unknown."

Piet shrugged. "OK, OK. Take it off again."

Shannon erased *Other* and then started at the top again beside Violet. "For means. I suppose she might have given Mal some drugs to make him groggy and confused and then took him for a walk. They have a dock. Maybe it was enough. She walked him down to the end of the dock and shoved him into the water." It gave Shannon the shivers to even contemplate it.

Emma tilted her head. "It was broad daylight, though. And you have three people saying she was at lunch with them for that time period, right?"

Biting her lip, Shannon thought about what she'd heard. "She stopped on her way back home for a few minutes. No one saw her. She said she felt sleepy or something like that, so she pulled over. It does throw the timing off. One thing, though: If we go with the dock scenario, how did Mal's coat end up floating around?"

Piet nodded. "That sounds like a forensics question. Maybe your friend Kal knows. Could his coat have come off if he didn't have it all buttoned up properly?"

Shannon nodded. "I may ask him. For now, let's keep going."

Piet stood up. "Let me keep going. You go sit down. You're looking pale."

She didn't argue and handed over her blue marker.

Piet pushed his glasses further up his nose. "Jennifer. What can we say about her? We know she wasn't where she told the police she was when her father went missing." He wrote: *time discrepancy/ no alibi.*

Emma took a handful of popcorn, but before eating any, she asked Shannon, "Would people notice her there? She was the Walkers' daughter. Could she have gone for a walk with her father, and no one noticed?"

"Maybe, but it sounds like she rarely went up there anymore, so probably the opposite was true. What if she called him and invited him to go for a drive? She could stop the car at the house, and then out he'd come. There are a few places they might stop and go for a walk where no one knew them."

Piet tilted his head. "How likely is that, though? If they didn't get along, would he really go out to meet her to go for a drive?"

Shannon frowned. "Maybe. If she said she wanted to make things up, and she wanted to take him somewhere neutral?"

Piet wasn't convinced. "And the drugs?"

"She slips something into a drink they buy while they're out and about?"

"Hmm. It's possible, but so many people might have seen them, don't you think?"

"Not necessarily. Not if they go somewhere they aren't known. Who notices two people out for an afternoon walk? She'd only do the deed if she were sure no one was around."

Emma nodded. "That's true. It's bold but not impossible."

Piet wrote: *She takes him for a drive to get away from the area. Slips something into drink.*

He turned back. "OK. Chris. He was at home when Mal died. Do we assume the police checked his alibi?"

Emma took a small sip, making her drink last. "I think we have to assume that, but maybe it was also a bit off. So, let's imagine he knows Violet's going out for lunch and zips down to his uncle. It's only what, half an hour?"

Shannon shook her head. "Less if you speed."

Piet hesitates at the whiteboard, not knowing what to write. "If he shows up, someone was bound to see him, wouldn't they? His car? Him, walking with his uncle? And again, did he push him off the dock? How did he drug him?"

Emma turned to Shannon. "You met him, right? What did you think?"

"I didn't talk to him for long. He's clearly very fond of Violet, but it sounds like he was even closer to Mal."

Emma raised her eyebrows. "Maybe he didn't like how his uncle treated his aunt?"

"I don't know. Why now? I can imagine him having that sort of reaction when he lived with them. From what Jenn said, it sounds like Chris did what he could to get along with everyone. I don't know why that would change now that he's out living alone, with a good career and life of his own."

Emma shook her head. "Like we said. Maybe he needed money for his business or his house. Whatever. He's in debt, and maybe he asked his uncle for a loan, and he gives Chris the same runaround that he did to Jennifer all those years ago."

Shannon nodded. "Could be, all right."

Next to Chris' name, Piet wrote: *Familiar with house. Easy to get uncle to go with him.*

Nate Stevens came next. Piet thought he was a definite possibility. "When I spoke with him at the funeral, this guy was pretty bitter."

Shannon nodded. "He knows where the house is. He lives on the lake himself these days." She widened her eyes. "Maybe he's even got a boat, and invited Malcolm to go for a ride. He has a thermos and gives him something to drink with drugs in it. When Mal's groggy, he pushes him overboard."

Emma joined in. "Maybe the hot coffee, drugs, or whatever made Mal hot, and he takes his coat off."

The three looked at each other. Piet turned back to the board and wrote: *Boat? Access to drugs? Lives nearby.*

Last on the list was *Religious Man*

Emma brushed popcorn salt from her hands. "Will you guys please eat some of this? I'm making a pig of myself. So, do we know anything at all about this man? Is it a man? Maybe it's a woman?"

Shannon furrowed her brow. "No. I'm sure Jennifer said it's a man. Aside from that, here's what I know;" she ticked them off on her fingers. "He felt entitled to own the Scriven collection for some reason. He was very keen to get the things Mal had. Based on third-hand information from Jennifer, who had it from Nate, Mal and this man argued."

Piet waited, and when Shannon finished speaking, he raised his hand in question. "That may have motivated this man to attack Mal, but looking at the whole picture of motive, opportunity and means, we're on means now. Did he know where Mal lived? Even if he did, was he there? Wouldn't a stranger be noticed?"

Shannon sighed. "Right. We need to know more before we can decide that."

Piet put a question mark beside Religious Man and set the marker down on the ledge of the whiteboard. "And with that, I think we should call it a night. You need sleep, and we all can mull over what we've got here."

Emma nodded. "Piet's right. Let's leave it there. We can discuss it tomorrow, but it seems to me we should talk to Nate Stevens. I don't like taking anything Jennifer said on trust."

Piet nodded and wagged his finger at Shannon. "That does not mean you are allowed to go and meet with him on your own. He may be dangerous. Got it?"

Shannon nodded. "Got it, Uncle Piet."

He frowned sternly. "Remember it, or I'll be forced to call your real uncle."

She held up her hand. "Scout's honour."

After her two friends left and Dusty had been out for her last tour of the yard, Shannon added a few more notes to the whiteboard under a new heading: Questions for N.S.

Who is the Religious Man?/ What does Nate know about him?

Where exactly does NS live? Owns a boat?

Did he get everything he wanted from Jennifer?

Where was he the afternoon Mal died?

Should I ask Kal some of these questions? Maybe they already looked at Nate Stevens. She opened her laptop and created an email for Kal, but then hesitated. *Should I or should I not?*

Chapter Twenty-Three

SHANNON DECIDED AGAINST SENDING a note to Kal and went to bed instead. Afraid Detective Khan may feel compelled to let his boss know his niece was meddling made her think twice. In the morning, she rose without a headache and felt more able to think clearly. She planned to do some work, but first, she followed her initial instinct and sent Kal an email note. *I trust him.*

Hi Kal,

Just wanted to let you know I'm feeling quite well again. Not perfect, but better than I was. The headache is gone, and I can breathe better. I'm on over-the-counter pain meds, and that's enough to manage.

My friends Piet and Emma visited last night, and Mal and Violet Walker naturally came up in conversation. Piet mentioned he had spoken with Nate Stevens (Mal's former business partner) at Mal's funeral. I'm sure I'm not supposed to ask this, but I know I can trust you not to mention my curiosity to Uncle Bob. Did you folks look at Stevens? It sounds like

Nate held a grudge against Mal for some business issues. I know he lives on Rice Lake as well.

That's it. Enquiring minds want to know!

Best regards
Shannon

After she pushed *send*, she dedicated herself to catching up on her email correspondence. She sent a note to her boss, Amanda Carter and offered to come to the office, but the response was almost instantaneous.

Stay home. Do what you can, but don't overdo things. Come in on Monday rested and ready to take on a new client. Amanda

She sent a few notes, including one to Rod, to ensure the Walker house would be ready on Monday for the Sullivans, and made a note to herself to pick up the housewarming gift she gave all her clients on closing. It was a handmade charcuterie board with the family name and address of the new home burned into it. The craftsman who made these beautiful pieces had left a message two days ago to let her know it was ready for pickup. Shannon felt she was returning to normal for the first time in days.

She'd been so busy with work that it was almost a surprise when she received a note back from Kal.

Hello Shannon,

I'm very glad to hear you are improving. I am less glad to think you are still concerned about the Walker case, but I can let you know that we did look at Mr. Stevens as part of our enquiries. At the conclusion of our interview with him, we did not have any unanswered questions.

Continue to rest, and we will speak soon.

Regards

Kal Khan

Shannon sighed. *Oh, Kal. You are a master at not revealing much. I'm forced to ask more, but maybe you're right. Time for a visit, my friend, since you aren't so cautious when we're talking.*

Thank you! I'm feeling a bit of cabin fever. How about dropping by for a cup of tea?

S

Hello again. I should be finished by five o'clock. Shall I drop by after that?

Kal

Perfect! See you later.

Shannon

After a bowl of soup and a short stroll around the garden with Dusty in the warm sunshine, Shannon realized she was more tired and achy than expected. *I'll lie down on the couch for an hour.* She took two ibuprofen and stretched out.

❦

Dusty's barking woke her. She sat up, confused and disoriented. "What is it, Dusty? Quiet."

Shannon heard the knocking and stumbled to her feet. She tried to smooth her hair as she crossed the small foyer to open the front door. "Oh, goodness. What time is it?"

Kal Khan stepped back as if to give Shannon space. "It's five-twenty-five."

"Oh, Lord. I slept all afternoon. I can't believe it. Come in, come in."

Kal folded his arms. He looked impeccable in a light grey suit and white shirt. "Perhaps it's not a convenient time for a visit. I can come another day."

"Oh, no, please do come in. I'm sorry I'm so frazzled. I never sleep like this in the afternoon, and it takes me a minute to… find myself."

He nodded solemnly and followed her into her flat. "You need the rest. You were right to sleep."

Shannon gestured to the sofa. "Please sit. Let me splash some water on my face, and I'll be right back to get that tea going."

When she returned, she was horrified to see Kal standing in front of her whiteboard. "Oh, no."

He turned to look at her. "You are getting more sophisticated. Last time, I believe you had sticky notes on your window to track your investigation."

Shannon flushed. "You've caught me again. I meant to take that down before you got here. Since you've seen it, there's no use in pretending it doesn't exist. Let me put the kettle on unless you'd prefer a cold drink?"

He smiled. "Tea sounds perfect."

"Green or black?"

"Whatever you're having."

"I think I need black tea. I have a nice Assam."

"That sounds good." He followed her to the kitchen. "Don't make food. You are supposed to be resting."

"I have to admit I'm a bit hungry. How about a no-work meal? Mammy sent me home with a pile of food all cooked and ready to be put in the microwave, and she always packs enough for two in each container." Without waiting for a response, she opened the freezer. "Lasagna. Would you eat that?"

He grinned. "Who doesn't eat lasagna?"

She nodded. "It's Italian food with an Irish twist. Instead of pasta, she uses sliced potatoes."

Kal raised his eyebrows. "I'm sure it's delicious."

Shannon put the dish into the microwave to heat, made two cups of tea and then led the way back to the living room. They stood sipping the tea as she took him through what the three friends had written the evening before.

Kal nodded. "You want me to tell you more about the interview with Nate Stevens."

"Will you?"

"It seems a conflict of interest."

She didn't try to persuade him, but let him consider her request for information in silence.

He picked up the red marker from the ledge of the whiteboard. As a response to the question *Owns a boat?* Kal wrote 'yes.'

※

The potato lasagna was hot, the cheese bubbling and aromatic. Kal added several notes to the board, and then they sat down to eat.

Shannon poured sparkling water for both of them, and she led him into a conversation about his motorcycle and plans for the summer. *I don't want him to think I only care about using him for information.*

Kal's eyes sparkled behind his dark-framed glasses when he spoke about his plans. "I'll take the bike and go to Ottawa. I was there as a child, but not since then. The city will be my final destination, but I will camp at Bon Echo Park and then at Fitzroy Provincial Park."

"Oh, it sounds like an amazing trip. How long will you be gone?"

"Two nights in Bon Echo and then three in Fitzroy, and on the way home, I plan to stay two nights in Silent Lake Provincial Park before returning to Port Hope. A total of seven nights away. I have the campgrounds reserved."

"Do you? What if the weather is bad?"

He grinned. "I have a rain suit and a good tent."

"Aren't you nervous about travelling alone like that? Just you and the bike?"

"Not at all. I'm looking forward to it."

She shook her head. "You seem so fearless to me. I'm in awe."

Kal frowned. "Don't be. When I first learned to ride a motorbike,

I was uneasy, but it seemed like an extension of riding my bicycle, and with practice, I became confident. Now, I know the feeling of each turn or road condition I encounter and manage them without thinking much about it."

Shannon nodded. "That makes sense. So, if going off on a road trip on that big bike doesn't make you afraid, what does?"

He smiled. "This."

"This? What does that mean? Eating my mother's potato lasagna?"

"No. That was the easy part. Socializing. I'm not good at it, and I know I can be awkward. It's how I've always been. My best friend in school was like me, except he was the only Jew in the class. He liked to play chess and study computers. I enjoyed those things, too. We didn't play sports. We didn't like school dances. And, of course, because he was Jewish and I'm Muslim, that made us an odd pair, and we tended to spend our time with each other and no one else. My grandmother encouraged me to make more friends, and there was talk about sending me to some youth group, but my father and my friend's father agreed to let us go to Kumon together after school instead. We both excelled in math, but it didn't help us with social skills."

Shannon laughed. "You're doing just fine as far as I can see. Are you still in touch with that school friend?"

"I am, but he lives in Waterloo, so we rarely see each other in person."

"Canada's Silicon Valley. Is he working in tech?"

"Yes. He has a good job."

"You didn't choose a career in computers."

"No. Somehow, a career with the police appealed to me more."

"Well, that's lucky for us." She stood and cleared away the dishes.

"I should be going. Thank you for supper. I enjoyed the visit very much."

"Thank you for coming." She followed him towards the door

and waved at the whiteboard in passing. "And for answering some of my questions."

At the door, he turned to her. "You are the brave one. I've seen it over and over again. You act despite your fears. Whether it's taking a ride on a motorcycle or confronting someone in the pursuit of what you believe is right, that's true courage. I'm helping you because I hope I can keep you from acting in a way that will lead you into danger." With that, he walked out into the darkening evening.

Chapter Twenty-Four

BY THE TIME KAL left on Friday evening, it was too late for the three friends to get together, and Piet had plans to meet Connor, so they decided to meet for brunch the next morning.

Shannon promised them omelettes in exchange for an hour of their time. "You both have lots to do on Saturdays, but it'll be worth it."

Piet's voice on the three-way call sounded hesitant. "Not too early, though, right?"

"How does eleven o'clock work for you both?"

Once they had agreed on the time, Shannon relaxed on the sofa, looking at the new bullet points. *Nate Stevens has a boat, but he has an alibi that Kal assures me is water-tight. A two-day antiquities conference in Gananoque where several people agreed Stevens attended.* She sighed, and Dusty crept from the foot end of the sofa to curl up on Shannon's lap. "I guess a room full of people isn't going to lie for him, so I have to take him off the list. He has a boat, though, Dusty. And he lives closer to Pengelly Landing than I thought. Hall

Landing is just down the road, only about a five minute drive." She shook her head as if her dog had been arguing with her. "No. Kal tells me they've validated his alibi. I'll take him off the list."

Shannon chewed her lip. "The good thing about removing him as a suspect is that I can now ask him questions." She stroked her dog's ears. "Every cloud has a silver lining, right?"

❧

Shannon went out to the grocery store early Saturday morning. She bought the ingredients to make a variety of omelettes. Old cheddar cheese, goat cheese, mushrooms, prosciutto, and fresh spinach went into her basket. She bought a bag of oranges to squeeze for fresh orange juice and two kinds of bread for toasting.

Before she started her prep work, she took Dusty for a walk, stopping to talk to a neighbour. "Your garden is always so spectacular, Mr. Byrne. Now I understand why. You put so much work into it."

He straightened his tall, lanky frame and stretched. "It's a labour of love. We'll have the place open again for the annual house tour, so we like to have it look good." He peered at her. "You look like you've been through the wars. What happened?"

"It looks worse than it is now. I was knocked down by a car a couple of days ago."

He widened his eyes. "Over at Tim Hortons?"

"That's it."

"Good Lord. I had no idea that was you. I heard it was deliberate."

"Really?" She frowned. "Where did you hear that?"

He shrugged. "Everyone's saying it. I heard it at the Timmy's when we had our morning coffee yesterday, but I heard someone else talking about it at the grocery store."

"My goodness."

"Is that wrong?"

"I'm not sure. The police haven't told me much about it. I know I was distracted and didn't watch where I was going, so I assumed it was my fault."

"Well, be careful. Either way, if you were hit because you didn't pay attention or someone is out to get you, you need to keep your wits about you. There are so many tourists around already. It wouldn't be someone from here, I'm sure."

Shannon smiled. "Thank you for the reminder, Mr. Byrne. We'll be careful, won't we, Dusty?"

※

Later, when Emma, Piet and Shannon sat down to their brunch, she told them what her neighbour had said.

Emma speared a piece of omelette, gooey with the two cheeses. "I knew it. You've rattled someone, Shannon."

"How is that possible? No one knew I would be there at that time."

Piet shook his head. "Your old nemesis, Jennifer certainly knew. And who knows who she told? Violet didn't go out because she was under house arrest, but Jennifer could have told anyone. Maybe she's in cahoots with someone else, so while she created an alibi for herself by visiting her mother, she could have had someone else try to take you out."

Shannon raised her eyebrows. "It all sounds very Mafia-like."

"That doesn't mean it's not true."

"I know, Piet. You're right. I haven't considered that she's got a partner. Still, I'm not convinced the accident wasn't just that, an accident."

They finished their food and took mugs of coffee into the living room to study the whiteboard.

Emma pointed to the new comments. "So, Nate Stevens is off the list. If he was away for two days when Malcolm died, he's in the clear. That's what Detective Khan is saying here, right?"

Shannon nodded. "Yes. He didn't know Mal and Nate argued, but he feels it's irrelevant."

Piet tapped on Jennifer's name. "What did he think about your conversation with Jennifer?"

Shannon sighed. "Well, like Uncle Bob, he believes it makes an even more compelling case against Violet. If Mal were as cruel as Jennifer makes him out to be, Violet would have even more motivation to get rid of him."

Emma nodded. "But you still don't believe it, do you?"

"No. For one thing, she's not strong, and Mal was a tall, heavy man. But more than that, I can't believe she's like that."

Piet took his mug into the kitchen for a refill of coffee and called out, "If we put Jennifer aside for a moment, who else is there? Chris? This mysterious religious guy we know nothing about?"

Shannon tapped on the board. "I want to know more about this mystery guy. I'm going to talk to Nate Stevens."

Emma sighed. "I bet Detective Khan told you not to."

"He told me to leave it to them. He always tells me that, but they aren't pursuing this. They're so determined to build a case against Violet."

Piet sat on the sofa and propped his feet on the coffee table. "You plan to phone Stevens?"

"I plan to phone him and see if he'll meet with me."

Both Emma and Piet groaned.

"I'll meet him somewhere public. I promise."

Piet sighed. "I'll go with you."

"He knows you from the funeral home. I don't want to put you in an awkward position." She held up a hand before Emma volunteered. "I don't need anyone. I'll meet him at Beamish House. That's public enough."

Piet nodded. "Somewhere that Connor can keep an eye on you."

Emma raised her eyebrows. "Connor? Who's that?"

Shannon smiled as Piet talked about his new friend. The meeting of the Walker investigation was over.

※

Nate Stevens was reluctant to meet with Shannon. "Why? Who are you, exactly?"

"A friend of the Walkers. I spoke with Jennifer recently, and it sounds like Mal had some interesting collectibles concerning local history. I wanted to understand more about that, and believe you are something of an expert on local history."

She heard his voice thaw. "I do have a wide knowledge of local history. I suppose Jennifer Walker, or Jones as she's called now, told you I recently bought some items from her about the Rice Lake sea monster, but I also have quite a collection about the Rice Lake sunken railway."

"See? As a realtor, I enjoy having interesting facts at my fingertips when showing clients around these communities, and you're the man to inform me."

"And there's a lunch in it for me, is there?"

"Absolutely. How about the Beamish tomorrow? They do a lovely lunch."

"Yes, I know it. All right. How's one o'clock?"

"Perfect. Look for my long red hair."

"No doubt we'll find each other. I'll see you there."

Shannon texted Piet and Emma: *"I'm meeting Nate Stevens tomorrow at the Beamish at one. Stay tuned for a report after that."*

Piet responded moments later. *"Connor's working tomorrow. He'll keep an eye open."*

She grinned and spoke aloud to Dusty. "I'm not sure what Connor can do, but it's comforting to know someone's looking out for me. Now, let's pack up these empty containers and take them with us when we visit Mammy and Da."

※

Her parents fussed over her when Shannon arrived at their home. Shannon insisted she felt fine. "Only a little sore around the ribs, so no making me laugh, Da."

Her mother caressed her daughter's hand. "What about the wrist?"

Shannon nodded. "OK. That's a little sore, too. It's my own fault. I keep forgetting and it's only when I try to use it, I'm reminded."

Her mother took the empty plastic food containers into the kitchen. "I'll put the kettle on."

Her father steered Shannon into the living room. He glanced towards the kitchen to ensure his wife was busy before leaning over to speak quietly. "Your mam's been on the phone to her brother."

Automatically, Shannon leaned in to speak in the same quiet tone. "Uncle Bob? What about?"

"Your accident. Bob admits it seems suspicious. They haven't found the car responsible yet, but more than one person said it looked like it aimed to run you down. I'm only telling you because your mammy wants to keep you here."

She raised her eyebrows. "Move in?"

He shrugged.

They heard her coming with the tea tray, and he held his finger to his lips.

As soon as the three of them were seated with mugs of tea, and Dusty curled up on the lap of Shannon's father in the worn recliner, Shannon began to tell them of her upcoming lunch with a local historian. She neglected to say he was connected to the Walker family but emphasized his local knowledge. "He's promised to tell me all about the sunken railway in Rice Lake."

Her mother frowned. "Do you not think you should take it easy a few more days?"

Shannon shook her head. "Good Lord, no. I'm going back to work on Monday, Mammy."

"Maybe just stay here for tonight, so?"

She laughed. "And miss my opportunity to chat with this man about local lore?"

"Sure, your da probably knows as much local history as anyone."

He shook his head. "I know many things, Mary, but nothing about the sunken railway in Rice Lake."

Her mother pressed her lips together grimly as if her husband had let her down.

Shannon smiled at her mother. "Mammy, you've been looking after me even when I'm home in Port Hope. All that food you sent with me is a godsend."

"I could feed you better right here at home." Mary Coyne protested.

"And I'm looking forward to the potato leek soup you promised me for an early supper, but then I'm going home again."

Her mother furrowed her forehead. "I didn't want to say, but your uncle Bob thinks you might be in danger."

Shannon nodded. "Well, it's good you've told me. Now, I'm aware, and I'll be extra cautious. I'll call Uncle Bob on Monday and ask him what he knows, right?"

"It's not enough." She turned to her husband. "Tell her, James. She should stay here."

He stroked Dusty as he spoke. "She's an adult, Mary. Of course, I worry, too. We have to have faith in her to be extra vigilant. Chances are that Bob's wrong. Just because you have an eyewitness say it looks like the accident was deliberate doesn't mean it was. He didn't say he knew for a fact it wasn't an accident, did he?"

Mary sniffed. "He wouldn't. He's a great one for being cagey."

"Well, then. We'll leave Shannon to make up her own mind." He turned to his daughter. "You know you're more than welcome to stay here."

"I know that, and I love you both for the care you give me, but I'll be going home after my soup."

Her mother rose. "I better get it heated, so. I want to be sure you get home in daylight."

※

For all Shannon's bravado, she was happy to get home in daylight and lock the doors behind her.

Chapter Twenty-Five

SHE RECOGNIZED NATE STEVENS from the photos she'd seen online. She waved at him when he hesitated at the door, blinking as his eyes adjusted after coming in from the bright sunlight. "Nate? Hi. I'm Shannon Coyne." She had already chatted with Connor and stifled a grin when she saw him lift his phone to take a photo of her with Stevens. She suspected he was sending it to Piet.

Nate Stevens shook her hand and sat down at the small round table. "Were you waiting long?"

"No, not at all. Long enough to glance at the menu. That's it." She slid it across the table. "Do you want to decide, and we order first?"

He raised one heavy white eyebrow. "Before you grill me with questions?"

She smiled. "I'm sure grill is too harsh a word. I have a keen interest, that's all."

The waitress came and took their orders: fish and chips with a glass of white wine for her and the Sunday special of prime rib roast with all the trimmings for him and a pint of Smithwick's to go with it.

When their drinks came, he took a deep sip and wiped his lips with the back of his hand. "OK. Fire away. I should tell you I spoke with Jennifer Jones this morning."

Shannon felt herself flush. "Fair enough. What did she tell you?"

"She claims you don't have a lot of interest in local history at all. She believes you are trying to prove her mother innocent in the death of Malcolm."

Shannon took a sip of wine and then lifted her chin. "Well, then. That saves time. Don't get me wrong; I *am* interested in the Rice Lake lore, but first, I'd like to know anything Mal may have told you about the religious person who wanted to buy the Scriven items."

Stevens leaned back in his chair and took another deep mouthful of his beer while he thought about her question. "I don't know much. He talked about it before we talked about the pieces I was interested in, so I didn't pay much attention. I remember he told me the man was very keen to get his hands on the Scriven collection because he wanted to make a point with someone. I didn't ask any questions, so I don't know what point he wanted to make."

Shannon waited, but Nate didn't add anything more. "That's all? You don't remember anything about where this man is from? Is he local or from somewhere else? Did Mal say what church he's affiliated with?"

"He must have been from within driving distance because they met once. The man went to see the collection in person. That's how Mal knew the guy was so keen. He made a joke about it. 'Keen as mustard,' he said. And then he laughed at his own joke and added, 'Mind, the brethren may not eat mustard.' You knew Mal, I gather? You'd know that no one enjoyed one of Mal's jokes like Mal did."

Shannon frowned. "I'm starting to realize I didn't know Mal as well as I thought. If you remember anything more, will you let me know?" She put one of her cards on the table by his glass.

He tucked the card into his shirt pocket and nodded. Then, the lunches arrived, and Nate opened his napkin with a flourish. "This looks delicious. I won't need to cook today."

As promised, Nate Stevens spent the rest of the lunch telling Shannon about the sunken railway in Rice Lake.

She finished eating before him. "You know so much about it. I've heard about it before, but mostly as something that people need to watch out for when they are boating. Is that true? Is it a hazard?"

"It can be. Some of it's marked, but not all of it. That's why Rice Lake is so interesting. There's a lot more to it than some people understand."

When the bill came, Nate made a half-hearted attempt to pick it up, but Shannon put her hand over his. "No. I said I'd take you out for lunch. This is mine."

He nodded. "I hope I've given you value for your money."

"You've given me lots to think about. I appreciate it."

As they waited for the waitress to get the credit card machine, Nate studied Shannon. "Are you an amateur investigator?"

"No, but I can't sit by and see a miscarriage of justice done."

"Did you think I killed Malcolm?"

She tilted her head. "Why would I think that?"

"You probably heard we weren't on the best terms. Especially when he promised me the Rice Lake collection and then tried to double the price. I wasn't pleased."

She nodded. "I know Violet didn't do it, so I've been looking at everyone in his circle."

He folded his arms across his chest and grinned as he considered her answer while Shannon took care of the bill.

When the waitress left them again, Shannon leaned forward to speak quietly. "You know how I feel, but I wonder what your thoughts are. Do you believe Violet did this?"

"Push Mal into the lake to drown him?"

"Yes."

"Not a chance."

"Why not?"

"He bullied her their entire marriage. She'd be too afraid of him to try anything like that. That's if you don't even consider how much bigger he was. If she did decide she'd had enough of him, she wouldn't take such a risk. He could have turned around and thrown her into the lake. No, she'd have to poison him or something, but I'm telling you, she's not capable."

"Thank you. That's what I think, too. What about the rest of the family?"

"Mal was understandably very proud of Chris. Despite losing his parents at a young age, Chris has grown up to be a solid citizen. He's a great architect. I love the design he did for the extension on my house." He laughed. "Jennifer, on the other hand…"

Shannon raised her eyebrows. "Is she capable?"

Nate Stevens shrugged. "I wouldn't want to get on the wrong side of her. She has a fierce temper, but I'm sure the police looked into her just as they did me. Jenn is abrasive and not my favourite person, but I understand why she is the way she is. She came good for me with the collection."

They stood and shook hands. He turned back to her before leaving. "Good luck. If I think of anything else, I'll shoot you an email. Violet and I didn't always get along. She claims I took advantage of Mal when we split up the business, but she only thinks that because it's what he said. She wasn't allowed to think anything else. I didn't blame her. I knew who Malcolm Walker was. He didn't respect women and assumed they needed him to do their thinking for them." He nodded a final time and left while Shannon went to the bar to speak with Connor.

The handsome bartender filled pint glasses with Guinness, tipping each glass at a 45-degree angle and filling the glass three-quarters full of the foamy dark brew. He looked at her as he waited for the two glasses to settle. "So?"

"That was worth the price of lunch."

"Grand."

The waitress ordered more drinks, and Shannon left him to his work with a smile and a wave.

※

Piet came downstairs moments after Shannon got home. She phoned Emma and put her on speakerphone. "OK, team. Here's what happened." She took them through her conversation with Nate, leaving out all the information about the sunken railroad.

Piet picked up a marker to update the whiteboard. "So, religious man sounds local, but what else do we know?"

Shannon opened her laptop. "I've been thinking about that joke Malcolm made."

Emma's voice was puzzled. "Keen as mustard? I've heard that before."

"It's what else he said about the brethren not eating mustard."

Emma was still puzzled. "I don't get it."

"The Brethren. That may refer to the church this man belongs to."

She typed in a few searches and then exclaimed, "Yes!"

Piet read over her shoulder. "Plymouth Brethren. You also found something called the Brethren Church. Why not them?"

"I'm trying to tie it to Scriven. I remembered reading something about when Scriven came from Ireland; he was a member of the Plymouth Brethren."

Emma's voice was sceptical. "Where do you go from here, though? You can't call up the pastor or whoever is in charge and say, 'Hey, we're looking for a man in your congregation who may have pushed Malcolm Walker in the lake to drown.'"

Shannon had her portfolio open and was jotting down some notes. "That's true, Emma. I think I'll start by finding a congregation around here. Then, I guess I'll have to figure it out from there, depending on how willing anyone is to talk to me."

Piet made a note on the board and then set the marker down. "It's a long shot."

Shannon nodded. "I know. Putting this brethren guy aside, I

forgot to tell you what Nate Stevens said before he left. I asked him if he thought Jennifer was capable of causing Mal's death. He didn't say no. He said Jenn has a fierce temper."

Emma agreed. "We know that already from your experiences with her. Did Detective Khan say why she isn't a suspect?"

"He wasn't convincing. He felt her alibi was solid; mostly, they didn't believe she had a motive. The house sale goes to Violet, so, in theory, Jenn has nothing to gain."

Piet frowned. "But she seems to have access to Violet's money. The house sale goes through on Monday, right?"

"Yes."

"What's to stop her from taking all that and disappearing?"

"Nothing, as far as I can tell. I felt sorry for her after I spoke with her, but you're right, Piet. Once she has her hands on the money, she could be out of here."

Emma asked a practical question. "But does she have access to that money? Just because Mrs. Walker assigned her to sign real estate documents on her behalf doesn't mean she can get into the bank account."

Shannon nodded. "That's true. Good point, Emma. I wonder how I can find that out without asking Violet outright."

Piet shrugged. "I can't see how unless you ask your pal, Kal. He might know."

"You're right. And by raising the question, I put the responsibility on the police to figure that out and prevent Jenn from getting away with Violet's money."

They parted for the evening, and Shannon decided she'd write a note to Kal right away. Tomorrow's schedule was packed with a day in the office and a visit to the Sullivans once she knew the house closing was successful.

Hi Kal,

Piet and I talked today, and he asked me a good question. I

didn't know the answer, so I'm throwing it over to you. Since Jennifer was given signing authority for the documents dealing with the sale of the house, does that mean she also has access when the lawyer disburses the money from the sale tomorrow?

I know the police looked at Jennifer Jones and eliminated her from your inquiry. I, too, feel more sympathetic to her since we spoke, but I'm still uneasy about what might happen when all that money is accessible.

Shannon

It was more than an hour later before she heard the ping notifying her of an email. She smiled to see it was from Kal.

I'm leaving Brampton now, so I won't have time to confirm tonight, but I will check first thing tomorrow morning. You are a kind person to worry about your friend Violet Walker in this way. I'll be in touch tomorrow.

Kal

Chapter Twenty-Six

THE MORNING MEETING AT the office drew to a close. Shannon thanked her colleagues for their concern and the notes and cards she received after her accident. She also thanked her boss, Amanda, for arranging the muffins they enjoyed during the meeting in honour of her return.

Amanda helped herself to a cranberry before Emma took the tray to put the few remaining pastries in the small kitchen by the coffee maker and kettle. Her jacket was snug, and she smiled at Shannon. "I probably shouldn't have this, but it's a celebration, after all. And the Sullivan sale closes today, doesn't it?"

"It does. I think they'll be happy at that house."

Amanda tore another piece of muffin and prepared to pop it into her mouth. "Wasn't there some scandal about that place?"

"The previous owner died in the lake."

She nodded, her mouth full of food.

Shannon took the opportunity to head back to her desk. "Now that you mention it, I better follow up to make sure everything is going according to plan."

True to his word, Shannon found an email note from Kal waiting for her when she returned to her desk.

Good morning Shannon,

You may rest easy. Jennifer Jones-Walker does not have power of attorney over her mother's financial affairs. They had one drawn up specifically governing the sale of the house. Kal

Shannon wasn't sure how he found out. *He must have called Violet and asked, which was probably awkward for him, but, God love him, he did it. Well, that's a relief anyway, but does it confirm that Jennifer didn't have a motive?*

She rolled her shoulders and got to work on the job she was paid to do. *Put all that out of your mind, Shannon Dierdre Coyne. There's work to be done.*

It wasn't until lunchtime, as she and Emma walked along Walton Street to Dreamer's Cafe for a bowl of soup, that they had a chance to talk.

Emma touched Shannon's arm. "How are you feeling?"

"I'm fine. I took a couple of ibuprofens this morning, and that's enough." She waved her hand to dismiss any further questions about her health. "I had a note from Kal. He checked, and Jenn can't get her hands on the money. Violet would need to give her some, and hopefully, Jenn doesn't bully her mother into doing that."

"I guess that takes her off our list, does it?"

Shannon led the way into the café to their favourite table with a view of Walton Street. "I don't know if I'm ready for that. Something about her keeps me suspicious, but I guess I need to focus on tracking this other guy to see where that leads."

They ordered their lunch and continued their conversation. Shannon pulled out her phone. "I found a number for the Plymouth Brethren."

"Did you? Have you tried calling already?"

"No, but they don't sound like the sort of people who could do a thing like this. Listen. This is from their website." Shannon read parts from the group's site to Emma.

"It sounds like they're pretty involved with charity and volunteer work."

Shannon sighed and put her phone away as their lunch was served. "I know. They sound like they keep to themselves, but so do the Mennonites and lots of other groups. I don't know if this line of research will lead anywhere, but I'll give it a go anyway. I'll call the number when I get home and see what they say."

After lunch, Shannon confirmed that the Sullivan sale had gone through, picked up the handmade charcuterie board, and headed to Pengelly Landing to congratulate them on their new home. As she drove, she called Violet Walker. "Hi, Violet, it's Shannon Coyne."

The elderly woman's voice sounded faint on the speakerphone over the road noise. "Hello, Shannon. Well, that house is gone now, and I suppose I'll be using the money to pay lawyer bills when I'm dragged into court."

"I still hope it won't come to that, Violet. You need to stay positive. I wanted to call you to be sure you know I'm not giving up on you just because the house sale is done."

She heard Violet sniff and knew she was crying. "Thank you. At least I have one person who believes in me."

"You have more than just me, Violet. I spoke with Nate Stevens yesterday, and he told me there was no way you would have done such a thing."

"Did he? That surprises me."

"He knows you haven't always gotten along, but he believes in your innocence. And then there's Chris, and I'm sure even Jennifer believes in you. She may not show it, though."

The older woman sighed loudly. "That's all well and good, but the police don't believe in me, and they're the ones that matter."

Shannon knew she was right. "I know, but like I said, I'm still asking questions. Violet, I might lose you in the hills here, so I'll let you go, but I'll be in touch soon. Try to think positive."

"Thank you, Shannon. I'll do my best."

※

Shannon parked along the road's edge to avoid all the activity in the driveway. She took her bag containing the house-closing gift and called out to Jessie who was playing with their toddler out of the way at the side of the house. "Hi, Jessie!"

The expectant mother rose from the plastic lawn chair to greet Shannon. "Hello. I wasn't sure we'd see you again, but I'm glad you came. We're so happy with the property. Thank you for nudging me along. I know we're going to have such a happy time here."

"I'm so glad to hear you say that. It truly is a beautiful spot." They turned and stood side by side, gazing out at the lake.

"Hello…hello." Shannon turned and waved automatically at the elderly woman coming through a gap in the tall privacy hedge.

Jessie Sullivan waved as well. "Looks like the neighbours are friendly, anyway."

"Oh, I'm sure they are. Many people live here year-round, and some, like you, come for weekends and vacations. It's good to get to know people, and you'll be comfortable knowing eyes are watching your place for you."

"As long as they aren't too nosy," Jessie said before putting on a large smile to meet her new neighbour.

The woman was small and slender, with short, curly white hair. Her hands appeared thin and fragile, but her grip was almost painfully strong when she clutched Shannon's arm as the closest person to latch on to. "Who are you?"

Shannon tried gently prising the woman's hand from her arm, but the neighbour held on tight. "My name is Shannon, and this is Jessie Sullivan. Jessie and her family have just bought the house. What is your name?"

"Mrs. Stewart. We've been here for generations, and I don't know you."

Shannon caught Jessie's worried glance as her boy shifted to stand behind his mother. "You're right, Mrs. Stewart. My family is not from around here, and neither is Jessie's, but they love the area and house and look forward to being your new neighbour. Isn't that right, Jessie?"

Her smile was less certain now. "Absolutely."

Mrs. Stewart frowned. "Where's Violet? Where's Mal? He'll tell you. I've been here for most of my life. They live here."

Shannon put her hand over the elderly hand on her arm. "Violet lives in Port Hope now, Mrs. Stewart."

"No. I saw her just the other day, and she didn't tell me she was moving. And Mal? He wouldn't like to live in the city. That's nonsense. Who are you again?"

Although she was elderly, the woman's voice had a piercing quality that carried. Nick Sullivan came outside, and his son scurried to him to be lifted. Mrs. Stewart removed her hand from Shannon's arm to turn and watch Nick approach. "Who are you? You aren't Chris."

Nick frowned, and Shannon answered the woman's question. "Mrs. Stewart, this is Nick Sullivan. He's married to Jessie, who you just met, and is also one of your new neighbours. Chris won't be coming here anymore because the Walkers sold the house to the Sullivans here."

"I just saw the Walkers. You're lying to me."

Nick put his arm around his wife's shoulder and carried his boy on his other arm. "Come inside, Jess. I need you to explain exactly how you want the kitchen renovated to Anja. She'd rather hear it from you than me."

Shannon handed the bag with her gift to Jessie. "Take this with you. I'll be in shortly." Mrs. Stewart stood staring after them until Shannon pointed to her house. "How about you show me your house? Or yard, if you don't want me inside. I see you have climbing roses. They must take a lot of work." She steered the woman back through the gap in the hedge towards her own home. *I can see Nick building a gate as one of his first projects.*

They had hardly come through the path in the hedge when Shannon heard a voice call out from Mrs. Stewart's house. "Mom. There you are. I wondered where you'd gone."

A woman who appeared to be in her sixties came through sliding doors and across a large deck. She linked her mother's arm through hers. "Have you been meeting the new neighbours?"

Shannon smiled. "I'm Shannon Coyne, the realtor, but yes, your mother came over and introduced herself, but she's having trouble believing that Jessie and Nick Sullivan are indeed the new neighbours. She feels quite certain that Violet and Mal still live there."

"Oh dear. Mom, we've talked about that." Her voice was gentle. "Mal died months ago now, and Violet, well, I'm not sure what's happening with Violet." She nudged her mother towards the house. "Why don't you go inside and get some lemonade for us? I'll be right in."

"I'm Liz. I'm sorry about my mother. I hope she didn't upset the new people."

"They're fine. I'm sorry your mother is confused. I'm sure that's hard for you."

She sighed. "It's so recent, I'm still trying to figure out what's happening. Up until a few weeks ago, she was perfectly lucid. At least, I think she was. I don't live with her here, to be honest, and I was away travelling for a bit, so she may have been worse than I realized."

Shannon had a sudden thought. "It sounds like you're aware that Violet is implicated in her husband's death."

Liz nodded. "My mother told me about Mal's death, and I heard from one of the other neighbours that the police believe Violet had something to do with it. It's unbelievable. She's such a sweet woman. She and my mother have been friends for decades."

"Did your mother speak to the police about Violet?"

She frowned. "On the day Mal drowned, you mean?"

"No, more recently."

"Not that I know of. Why do you ask?"

"The police have an eyewitness that puts Violet here when Mal went missing, despite friends saying she was at lunch for most of that afternoon."

Liz widened her eyes. "I can't see Mom saying anything to contradict Violet's friends."

"When your mum came over to talk to the new neighbour, she said she'd seen Violet recently. It's obvious now that she's confused, but if you say this change has happened recently, she may have seemed quite lucid talking to the police."

Liz put a hand over her mouth. "No. I can't believe Mom had the wherewithal to contact the police and give them a statement."

"You were travelling. When were you away?"

"I went to Japan. I just got back this week after being away for a month. My brother checked in on my mother a couple of times, but I'm not sure what he would have noticed. He picked up groceries, and I suspect that's as far as it went."

Mrs. Stewart came to the door and called her daughter. "What did you ask me to do? I can't remember." Tears trickled down her cheeks.

Shannon pulled a business card from her purse. "Will you call me later? I'm going to ask the police if your mother is the eyewitness. Go on. She needs you."

Liz nodded and clutched the card. "I'm coming, Mom. Don't worry. It's nothing to be upset about."

Shannon watched as she trotted to her mother and hugged the distraught elderly woman before the two of them went into the house.

Chapter Twenty-Seven

SHANNON WAITED UNTIL SHE was home again before contacting Kal. This time, she sent an email note asking him to phone her when he had time.

He called as she prepared some pasta for her supper. She turned the stove with its pot of boiling water off. "Hi, Kal. Thank you for calling."

"My pleasure. How can I help you?"

She told him about her encounter with Mrs. Stewart. "If your eyewitness is not her, I don't expect you to name them, but if it is her, I thought you should know she's unreliable."

Kal took a few seconds before answering. "Yes, that's the name of the witness. I didn't speak to her myself. One of my colleagues went, but it sounds like I should do a follow-up with her."

"Yes, I think you'll be glad you did. I can imagine she came across as credible, but I suspect she was already in the first stages of this dementia. I'm not an expert, but I remember hearing a lot about it when I worked at the seniors' centre all those years ago. It can come on quite quickly and may even be temporary. I hope to hear from

Mrs. Stewart's daughter, Liz, later, and I'll encourage her to take her mother in for a physical exam as soon as possible. An infection or some other physical cause may have triggered the condition."

"I'll connect with Mrs. Stewart and, if necessary, will go to see her in person or ask if her daughter can bring her to the station to go over the statement."

"Thank you, Kal. That makes me feel better." *Should I say something about the Plymouth Brethren? No. I'll wait until I know more.*

After disconnecting her call with Kal, Shannon checked the website again and called the number for general enquiries. She left a message, simply saying she was interested in hearing more and asking someone to please call her.

Shannon returned to her supper preparations when Dusty began a low growl at the door. When Piet or someone else Dusty knew and liked was on the other side of the door, she had a high-pitched, excited bark. This sound set the hairs on the back of Shannon's neck standing.

She turned the stove down and went to the door. She heard firm knocking on the outside door and she opened her apartment door a crack to peer out.

"Shannon? Are you home?"

She flung open her door and crossed the foyer to pull open the outside door. "Uncle Bob!" She stood on her toes to kiss him on the cheek. "Come in."

"Sorry. I should have phoned, but I was already here when I thought of it."

Leading him into the living room, Shannon invited him to sit. "I'm making spaghetti for supper. Shall I throw in some extra pasta? Will you stay?"

"No, no. I have to pick up some messages on the way home, and Sarah's waiting for me."

Shannon smiled to hear his Irish way of saying, 'No, thank you.' She doubted her Aunt Sarah was waiting for her uncle to pick up *messages*, the Irish way saying groceries, but she nodded and sat down. "What brings you here, then?"

"I wanted to let you know we are convinced that your accident was not, in fact, an accident. We've seen footage from a security camera nearby, and between that and the witness statements, I feel this person intended to knock you down."

Dusty sensed Shannon's distress and hopped up to lie across her lap.

Shannon shivered. "I thought Mammy was making too much of it. Can you tell what sort of car it is from the security video? Or better yet, a licence plate number?"

"I'm afraid not. We can't even tell if it's a man or a woman. They're wearing a ball cap, and the black and white footage is too grainy to make out anything more."

"Good Lord. What do you advise me to do?"

"Have you upset anyone recently?"

"No. Of course not."

"I didn't think so. It may have been a joyrider doing it for kicks. It's impossible to know. All I can tell you is to be very watchful. Don't go out alone at night. Lock your doors."

She sighed. "I do all that anyway."

"Just keep doing it, then. You may have been in the wrong place at the wrong time, but I don't know for certain. It's obvious there is some damage to the car, so we're canvassing local body shops. We're showing photos to all the staff and some of the regular customers of that Tim Hortons in case someone recognizes the car or person. We're searching for them, but I owed it to you to tell you what's happening to ensure you keep your eyes open."

She nodded. "Maybe the person confused me with someone else. I never go there, so it's unlikely they were after me."

Uncle Bob stood. "All right. I've said my piece, and I'll go now. I'm trying to keep it low-key when I talk to your mammy. I know my sister, and she'll be out there hunting for the culprit herself if she thinks it would help."

Shannon picked Dusty up and cuddled her dog as she walked her uncle to the door. "Thank you for coming, Uncle Bob. Next time, though, you know there's a buzzer you can push that will ring in my flat, so I know who's thumping on the door."

He laughed. "I'll try to remember that in the future."

❧

Shannon wasn't in the right mood to take Dusty for a walk after supper, so she confined their stroll to the back garden, ignoring the faded Muskoka chairs and wrought-iron table with one leg lying on the ground, having been broken when someone sat on it last summer.

The phone rang while she was scuffing at some weeds. *We need to hire someone to look after this yard properly.*

She didn't recognize the caller's number. "Shannon Coyne speaking."

The woman's voice was warm and friendly. "This is Helen Brown calling from the Plymouth Brethren Christian Church. You left a message looking for information. How can I help you?"

"Thank you so much for calling. This may seem like a strange question, but is there a congregation near Port Hope, Ontario?"

Her voice grew more animated. "Are you considering joining us?"

"Well, no. I'm looking for someone in particular who expressed an interest in a collection of Scriven material."

Helen's voice flattened. "Oh yes. And are you the one selling this material?"

"No. Someone I know told me about it, and I just wondered if that man is still interested."

The woman sighed. "I know who you're talking about, and quite frankly, he's in temporary isolation."

"I'm sorry? Is he in hospital?"

"No, it just means we don't share fellowship with him right now. We suggested he might find a better fit for his values elsewhere."

"Oh. I see. His values didn't coincide with the Church's?"

"He was very vocal against our work with the Rapid Relief Team."

Shannon recalled the name. "I read about that. It sounds like the PBCC does good work with providing support in crisis situations. Who could argue with that?"

"Indeed."

I'd be very interested in connecting with him. Do you have a phone number or email address for this man?"

"We don't give out that kind of information." She relented then. "You can find him any time you want to at the hardware store north of Port Hope. He's the proprietor."

Before Shannon could ask for more specifics, the woman had hung up.

※

Piet's phone went directly to voicemail. "Piet, it's Shannon. I heard from the Church people. Call me when you get a chance."

Filled with nervous excitement, she went online and searched all the hardware stores in the area to see if she could figure out which was owned by the man she wanted to find. *Although it's possible, I can't imagine it's part of a chain. Are there any independents? Here! This must be it.*

There was a rudimentary website for the shop located in the middle of farm country. The one-page site simply displayed a few bullet points listing the services offered: farm machinery repairs, welding, tractor parts for sale, and locksmith services. *Locksmith! That would explain how someone broke into the Walker house without it looking like a break-in. All right, Mr. Andrew Noble, Proprietor, who are you?*

She scanned other hardware-type stores in a wide circle north of Port Hope, but no other place seemed as compelling. Next, she searched for his name, hoping to find a photo of the man, but he was a ghost. There were no references to him. *That really convinces me. He doesn't spend his time out and about getting his photo taken.*

When Piet called and told her he was home from work and she

was welcome to come up for a cup of tea, she had made and abandoned several plans to meet Mr. Noble. Her head ached, and she was glad to go up to see what ideas her friend might have.

"Come in, " he called out over the whistling kettle. Is chamomile OK?"

"Perfect."

Curling her legs up under her, she tucked herself onto his sofa. She wrapped her hands around the mug he handed her and, enjoying the fragrance of the steaming tea, she told Piet about her uncle's visit and what she had discovered about the man she believed was the mysterious 'religious man.'

Except for a few exclamations of 'oh' or 'oh, dear,' Piet listened until she finished. "It's scary to think someone deliberately tried to run you down."

She nodded. "I know. I guess I have to be extra careful, but I still think it was random. No one is specifically after me. I was just in the wrong place at the wrong time."

"You can't know that. Maybe you've gotten closer than we realize to Malcolm's killer."

Shannon shook her head. "I don't think so. Let's say that's true. Let's say it's Jenn, who you and I both mistrust; how does it help her to run me down?"

"I don't know. Maybe you're right, but don't take any crazy chances."

"I won't. Believe me. Now, let's talk about Andrew Noble." She gave him a rundown on the ideas she'd had.

Piet laughed. "You're right; I can't see him coming to have lunch with you or, even talking to you on the phone. Why would he? What's in it for him?"

"I don't know. So what's your idea?"

He shrugged. "Let's take him some business."

"I don't happen to have any farm machinery in need of repair. Do you?"

"No, but he does welding, right?"

Shannon widened her eyes. "The darned table from the back garden."

"Exactly. The one you complain about every time you see it."

"Great idea. When can we go?"

"I can go in the morning. I have an afternoon and evening visitation tomorrow, so I have to be at work by one o'clock."

She grinned. "Plenty of time. Farmers are up early. If we leave here at nine-thirty, that will get us there before ten and out again by ten-thirty."

Piet nodded. "And what exactly do you expect him to tell you?"

"I want to see his reaction when I ask him about the Scriven collection. If he doesn't know what I'm talking about, I'll be able to tell."

"And what if he looks guilty? Then what? Will you go to the police?"

"I will. I promise."

They went out together to carry in the small iron table and Shannon wiped it down to ready it for the morning.

Chapter Twenty-Eight

THEY TOOK PIET'S NISSAN Rogue up to find Andrew Noble's repair shop. The rain beat down steadily, and Piet grumbled about the poor drivers who all raced around him on Highway 28. "Doesn't anyone slow down for the weather anymore?"

Knowing she, too, had a heavy foot, Shannon didn't comment on Piet's driving but kept her eyes glued to the GPS on her phone and remained silent unless it was to give her friend directions.

"OK, turn left in five hundred metres."

Pete slowed down. The only landmark on the four corners of the rural road was a Township of Hamilton Forest Fire Hazard sign with the arrow pointing to orange. "You'd miss this easily enough, wouldn't you?"

"I suppose most people turning here will know where they're going."

"True." At the same moment, they both spotted the hand-painted sign at the end of a long farm driveway. Piet turned and drove up the gravel lane, bypassing the farmhouse and stopping in front of a long, low building. The barnboard walls were faded, but the site was tidy outside.

Piet looked at Shannon. "Well?"

"Let's go." She took the leg, and Piet carried the table to the open double doors. She called out when she got close. "Hello?"

The man wore a grease-covered dark blue set of coveralls, holding a mug in one hand and a wrench in the other. He had been studying a John Deere tractor. The classic green of the body was in good condition, but the yellow wheels showed its years. The man himself was not unlike the tractor. When he set down the wrench and came forward to greet them, he moved with the fluidity of a thirty-year-old, but his bald head and lined face put his age closer to sixty. His hooded grey eyes assessed them as he came to look at the table Piet held.

"You folks want this welded, I suppose?"

Shannon handed him the leg. "If it's possible."

He looked at Piet when he answered. "Not sure it's worth it, but sure, I can do it."

Piet nodded. "How much would it cost?"

"Hundred."

Piet glanced at Shannon. They had only paid eighty for the table at a yard sale.

She stepped closer to the man. "Yes, please, go ahead."

He pointed to a back wall. "Set it there, then."

Shannon took back the leg, and together, she and Piet took the table to the designated spot.

Piet mumbled. "Now what?"

"Leave it to me."

They returned to the mechanic as he set his empty cup on a workbench.

Shannon glanced around. "You look like you do all sorts of skilled work, Mr.?"

"Noble."

"I heard about you from someone who knows you, so we thought you might be just the person we need."

He frowned. "Oh?"

"Yes. Helen Brown."

He blinked several times. "You're not members."

She smiled. "No, we're not, but I was interested in their volunteer work. I've been involved in volunteering for years with different groups."

Noble scowled. "We don't need outsiders."

Shannon took a deep breath. "Did I understand correctly that you, yourself are in temporary isolation?"

He paled. "What if I am? I'm going back soon."

"Are you? How will you manage that?"

His mouth was a grim line. "I have something they want. They'll take me back. You can be sure of that."

"Do you have the Scriven collection, Mr. Noble?"

His mouth fell open. His voice was low. "Are you a witch? You can't know about that."

"But I do know, Andrew Noble. I know you are also a locksmith, aren't you? Did you let yourself into Malcolm Walker's house to help yourself to the collection?"

His eyes blazed. "It wasn't his collection. The original page where Joseph Scriven penned the words for *What A Friend We Have In Jesus* belongs to us; to the Exclusive Brethren."

At this confession, Piet put his arm around Shannon. "We need to leave, right now."

Noble picked up the wrench again. "Yes. Get out of here. You have no right to be here."

Shannon held up her hand. "Fine. We're leaving."

They hurried to the car as Andrew Noble stood outside the workshop glaring at them.

Piet's tires spit dirt as he turned the car faster than he normally would, and sped back down the laneway. "Oh my God. He's one scary dude."

Shannon was giddy with what they had discovered. "Somehow, I doubt we're getting our table back."

"Not repaired, anyway." He turned to glance at her. "Did you notice he drives a black car? That's what's parked beside the building. Isn't that the sort of car that ran you down?"

✤

They had stopped on a hill on the side of the road to phone Kal Khan. Shannon knew the two of them must sound on the verge of hysteria, but Khan asked questions with his usual calm, serious manner.

By the time Piet pulled into their driveway, he had regained his composure. "One thing I'd say about that detective. He knows how to calm a person down."

Shannon agreed. "And he always takes things seriously. If I had called my uncle instead, he'd have been annoyed to know I'd been investigating even when he continually told me not to, and he'd have talked to me like I was a foolish little girl."

Piet turned off the engine. "He probably sees you as a little girl. You're his niece, and he's known you since the day you were born. It's hard to see someone in a different light than he's used to."

She sighed. "I know. He was very kind to me when he was explaining how he believed the car hit me on purpose. Uncle Bob was clearly concerned about me, but that's another reason I like to talk to Kal. He's concerned about my well-being, too, but he can still be objective."

Piet stopped at the base of the steps leading up to his flat. "Go on in. I want to hear you lock the door behind you."

She smiled and gave him a final wave before closing the door behind her and locking it. Dusty spun circles around her. "Yes, sweetie, yes. I'll let you out." She wandered around the yard after Dusty. *I guess we'll need to start going to yard sales again to replace our table.* Shannon frowned when Dusty stopped with her nose lifted in the air, and began a shrill barking.

"What is it? What do you hear that I can't?"

Dusty stopped and cocked her head in Shannon's direction. "I don't know what you want, little girl."

With a last series of high-pitched barks, Dusty turned, trotted back to the open French doors, and disappeared into the apartment.

Shannon followed and went straight through to the kitchen window and peeked outside, remembering how vulnerable she felt when someone broke in through that window the previous year. She bit her lip as she heard a car door slam and, by craning her neck, was just in time to see a black Chevrolet Trax disappear up the road. *Don't start getting paranoid. Didn't I read that black is Canada's most popular car colour after white?*

Shannon checked in with work and scheduled an appointment to visit a new client late afternoon. The older couple was downsizing and looking for a small bungalow in the town of Port Hope. Their son was taking over the family farm, so they were looking to buy a home but not sell. She reassured her boss. "Don't worry, Amanda. I'm fine with that. In fact, it makes things easier. Their timing is probably flexible, without the pressure of selling first."

Focused on preparing the paperwork for her meeting later, she almost forgot about the morning drama when Kal phoned.

She put the phone on speaker. "Hi, Kal. Were you able to meet Andrew Noble?"

"Yes, I met him, and I'm happy to say he was quite forthcoming."

Shannon took a deep breath. "Did he do it? Did he kill Malcolm Walker?"

"Oh, no. He claims he had nothing to do with that. No, he admitted to stealing the documents pertaining to Joseph Scriven. He anticipated our arrival and had the items ready to hand over. He was charged with theft and is on his way here to the station now."

"I see. He admitted to the theft but not the killing. Will you investigate him for that? He might be holding back."

Mr. Noble provided me with evidence to show he was at a farm auction in Alliston on the day Mr. Walker died. The auction ran until five o'clock. He bought several tractor parts and, after the auction, went to Barrie to buy a 1965 black Citroen to fix up. He carried it home in a trailer since it wasn't drivable."

"Oh."

"I'm satisfied that he's telling the truth, but of course, we will follow up with both the auction house and the man who sold Mr. Noble the car."

Shannon rubbed her head, which was pounding. "Thank you, Kal. I thought this was it."

His voice was sympathetic. "You did solve a crime. I have no idea what the value of this document is; this page contains what appears to be the original manuscript for the lyrics of the hymn entitled *What a Friend We Have In Jesus.* It is signed by J. Scriven and dated 1846."

"Sounds authentic, and of course, I'm glad to have caught a thief, but that's not what I was trying to do. I want to prove Violet Walker is not responsible for her husband's death, and I've failed miserably with that."

There was a pause, and then Kal spoke again. "I shouldn't say anything, but since you are the one who discovered the problem, I'll let you know that we have eliminated the eyewitness statement from our inquiry as unreliable."

"Oh, that *is* good news. Thank you for telling me, Kal. What does that do to the case?"

"It makes it more difficult for the Crown to prove, but the investigation is ongoing."

"I understand." Shannon glanced at the clock. "I better run. Thank you for calling."

Chapter Twenty-Nine

SHANNON DROVE NORTH TO Welcome and then west. Zig-zagging along the country roads, she was reminded of her motorcycle ride with Kal. *It's such pretty countryside out here, but I admit it was more exciting on the back of the bike instead of safe in my comfortable car.*

She pondered why she had experienced such an adrenalin rush on the motorbike while driving her car was almost boring in comparison. *Was it the danger of being on a motorbike? Maybe.* Her thoughts went back to what Piet had said when he encouraged her to go for it: something about facing her fears. *Does it make you more able to do something if you have to steel yourself like that? I think so. The adrenalin helped overcome my fear, and then I felt great.*

Shannon shook her head to organize her thoughts for the coming meeting, but she felt something about facing her fears was important. She set it aside for later.

In the rolling hills typical of the area, the two-and-a-half-storey white farmhouse with its red metal roof looked picturesque. Behind the house, a faded red barn stood in the shade of several towering old maple trees. She parked in the yard and smiled when a border collie came racing up to greet her, his waving tail belying his frantic barking. A woman who looked to be in her seventies came out on the porch and called the dog firmly. "Monty, come."

With a final bark, the dog turned and trotted to the woman, passing her into the house.

Shannon held her hand out to greet her new client. "Mrs. Smith? I'm Shannon Coyne."

The woman, whose snow-white hair was cut in an attractive short bob and blue eyes matched the stripe in her crisp cotton shirt, firmly gripped Shannon's hand. "Call me Sandy. Please come in. Don't be nervous about Monty. He has a lot to say for himself, but he's very friendly."

"I love dogs. I have a cocker spaniel named Dusty. She's the love of my life."

Sandy nodded as she led the way to the large farmhouse kitchen. "You don't mind sitting in the kitchen, I hope?"

"I grew up on a farm. I feel right at home here."

As Shannon talked about her childhood home and the continuing improvements her father and sister were making, Mr. Smith came into the kitchen. He moved slowly, feeling his way through the doorway to the chair at the head of the table.

Sandy introduced him. "This is Ron."

He nodded. "Hiya."

Shannon smiled at the contrast between Sandy and her husband. As she pulled the papers from her portfolio for their signature, she tried to draw them out. "You're looking for a smaller house. That will be a big change after living in this beautiful home. How long have you lived here?"

Sandy nodded. "It will take some getting used to, all right. Ron grew up here. He took the farm over from his parents."

He grumbled. "My parents lived here till they died. They didn't *downsize*." He said the word as if it left a bad taste in his mouth.

Sandy laid her hand over his. "It's different these days. The kids have their own life to lead, and more than that, you know the stairs are getting too hard for you."

"I'd manage."

Shannon saw on Sandy's face that they'd had this conversation many times already. "I'll do my best to find you a home that will bring you joy."

Before Sandy could speak, Ron answered. "No joy in losing your eyesight and having your legs cripple up."

Shannon bit her lip. "I'm sorry to hear you aren't well. It sounds like a smaller home will be just the answer to make life easier for you." She turned to Sandy. "Tell me what you're looking for, and I'll get started."

Shannon led the conversation and took notes about what they needed and wanted. For her, a garden would be nice, and for him, a walk-in shower was necessary. Wide doorways, main floor laundry, and two bathrooms would be convenient if possible. Shannon promised she'd get to work to see what was out there when they finished. Ron sat with his arms folded across his chest as Shannon stood. "Goodbye, Ron. It was nice meeting you."

He nodded. "Bye."

Sandy walked Shannon out to the car. "This is hard on Ron. The idea of moving out is hard on him."

Shannon took a breath. "Your kids aren't open to your remaining here?"

"Oh, they'd be fine. We all get along, but the reality is that the house just isn't suitable for Ron anymore. He has terrible arthritis in his knees. He's already had a hip replacement, and he said he won't go through knee replacements. But the worst is his eyesight. It's been going for a long while, and now the doctors say it's likely he'll lose it completely within a few months."

"That's heartbreaking to hear. Is it possible to renovate a room or two on the main floor to work as a suite for the two of you?"

Sandy tilted her head. "You're not like any real estate agent I ever met. Shouldn't you be trying to sell me a house?"

Shannon smiled. "I want to find a solution that works for you and your family. If a new house is the answer, I'll do everything I can to find it for you. I'm just not sure that is the answer. Have you considered this option?"

Sandy frowned. "It's come up in conversation, but we haven't spent any time really discussing it. We don't have a lot of savings for something like that. Micky, our son, is getting a mortgage because the house will be his, and then we'll have the money to buy another house. I don't know about getting money if he isn't going to get the house, and I can't imagine anyone lending us money at our age."

Shannon laid her hand on Sandy's arm. "Why don't I get more information? I'll certainly start looking for houses that will suit you, and at the same time, I have a friend who is a mortgage broker, and he may have some creative ideas for you. I just wasn't sure if it was an option in case your kids were looking for the privacy of having their own space."

"Micky is letting me say that, as a way to get Ron into a safer place." She swallowed. "He'd do anything for his dad."

"He sounds like a very caring son. You talk to him, and I'll reach out to my friend. Sandy, together we will find something to satisfy all of you."

※

On the drive home, Shannon turned her thoughts to Violet. *I should visit her. I wonder if she knows the eyewitness statement is gone.*

She pulled over on a hill and phoned. "Hi Violet, it's Shannon. I just wanted to check in on you. How are you managing? Shall I come for a visit?"

"Hello, Shannon. It's kind of you to call. I'm too tired for more visitors this evening. My lawyer just left. She told me that the police had decided the eyewitness was, let me think what she said, yes, she said they were unreliable."

"That's great news, Violet. I can understand you must be exhausted by it all. How about I drop by tomorrow? Perhaps I can bring you some groceries?"

"Thank you. I have everything I need. Chris and Jenn have created a schedule, so I'm kept well stocked."

"That sounds good. I didn't think Chris and Jenn got along very well. It's good to hear they've put their differences aside."

"For now, anyway. Chris has even been phoning Jenn, which is surprising, but nice. I don't need anything, but I'd like to see you for a visit. Maybe tomorrow around eleven?"

"Perfect. I'll see you then, Violet."

She went straight home, thinking about the Smiths and their son Micky and Violet, with Chris and Jenn getting along for her sake. She remembered how her mother dropped everything to come to the hospital and then wanted to keep her safe back in the security of the farm. *Family. Where would we be without them?*

Chapter Thirty

SHANNON CALLED EMMA TO tell her how the visit with the new clients went. "I'm not entirely sure I'll be selling them a new house. You don't need to tell Amanda that, but I seriously feel there's a better option for them."

"So, that's the client update. I know you want to talk about the Walker case. Tell me what's new there."

Shannon laughed. "You know me too well. You know I tracked down the man we were calling Religious Guy?"

"Yes, you told me, and you said you and Piet were going to see him. That's what I want to hear about."

"It was a bust, I'm afraid."

"Oh? He wasn't the right person?"

"He was the right person for the theft. He broke into the Walker house and stole all the Scriven memorabilia, but he didn't kill Malcolm." She gave Emma all the details, to the sound of her friend's gasps and occasional muffled 'oh.' Shannon imagined Emma holding her hand over her mouth when she listened to the story of

Andrew Noble's confession of the theft and Piet hurriedly hustling Shannon away.

Emma's voice trembled. "Why do you sound so disappointed? You caught this man. You did everything to track him down. You did a great job, Shannon."

"I'm proud of that. Of course, I am, but he's not responsible for the murder. That's what I wanted to hear. Kal tells me there is no way Noble did that."

"I see. I know you don't want to hear this, Shannon, but is it possible you're wrong? Maybe Violet did kill him? People change over the years. Maybe she just isn't the person you knew years ago."

Shannon sighed. "Or maybe I never really knew her. I don't know what to think anymore, Emma. I'm going to visit her tomorrow, and then I'll make up my mind."

"Whatever happens, you did everything you could and more than anyone else would have done to get to the truth."

"Thanks, Em. You're always such a great supporter."

※

Wednesday morning was the sort of morning Canadians spend the winter longing for. A bright blue sky with scudding fluffy clouds served as the backdrop to flourishing trees and gardens. A gentle breeze ruffled Shannon's long red hair as she walked from the car to the door of The Manse, Violet Walker's home.

The receptionist smiled at the bunch of pink peonies Shannon carried. "I saw you coming and called up already. Go ahead. Violet is popular today."

The door to Violet's apartment was open. Shannon called out as she stepped inside. "Hello, Violet. It's Shannon."

Despite the sun streaming in through the windows, the elderly woman's face was cheerless. The furrows on her forehead were deeper than what Shannon remembered, and her round face had collapsed in on itself, giving her a wizened appearance. She looked old and tired but smiled as Shannon held out the flowers.

Violet closed her eyes and inhaled the scent, smiling. When she looked at Shannon again, she nodded. "We always had peonies in the garden out back at Pengelly Landing, but they didn't have a scent. These are wonderful. Thank you."

Shannon smiled. "You're welcome. I thought I'd bring a bit of the June day inside to you but without the ants."

Violet chuckled, and her eyes sparkled. "I knew the ants were good for the flowers, but I didn't want them in the house, so I enjoyed them outside."

"I got these at a florist, so no need to worry."

Shannon was startled to hear Chris's voice. He had been behind the wall separating the kitchenette from the door foyer. "Shall I get you a vase for those, Aunt Violet?"

"Yes, please, Chris. Shannon, come in. Chris put the kettle on when they called up from downstairs to say you were on your way."

Shannon closed the door and came in. "Hi, Chris. Nice to see you again."

He smiled and filled a vase with water for Violet. "And you. I hear the lake house is sold now. It's hard to say goodbye to it, but we all need to move on."

Violet snipped an inch off the bottom of the stem of a peony before setting the flower into the vase. "Easy for you to say. Move on. I'd like nothing better, but here I am, a prisoner in my own home for no reason."

Chris rested his arm across her thin shoulders. "I'm sorry, Aunt Violet. That was thoughtless."

She sighed. "Don't mind me. You've been wonderful with all the help you've given me. Always coming all the way from Peterborough down here. I especially like that you and Jenn are friends now."

Shannon raised her eyebrows. "That's great to hear, Chris. I'm glad you two have come together to help your aunt."

He carried the vase for his aunt into the living room, speaking quietly to Shannon. "I wouldn't quite say we're friends, but we're learning to get along better for the greater good."

Violet scooped the small pile of inch-long stem ends and threw them into the garbage before following her nephew and Shannon. "Chris would do anything to help, " she smiled at the young man. "You went through such a tragedy, but I have to say, Mal and I were lucky to have you come into our lives."

Chris nodded but didn't return her smile. "Tea all around?"

Shannon nodded. "I'd love a cup, thank you."

When they were all seated with mugs of tea, Shannon addressed Violet. "Is there any further news on your case? You told me your lawyer told you the Crown set aside the eyewitness statement. Does your lawyer believe they'll drop the charges?"

The old woman frowned, deepening the network of wrinkles. "No. She told me not to get my hopes up too much, but she's following up with them to get more information about their case." She frowned. "Disclosure, I think she called it."

Chris set his mug down on the coffee table. "They can't prove anything. They'll have to let you go."

Violet nodded. "Of course, they can't prove it because I didn't *do* anything wrong."

"That's what I mean. They can't prove something that didn't happen." He turned to Shannon. "You were doing some inquiries, weren't you? How's all that going?"

She bit her bottom lip. "I wish I had some good news to share with you, but I don't. I thought I was on to something when I discovered a part of Mal's collection was missing. But it didn't lead to anything other than finding the thief."

Violet widened her eyes. "What? What was stolen, and who stole it?" She closed her eyes. "Please don't say Jennifer."

"No, no." Shannon didn't mention the sale of the Rice Lake Monster collection. "No, this was a collection of documents about Joseph Scriven."

Violet frowned. "That name is familiar, but I don't remember why."

"He wrote the poem that became the lyrics for the hymn *What A Friend We Have In Jesus*."

"Of course. There's a monument to him in Port Hope."

"That's right. Mal had an original document with the poem, signed and dated by Joseph Scriven."

Chris sat forward on the edge of his chair. "And you found the person who stole that?"

"Yes. It's a man named Andrew Noble. He's part of the same religious sect that Joseph Scriven was originally from. He believes the documents belong to his group and felt justified in taking them."

Chris sucked in his breath. "That's it, then. Probably Uncle Mal didn't want to sell them to him, and he got rid of Mal to get them for himself."

Shannon nodded. "That's what I thought too, but the police feel he has a solid alibi."

Chris slapped his knee in frustration. "No. They haven't looked hard enough. Anyone can fake an alibi. They must have the evidence if they found the documents."

Violet rubbed her head. "I thought you were going to say Nate Stevens stole them."

"No. I thought that, too, but he wasn't interested in them. He only cares about Rice Lake memorabilia. He was the one who steered me to this Andrew Noble guy, though." She turned to Chris. "You're right. Noble wanted to buy them from your uncle. Mal was prepared to sell them, but not at a price that worked for Noble."

Chris stood up to pace. "I'm calling the police. This is a breakthrough."

Shannon frowned. "I understand your frustration. I feel the same way. Why don't you talk to Violet's lawyer, Chris? She'd be the best person to challenge the police on it."

He raised his eyebrows. "Don't you have a connection with the police? I thought you talked to them all the time?"

She flushed. "My uncle works there, but I'll be honest with you. He doesn't like me getting involved. He considers it meddling."

Chris's face reddened. "I thought you were someone we could trust to help. Aunt Violet told me you were. Did you lie to her?"

Violet looked startled as her words were twisted this way. "That's a bit harsh, Chris."

"It's not." He glared at Shannon and shook his head. "I see we can't rely on you for help."

Shannon stood up and crossed her arms across her chest. "I already talked to the police about this man. That's how they knew about him and his theft of the Scriven documents."

Chris stepped closer and loomed above her. "Right. And that's enough, is it?"

She took a deep breath. "No, but I don't know what else to do. If there's something else for the police to discover about the man, I believe they'll find it."

Violet put her arm around her nephew's waist. "Chris. Calm down. It isn't Shannon's fault the police haven't found the real killer yet. I'm grateful for the effort she's taken. Let's hope the investigation discovers something new." She turned to Shannon. "It's a good suggestion to put it into the hands of my lawyer. She'll know best what to do with this."

Shannon nodded. She felt Chris simmering. "I'll leave you in peace now. If there's anything that I believe I can do to move the investigation forward, I'll do it. Don't worry. I haven't given up."

Violet walked with Shannon to the door. "Don't be upset by Chris. He's a good man."

"I see how much he cares about you and share his frustration. I'll keep thinking about it all. Don't give up hope."

"I'm trying to stay positive. It's not easy."

Shannon hugged Violet. "I know. Hang in there. You have truth on your side."

Violet nodded. "I hope it's enough."

Shannon heard the woman's deep sigh as she closed the door.

This evening, I need to relook at my board. I'm missing something. Is Chris right? Maybe I missed something about Andrew Noble or Nate Stevens—someone other than Violet.

Chapter Thirty-One

WHEN SHANNON ARRIVED AT the office, Emma greeted her with a few pink message slips: "Here you go, and Amanda asked if you could go see her when you got in."

Shannon nodded. "I'll do that first." She leaned in close to her friend. "Am I in trouble?"

Emma lifted one shoulder in a small shrug. "Mrs. Smith called a little while ago and spoke to Amanda."

"Oh, yikes. OK. Thanks for the heads-up." Shannon felt her armpits tingle with perspiration. Her antiperspirant had barely held after her stressful encounter with Chris Walker.

She walked down the hall, past the glass cube of their meeting room, to her boss's office at the end. The building was a heritage brick on the outside, but the inside was modern and bright.

She tapped on the doorframe, and Amanda Carter looked up from her laptop. She removed her burgundy tortoise-shell oversized glasses and gestured to a chair opposite her. "Come in, come in. How are you feeling these days?"

"I'm good again, thank you. If I sneeze, I feel the ribs, but aside from that, I hardly feel it anymore."

"That's great. I wanted a word about the Smiths. You went to see them last night about finding them a new home."

Shannon swallowed. "Yes, I did. You know how it goes with a new client. You try to find out everything you can about their situation, so you start on the right foot to end up with a happy client."

Amanda held up her hand, and Shannon stopped talking. "Mrs. Smith spent the entire phone call raving about you."

"Oh?"

"She told me you were one of the most helpful people she'd encountered in a very long time. She mentioned how upsetting things have been at home and felt pressured to move as the answer to keeping her husband safe. I understand you found them a mortgage broker who is working with them to refinance the property to renovate the home."

"I didn't hear how that went."

"It sounds like it will work out for them."

Shannon licked her lips. "I'm sorry, Amanda. It looks like I lost us a client."

Amanda studied her for a moment. "Mrs. Smith called me to get the contact details for our head office. She and her family are very moved by your willingness to find a solution, even if it means losing a sale. She wants to let our boss know."

Shannon took a deep breath. "How will that go over? It's nice that someone has good things to say, even if it isn't a sale. It's something, anyway. It doesn't help keep the lights on, but it's something."

"It's everything, Shannon. Your decision to put their needs first already led to another client. Mrs. Smith told someone at her morning coffee club who happens to be selling their home and was looking for a realtor, and now they've come to us." Amanda handed over a client contact sheet. Please give Margaret Bell a call."

Shannon took a breath. "That's wonderful news. I admit I was a bit worried after I suggested the renovation route."

Amanda shook her head. "Karma, Shannon. It's not easy to go against your own best interests, but it usually works out."

Shannon stood and took the page from Amanda. "Thank you, Amanda. I appreciate your support."

"This is a job about people, Shannon. Not about houses. You understand that, and you'll go far."

"Thank you, Amanda. That means a lot to me."

Back at her desk, Shannon first called the Smiths to thank Sandy for her glowing recommendation. "It sounds like things are going to work out for you. I'm so glad."

"It's not a done deal yet, but your friend, Max, believes there's a way to make it happen. We've started talking about how we can divide the dining room in half, use it for the bedroom, take the old parlour that we rarely use, and turn it into a small sitting room. Since the parlour backs onto the kitchen, Ron is sure we even have room to carve out space for a small bathroom."

"And your son and his family are willing to make these changes?"

"Oh, Shannon, they're so excited. Maybe even more than us. It'll be so nice to stay where we can still be together. It's easier for us, certainly, but also easier for them since I help out with babysitting. Also, they won't need to run around fetching and carrying for us if we live elsewhere." Shannon heard Sandy gulp, the tears in her voice. "The best thing is how Ron suddenly has a new lease on life. He was ready to give up, and now he's got a project to help work on. It's so good for him."

Shannon smiled to hear the excitement in Sandy's voice. "I'm looking forward to seeing it when you're all finished. Thank you for passing along my name to your friend Margaret Bell. I'll contact her now and get the ball rolling."

It was after five by the time She arrived home. Dusty danced around her feet, keen to go for a walk.

Shannon changed into a comfortable pair of light sweatpants and a T-shirt. She bent to ruffle Dusty's ears as she clipped the leash on. "All right, little lady. Let's go stretch our legs."

They turned left at Ridout. Shannon took her time, allowing her spaniel to sniff at every interesting scent she encountered while her mind busied itself thinking about the Walkers. Dusty led the way when they reached the corner of Thomas Street to head towards the green space surrounding the Port Hope Lions Recreational Centre. Heading east around the long, low structure that housed the Lions Centre and Branch 30 of the Royal Canadian Legion, Shannon lost track of the time. It wasn't until she had circumvented the building and was walking along the perimeter of the park's west side that she noticed how the light slanted through the trees, casting long, deep shadows across the path. She shivered despite the warm evening. "Let's pick up the pace, Dusty. It's dinner time. You're ready for yours, right?" She tugged at the leash when her pup stopped yet again to sniff a bush beside the trail. Dark, heavy rain clouds lumbered overhead. The playing fields were deserted this Wednesday evening, as supper time had taken parents and their children home.

Shannon swallowed when she noticed the lone car parked near the entrance to the Legion. *Probably the bartender getting set up for darts night or something like that. It's red, not black, so don't be paranoid.*

Dusty decided she'd had her fill of sniffing and trotted beside her mistress, nose in the air.

"Good girl. That's it. We don't want to get caught in the rain, do we?"

Dusty stopped and stared across the parking lot. Her hackles rose, and she gave a deep, warning growl.

"Dusty, don't. You're as bad as me, seeing goblins where there are none." Shannon pulled her phone from her back pocket. "Come on now, let's keep going."

When alarmed, the small dog had a surprisingly deep-throated growl, and she continued to rumble as they walked on.

Shannon dialled Piet's number but was sent directly to voicemail. She spoke loudly: "Hi there. How are you? I just thought I'd check in." She pretended to listen as she neared the parking lot on her way back to Thomas Street.

The car's lights came on as she passed the front of it. "Oh!" She spoke aloud. "Someone is sitting in the car. They've been watching me." The phone beeped to indicate she'd reached the end of the time to record a message, but she continued speaking as if conversing.

Her heart pounded, and Shannon clutched the phone but gave up the pretence of speaking with anyone. She began to jog the last short distance across the parking lot towards Thomas Street. She heard the car engine start and sprinted, stopping only when she reached the first house. Dusty sat down, unaccustomed to running unless it was to chase a ball, panting in time with her mistress as Shannon leaned over, hands on knees. *Oh my God. My ribs feel it now.*

She stood and stared back where she'd come from. The car had disappeared, leaving by the main entrance of the parking lot onto Strachan Street.

When her breath slowed and her heart stopped pounding, Shannon continued her journey back home. She turned to walk along the busier Walton Street and shook her head. *Good Lord, what was that all about? Some person sitting in their car, probably just finished work at the Lions Club or the Legion, making a call or looking something up. Probably never even noticed me. I've allowed myself to get spooked and won't do it again.*

Despite her determination, she glanced over her shoulder more than once on the walk home, locking the door securely behind her when she arrived back into the safety of her apartment.

❦

It was nine-thirty that night when Piet called her. "Are you all right?"

She heard his breath puffing and pictured him walking at his usual fast pace. "I'm fine. I'm sorry. I should have left you another message."

"We had a viewing tonight, so I had the phone shut off, but when I listened to your message, you sounded so…"

"Crazy?"

He laughed. "Not crazy, but distraught. I didn't know what to make of it. You said you were checking in, and then your voice went up a whole octave, and you said there's a car, and someone was watching you. What happened?"

"My imagination is what happened to me." She went on to describe her panic attack.

"But you're OK now?"

"I'm fine. Are you on your way home?"

"I planned to go to Connor's place, but I'll cancel if you need me to come back to the house."

"No, please don't. You go ahead. Have a nice evening."

Shannon poured herself another glass of wine and studied the whiteboard.

Chapter Thirty-Two

AFTER A NIGHT OF wind and rain driving against her windows, Shannon rose from bed feeling groggy and stiff. Her ribs ached after her run the previous evening, and the storm's low pressure triggered a headache. *OK. Maybe one too many glasses of wine didn't help.*

She let Dusty out back, and the spaniel came scurrying back into the house as quickly as possible after doing her morning business, looking bedraggled.

Shannon quickly threw a large towel she kept by the French doors over the dog and gave her a good rub-down before Dusty had a chance to shake herself. "Oh no, you don't. I'm not in the mood to start mopping the floor after you."

After a breakfast of yogurt and a banana, she took a long hot shower and decided she'd be fine. *Pull yourself together now. You've got a busy day ahead between the usual monthly meeting and then a visit out to the new client's house; there is too much on to mope around.*

The whiteboard with its notes stopped her in passing. She'd made a few more notes on it last night, but as she looked at the comments, there didn't appear to be anything actionable. *It's all just speculation. Jennifer suddenly takes more interest in helping out with her mother. Maybe she found a conscience? Chris is working with Jenn. Maybe he's prepared to put up with her because he loves his aunt? Nate Stevens argued with Mal and ended up with exactly what he wanted after Mal's death. Coincidence? And then there's Andrew Noble.* She had put two checkmarks beside his name. *He went to this auction and then up to Barrie to buy that car. I can't believe his time was tracked there. Did people know him, and even if they did, how can anyone be sure about his whereabouts the whole time? He's a fanatic. He broke into a house to steal those Scriven documents. Why are they so important to him? If Mal made fun of him, did he lose his cool?*

As Shannon drove the short distance to work through the rain, she made up her mind. *Chris is right. Andrew Noble bears looking at further.*

❧

After the office monthly meeting, Shannon invited Emma out for lunch. "Let's go to Dreamer's Café. The rain's stopped, but I'd love a good bowl of soup."

"Perfect. All I had in the fridge were stale bagels, so I planned to go out for something anyway."

Their two favourite tables by the front window were both taken, so they settled for a cozy spot tucked against the wall with its mural of a French café street scene. They ordered lunch: lobster bisque for Shannon and a turkey panini for Emma, each with a latte to start.

Emma took a sip of her drink. "That was so nice of Mrs. Smith to call and compliment you even though they aren't listing a house now."

Shannon smiled. "I know. I thought I'd be in trouble, but it worked out. I was embarrassed at the fuss Amanda made in the meeting, though."

Emma shrugged. "Amanda's a good boss. She likes to be sure people get credit when possible."

"She is. Just another reason I love this job."

Emma set her cup down. "So, what else is going on with you? You seemed distracted in the meeting. Something to do with Violet Walker, I bet."

She nodded. "Yesterday, I saw Violet and Chris Walker."

"The nephew. Did something happen to upset you?"

By the time Shannon told Emma a short version of both her upset with Chris's anger and the subsequent panic attack later in the day, their lunches were served.

Emma stared at Shannon before picking up her panini. "What an awful afternoon. It was a red car, though. You didn't think it was the same that hit you because that was black, right?"

Shannon stirred her soup. "I know. It was crazy. I just got freaked out for no reason aside from Dusty's growling. I have no idea why she did that. She's usually oblivious to cars when she's out for a walk."

"You were upset because Chris Walker accused you of not doing enough. I don't see him doing anything to find out what actually happened to his uncle. How dare he say things like that to you?" Emma took a large bite, satisfied she had put the matter to rest.

After a few spoons of soup, Shannon rested her spoon. "I don't know. I think he's right."

Swallowing, Emma raised her eyebrows. "About what?"

"I think the police gave up too quickly on checking Andrew Noble out."

She put down her half-eaten sandwich. "Shannon Coyne. I know that look. What are you planning to do?"

Shannon took a breath. "I'm going to go up and talk to him further."

Emma widened her eyes. "No. You are not going up there again."

"I have to." Shannon's voice was animated, her soup forgotten. "Don't you see? He could easily have gone to see Malcolm late in the morning or early afternoon before going to this auction. I checked it out. It's just under two hours from Pengelly Landing to where the auction was. He phones Mal and tells him he's willing to pay the money for the Scriven documents, but he wants to have a private meeting. Mal tells him his wife is going out for lunch, and they'll be on their own any time after eleven or whatever. Yer man gets there and lures Mal outside by admiring the view. He makes sure there are no prying eyes and throws him off the dock, but he doesn't have time to go in to get the collection. Maybe he sees someone or wants to make sure he gets to the auction in lots of time to make sure people see him. He comes back later when he realizes the house is being sold, and breaks in."

Shannon finished her cooling bisque in triumph as Emma considered the scenario.

"No. There are way too many problems with that. Didn't you tell me Mal had drugs in his body?"

"He had lots of ailments. For all we know, he took those drugs all the time."

"His wife's drugs? And she didn't know?"

"So maybe he just happened to take them that night because he was feeling rotten. In fact, maybe he was wobbly, and Noble saw his chance. It wasn't premeditated, but Mal made him angry. It sounds like Mal did that to people."

"I have a hard time imagining he'd go through all that and leave without the collection he so passionately wanted."

"He panicked."

Emma sighed. "So, what's your plan? You're going to go see him and spell out that story to him to see his reaction? That's nuts, Shannon. Let's say you're right. You can't take that chance."

Shannon pursed her lips. "What do you recommend, then?"

"I recommend you call your uncle or Detective Khan to tell them what you think. You said Noble has an alibi."

"Right, the auction and then he bought an old car."

"They must have a reason for believing it."

Shannon frowned. "I'll think about it."

Emma nodded. "I have to go back to the office, and you need to go see your new client."

They paid their bill and parted ways outside the café. Emma grasped Shannon's arm. "Please, Shannon. Promise me you aren't going to talk to that man."

She gave Emma a quick hug. "Don't worry about me. I'll be fine."

Chapter Thirty-Three

SHE DIDN'T HAVE TIME to think about Noble again as she made her way to Mr. and Mrs. Bell's home. Nestled on two acres, the property was carved out of the surrounding farmland. The house itself was a rectangular two-storey white building with a free-standing two-car garage next to it.

Mr. Bell met her at the front door as his wife pushed their barking Great Dane into a den. He held out his hand. "Hello. I'm Sydney Bell."

She shook his hand. "I'm Shannon Coyne." Shannon pulled out a card and handed it to him as his wife joined them. "You must be Margaret?"

The woman was about an inch taller than her husband. She pushed her glasses up and tucked a tendril of hair behind her ear. "I am. Please, call me Marg. Sorry about the ruckus. King will settle down in a minute."

"I love dogs. Don't lock him up on my account."

Sydney shook his head. "He's friendly but overwhelming. He'll go for a nap in a bit."

Shannon followed the couple to the kitchen, where Marg immediately went to the coffee pot and held it up. "Coffee? Or something else?"

"I'm fine for now, thank you." Shannon opened her portfolio and spent the next hour reviewing the paperwork and discussing the house and the couple's expectations. When Marg took Shannon on a tour of the house, Sydney let the dog out, and the two of them went outside.

Shannon admired the hardwood floors and large windows. "It's a beautiful house. A real family home."

"It is. That's why Sandy Smith and I always got along so well. Our families and lifestyles are so similar. Our boys played hockey together. You know. All that sort of thing."

Shannon smiled. "They seem like a lovely family."

"Oh, they are. I'm glad it will work out for them to stay together in the house. Their son is so good. I know he'll be happier having his father close by in order to keep an eye on him."

"Your kids live nearby?"

"One lives in Toronto now, and the other son lives further north near Parry Sound. They're both still close enough to get together regularly, but they have their own lives, which is fine. This house was a happy home, but now we're ready to find a smaller place. Make life easier on ourselves." She smiled. "Let the boys host the big dinners going forward."

Shannon made some recommendations for decluttering. "The rooms are so nice and spacious. If you take some of the extra furniture out, the space will show better."

By the time she left the Bell home, it was supper time, and she decided to swing past the Schnitzel Shack to pick up some take-out schnitzel with a side of red cabbage and apple. The serving was always so generous; she generally had enough from the leftovers for lunch the next day.

❦

Dusty went out into the back garden while Shannon portioned out her schnitzel and poured herself some sparkling water. She fed her dog and then studied the whiteboard as she ate.

Emma's right. I can't talk to Noble by myself. I doubt if Piet will go with me. I guess the sensible thing is to talk to Kal.

She finished her supper, cleaned up and wrote a note to Kal. Writing out her theories as she had explained them to Emma made her wonder if her friend had been right. *OK, there are some holes in it, but it's still worth asking.* She closed her note with a request for Kal to phone her when he had a chance, and she sent it off.

Her favourite television show, Coronation Street, had just finished at 7:30 when Kal called.

"Hi, Kal. Thank you for calling. I know I'm probably a nuisance by now, but I feel like there are too many unanswered questions when it comes to Andrew Noble."

She heard the smile in his voice. "They are unanswered in your mind, but not mine."

"Are you allowed to tell me why you are convinced of Noble's innocence?"

"We have CCTV film showing Noble at the auction. He arrived at noon and spent quite a bit of time wandering around, looking at all the items going up for sale. He bought lunch at the canteen in the auction house and then he was present for the bidding until he bought all the items he was interested in. There are several cameras around the auction barn. They've had too many thefts in the past and recently upgraded their security system."

"Oh. And you could track him for the whole time."

"Yes, we could."

Shannon felt her shoulders slump. "Well, that's that, then."

Kal's voice was kind. "Shannon, I know how much you want to prove Violet Walker is innocent, but we've looked at everyone else in Malcolm Walker's life, and she really is the one who has the motive, the opportunity, and although she's not a big, strong woman, with the quantity of drugs in her husband's system, we are sure she was able to do this. Maybe it was spontaneous. I don't know. The best help you can give is to convince her to talk to us. She should explain what happened."

Shannon sighed. "Thank you for telling me about Andrew Noble. I'll think about what you've said, Kal. I'll let you go now."

From the safety of the sofa, Dusty followed her mistress with her eyes as Shannon paced back and forth. She drew a line through Andrew Noble's name. She muttered, "Fine. You're a thief, but apparently not a killer."

Nate Stevens. You were away, and I'm sure that's also a watertight alibi. So, who's left? Jennifer and Chris.

Shannon spent the evening toying with those two names, and before bed, she knew she had the answer.

She called Piet and got his voicemail. She left a message. "Hi Piet. I've done some more thinking. I'm off to bed now, but can you come by tomorrow after work? I need to run this past you before I make a fool of myself again by talking to Kal Khan. Let me know."

❧

As Shannon got ready to take the Bells house shopping, she muttered. "If Piet calls before I get to the office to meet Marg and Sydney, I'll give him the highlights of my thinking."

She phoned him as she drove, but it went to voicemail again, and she didn't leave a message.

Mr. and Mrs. Bell waited in the parking lot for her, so she couldn't talk to him when Piet called back as she pulled in to work. "Hi Piet. Thanks for calling. My clients are waiting for me, but will I see you after work? I should be home by five."

"I finish work at six today and will come down as soon as I change."

"Thanks, Piet. I have some leftover schnitzel. I'll make sandwiches, some veggies, and dip. See you then."

She bounced out of her car to go and chat with her clients. They had already agreed to each drive their own cars, but the Bells would follow her. Shannon handed over the printouts of the two listings they would visit. "I think these have what you're looking for, but this one might be a little too far out. It's close to Grafton, but the property is beautiful."

Marg nodded. "We're willing to look at it, but I suspect you're right. We have a long list of wants, so finding everything in one house will be hard. We've been looking, so we know."

Shannon glanced at her watch. "Let's get going, then. I said we'd be there at ten."

※

The Bells were very thorough as they walked through the first home. When they left, Shannon treated them to lunch at the Buttermilk Café in Cobourg, where they discussed the positives and negatives of the house. Sydney was enthusiastic, but Marg felt the property was too large. "We're supposed to be downsizing. It still has a lot of lawn to cut."

"That's what I like about it."

Shannon smiled to hear the couple debating. This was usually the way it went. One person saw a feature as something to love, and the other found it to be a drawback.

"Right. Shall we head over to the next place, or are you ready to put in an offer on this one in Precious Corners already?"

Marg shook her head. "Let's go. I'm not ready to make a snap decision. Sydney hates shopping, even for a home." She stroked the back of his hand fondly.

He smiled sheepishly. "That's probably true. Maybe I should let you two go on your own, and when Marg picks a place, I'll go look at it."

Marg laughed. "No chance."

He stood up and gave her a mock salute. "Yes, dear. I'm ready to do my duty and go house shopping with you."

Shannon thought about the couple as she merged onto the 401 Highway, glancing in the rearview to ensure they were behind her. *They are a nice couple. They've been through so much together and obviously still enjoy each other's company.* Her mind turned to Violet and Mal. *I thought they were a great couple, but now it seems I was wrong. I can see the difference now. Violet and Mal never laughed together like Mammy and Da do.*

The second house appealed to Marg and Sydney, but by the time they left, Marg made it clear that the location didn't suit her. "If we want to visit Toronto, it's an extra hour's drive."

They went their separate ways, with Shannon promising to keep looking. "I know better now what's important and what isn't. Don't worry. We'll find it."

Sydney patted her on the shoulder. "We have faith in you. We're in no rush. We have those few things to do in our house before getting it on the market anyway, so there's plenty of time."

Shannon was pleased that the second viewing hadn't taken as long as the first. *I have time to take Dusty for a quick walk before Piet comes over. Poor girl's been cooped up a lot lately.*

She drove automatically, her mind on her whiteboard, and planned how to present her theory to Piet. *I don't know why I didn't see it before. If Piet agrees with me, I'll take Kal or maybe even Uncle Bob through it. They'll have to see it.*

Chapter Thirty-Four

"OK, PUMPKIN. YOUR UNCLE Piet's coming over in a bit, so we can't stay out long, but there's time for a short walk. We'll go down to the Commons Park. It's close by and nice and quiet. How's that sound?" She left her flat door unlocked in case Piet arrived before she was home.

Dusty yipped joyfully as Shannon clipped the leash on her, and they set off. Shannon's mind was wrapped up with the Walkers. She didn't notice the same red car that had prompted her panic attack the previous day sliding away from the curb where it had been parked. Although Dusty looked back a couple of times, Shannon failed to see as it slowly crept along the quiet street behind her.

They walked briskly across the main street and headed towards the nearby park. The small ballfield was empty, and the houses fronting the parkette were quiet. No sidewalks edged the grassy square, and as Shannon stopped to allow Dusty time to sniff a particularly interesting spot, she was startled to hear her name called.

She turned to face the red car stopped beside her. Her heart lurched as she recognized it from the previous day. The passenger window was down, and Shannon bent over to peer into the dim interior. "Oh! Chris. Hi."

He got out of the car and came around to stop her as Shannon began to move away. "I was going past and noticed you walking, so I thought I'd check to see if you'd heard anything further about that man you told us about."

Her heart thudded. Shannon tried to think of a way to leave, but Chris suddenly bent down and picked up Dusty.

"What are you doing? She doesn't like to be picked up, especially by strangers. She might nip you."

Chris opened the back door of his car and tossed the barking, wriggling dog into the back.

Shannon yelped along with her dog. "What in the world…"

Chris flipped his jacket aside to reveal a knife in a sheath attached to his belt. "Don't make a fuss, Shannon. Don't yell. Don't try to attract attention. I'm sure you don't want anything to happen to your little doggy."

She swallowed. "What do you want, Chris?"

"I need you to come with me. Get in the car."

Resisting his nudge, she reached for the back door handle.

"If you try to open that door, you'll be sorry." He slid the knife partially from its leather holder. The sun glinted through the trees on the wickedly sharp-looking steel.

Chris opened the passenger side door. "Hand over your phone and then get in. I won't tell you again."

Shannon pulled her phone from her back pocket and handed it to him. He powered it off and nodded again towards the open door. She got in, her heart thudding in her throat.

When her mistress sat in the car, Dusty calmed down, exhausted by her frenzied barking. Shannon reached back across the back seat and fondled the dog for a moment. "Good girl. Everything's fine. You lie down now." *If you don't, this madman might throw you out of the car, and that will kill me.*

At the park's edge, Chris made a U-turn to enable him to stop beside a garbage bin, into which he dropped Shannon's new phone.

All thoughts of somehow getting her phone from him died. *Now what?*

For the moment, she concentrated on staying calm. *Don't throw up. He won't kill me.* Her next thought was: *But he killed Malcolm Walker. The second time is probably easier.*

Chapter Thirty-Five

PIET CALLED SHANNON ON his way home, surprised when it went straight to voicemail. *She might be in the backyard.* "I'm on my way. Sorry, I'm a bit late. I'll be there by 6:30 and can't wait for that schnitzel sandwich you promised me. See you soon!"

Her car was in its usual parking spot, so he called through her door on his way past and up the stairs to his flat. "Back down in a few minutes."

Piet took his time getting changed into sweatpants and a T-shirt. He fed Caesar, talking to his tabby cat as he spooned a seafood mix onto a saucer. "I know, I'm leaving again. Shall I take you down with me? You can hang out with your pal, Dusty for a bit?" Piet decided there was no rush since Shannon planned to serve cold food. He sat down to call his friend, Connor, while Caesar leisurely nibbled at his dinner. When Caesar finished eating, Piet said goodbye to Connor, promising to call again later.

Caesar nestled into Piet's arms, and they went down to Shannon's flat. He murmured to his cat. "Your breath is disgusting. Don't breathe on anyone, or you won't be invited back." Caesar butted his head against Piet's chin and purred.

Piet tapped on Shannon's door and pushed it open. "Hiya. Your boys are here." He frowned when Dusty didn't come galloping to the door to greet him. He set the cat down on the sofa. "Are you two outside?"

He went to the French doors and looked out. *No. Not there. Where are you, girl?* Pulling out his phone, Piet dialed her number, and again, it went straight to voicemail. *OK. It's 6:45, and you aren't here. That's not like you. But Dusty's gone too, so you must be out for a walk. Weird, but nothing to worry about.*

He scooped up Caesar, who had curled up on the sofa and was contentedly giving himself a post-dinner bath. "Sorry, buddy. You're going back upstairs. I think I'll go for a little walk to see if I can track them down."

Minutes passed as Piet took his cat back upstairs, exchanged his slippers for sneakers, and stopped again at Shannon's flat to leave a scribbled note saying he was out looking for her. "Please call me when you read this. Getting worried, babe."

Chapter Thirty-Six

CHRIS GRIPPED THE STEERING wheel so tightly that Shannon saw his knuckles were white. *He's panicked.*

"Where are you taking me, Chris?"

"You'll see."

"I guess the bigger question is why?"

"You know."

"I don't. I know you killed your uncle, but I don't know why, and I don't know why you've taken me. None of this makes sense."

He stared out the window as he drove, as though he hadn't heard her.

She tried again, keeping her voice as calm as possible. "Are we meeting Jennifer?"

He snorted. "Jenn? Ha."

So, they aren't doing this together. I didn't think so. It was hard to imagine them collaborating on something like that.

He shouted. "Don't talk. Just be quiet!"

Dusty barked, and Shannon leaned her arm back to comfort the frightened dog, murmuring, "Shhh. It's all right. Quiet, now." The dog subsided to a low growling, and Shannon continued quieting her until the growling stopped, and she curled up again. "Good girl. Good, quiet."

Pulling her arm back, Shannon considered what to do. *Keep talking? Or sit here quietly, waiting to see what happens? Maybe he'll pull over, and I can catch someone's eye and tell them I need help.* She decided to be quiet as he drove.

The sun was still a long way from setting. *Last night, it was almost nine o'clock.* Shannon watched the familiar buildings along the route. Going east, but where?

As they went past the Tim Hortons where she had been struck by a car, she turned to look at Chris. "Was that you that ran into me?"

"Yes."

"Were you trying to kill me?"

"Maybe. I wanted to shut you up. I knew it was a matter of time before you figured it out, and I guess I panicked."

"Everyone said it was a black car."

He snorted again. "You never heard of Kijiji? You can sell anything there. That car, with its broken headlight, is in Calgary by now. A guy bought it for his son, who was heading there for school."

"And you bought this one."

"Yup. It's not as good as my last car. I miss that one, but no one was looking for a red Mazda."

"You were outside the Legion yesterday."

"Yup."

"You wanted to run me over again?"

"Maybe. Now shut up and let me think."

He's looking for something specific. What? Where? And why?

Chapter Thirty-Seven

PIET GOT BACK TO Shannon's apartment at seven-fifteen. He had called Connor as he walked. "I don't know what to do. We've been here before. She's in trouble. She must be."

"I'm coming over. I'll be there in ten minutes. Just stay calm. We'll figure this out together."

His friend's musical Irish lilt helped to settle his nerves, but he waited for his friend to arrive with the door open.

When Connor arrived a few minutes after Piet did, he came brandishing a bottle of brandy. "Have a dram first. You can't do anything until you're calm."

Piet found two glasses in Shannon's buffet. "Thanks for coming. I think I need to call the police."

"Let's look around first. Maybe there's something here you've overlooked. Some hint of where she's taken herself. Maybe the dog's hurt, and she's gone to the vet?"

Piet nodded. "Yes, of course. That's possible. We'll take a quick look."

Connor stood in front of the whiteboard. "What's all this, then?"

"It's about that murder we've been working on."

"Right. The Scriven business?"

"Yes. See, here Shannon's drawn a line through that fella's name. That's why I came tonight. She planned to take me through her current thinking."

"No shortage of ideas, then?"

Piet smiled. "No. She's great at seeing things other people don't."

"OK, take me through it."

"This. Well, this is new." Piet frowned to see two red circles drawn around Chris's name. "She's discovered something about this guy, but he has no motive. We eliminated him early on."

Connor tilted his head. "I can't make heads nor tails of it. Can you?"

"I can tell she's had some sort of epiphany about Chris, but I don't know why."

Connor wandered off around the small apartment. "I don't see anything else to steer us in the right direction. Do you think it's because of this that she's missing?" He waved his hand at the board.

Piet nodded. "It must be. I'm calling her folks to find out if they know anything."

Connor kept circling around the apartment as his friend called Mary Coyne.

"Mrs. Coyne? Hi, it's Piet Van Loo here. No, nothing to panic about. Shannon's healing well after her accident. It's just that, well, we planned to get together at her place this evening, but she's not here and is not answering her phone, so I figured I better check with you."

Piet nodded as Shannon's mother spoke. "You'll call them? I hate to say it, but I think it's a good idea. I'll wait here in her flat until they get here. Thank you."

Connor raised his eyebrows. "She's calling the police?"

"Yes. Her brother is the Detective Sergeant. After Shannon was hit by a car a couple of weeks ago, Shannon's folks tried to get her to stay with them because this police sergeant said it might not be an accident."

Connor's mouth dropped open. "I thought all this investigation she was up to, was more of a lark than anything. Good God. Someone tried to run her over on purpose?"

"They haven't proven that yet, but yes. Even Shannon told me she was worried."

"But not worried enough to stay where it was safe with her parents?"

"That's not who Shannon is. She has a life to live here in Port Hope, not out at the farm."

Connor shook his head. "Jaysus. Let's hope she continues to live it." He saw his friend pale. "Ah, no. Sorry, sorry. I didn't mean that. I'm sure she'll be fine."

Piet gulped. "I'm not sure."

"If the police are on their way, should I go?"

"No, please stay, will you?"

"I will, of course."

Kal Khan arrived first. He shook Piet's hand and nodded to Connor, who sat in Dusty's wingback chair by the French doors. "Tell me everything."

"Do you want to wait for your sergeant?"

"No. Let's not waste a minute." He pulled out his notebook, and Piet began.

Chapter Thirty-Eight

CHRIS DROVE EAST ALONG Highway 2, past Betty's Pies and Tarts, where Shannon had so recently bought butter tarts to take home. She swallowed a lump in her throat, thinking about her parents.

He slowed and turned left on Theatre Road. Shannon frowned. *Does he have a house along here?* In minutes, he slowed again. She watched him look in the rearview mirror, confirming the road was empty behind and in front of them. There were no houses along this stretch of road; scrub bushes and farmland made the spot perfectly isolated and ideal for the location of the old, abandoned drive-in theatre. Chris turned in and switched off the car, pocketing the keys. "Stay there. You can't run faster than me."

She knew he was right. She watched him move one of the wooden sawhorses that served as a roadblock into the old theatre land. He trotted back, drove the car through, and then returned to replace the sawhorse.

The large white "For Sale" sign was battered and peeling. No one had taken an interest in this property for a long time. Chris edged the car to the right, around the large concrete structure across which the rusting iron scaffolding crawled, spider-like, still holding up a screen that no one watched anymore. He bumped along the weedy, broken pavement, past the blue and white hut where the ticket seller would have hunched, taking in grubby coins and bills from excited

teenagers crammed into overfull cars. He let the car come to rest beyond the rusting barrier separating the parking area from the entrance road. Hidden from the sight of any passing vehicles, Chris leaned back and sighed.

Shannon rested against the passenger door and studied her captor. "Now what?"

He pulled a bottle of Crown Royal from under his car seat and broke open the seal. "Uncle Mal gave this to me last Christmas. I'm not much of a drinker. I don't know why he gave it to me other than he liked it." He took a deep drink and then coughed and sputtered, his face flushing with the effort.

When the coughing fit passed, he pulled out a bottle of pills and took two with another smaller swallow of whiskey.

"What did you take, Chris?"

He shook the half-empty bottle of pills. "Another gift from Uncle Mal. His diazepam."

Shannon sucked in her breath. "I thought the drugs in his system were Violet's?"

"No. He had his own prescription, but no one knew because he had gone to a different doctor." He held out the bottle. "Here. Take two."

She shook her head. "No, thank you."

He glared at her. "There are more than 20 pills left here. That's ten for you and twelve more for me. It's not a big overdose, but it should be enough."

Her lips were dry. "Enough for what?"

He stretched his mouth in a large, toothy parody of a smile that sent shivers down Shannon's spine. "To do us each in, of course."

The grin disappeared. "Take them." He rested the bottle on the car seat between his legs and slid the knife from the leather sheath on his belt.

Shannon held out her hand, and he tapped 2 round yellow pills into her palm.

Chris peered at her. "Don't drop them, or I'll take the shortcut to your demise." He laughed and waved the knife. "Short *cut*. Get it?"

He'll make sure I have them in my mouth. She put them in her mouth and rested them on her tongue.

"Open your mouth."

She opened it, and when he nodded, she closed her mouth again, sliding them into her cheek. "I need a drink."

He handed the bottle of whiskey to her. "Don't drink much. This is mine."

She held the bottle by its neck, her fingers curled around the top, and when she tipped the bottle up, tongued the pills to the front of her mouth. She coughed, as he had done with the first sip, and the softened pills went into her fingers. She shoved them inside the neck of her mock-neck T-shirt in one fluid movement.

He barked at her. "Show me your hand!"

She opened her hand. "I swallowed them."

He nodded and took two more pills himself with a large gulp of whiskey. "This grows on you. I may come to like it."

"We're going to be here a while. Tell me what happened."

"You wouldn't understand."

"I think I would. You loved your uncle. He was good to you."

He nodded. "I loved him even more than I did my real dad. I hardly knew that guy, but Mal made a real effort with me. Took me everywhere. Taught me things. Brought me here. Just him and me, sitting here in the dark, eating popcorn. He never took Jenn. This was our place. Sitting in the dark, we could talk about anything. Girls, work, responsibility."

That's why we're here.

"Responsibility." Chris slurred as he struggled to repeat the word.

"When Mal got sick, he turned to you, didn't he?"

"He hated looking weak in front of the women. He could only relax with me."

"He asked you to help him die, didn't he?"

Chris peered through the dusky light at her, and growled. "Hold out your hand."

"Why kill me, Chris? I wanted to free your aunt. The truth. It's all I ever wanted."

He became more agitated. "Hold out your hand."

She did as he ordered, and he tapped two more pills out. He blinked several times as he watched her. Shannon opened her mouth and put a pill on her tongue, showing him it was there.

"And the other one."

She tongued the first pill to the side, made a show of swallowing, and then opened her mouth to place the other one on her tongue as she retrieved the first one back out. She pushed that one down between the car seat and back while she pushed the second pill to the front between her teeth and bottom lip.

Satisfied she had taken the pills, he turned to stare out the front window at the darkening theatre. Shannon turned away and flipped the pill out of her mouth, hoping it landed somewhere he wouldn't notice. She felt queasy and lightheaded. *The whiskey or the pills? Or adrenalin?*

Shannon heard Dusty turn in the back seat several times and knew she was getting restless. "Well, Chris? Why me? What did I do to make you hate me?"

Without looking at her, he mumbled his answer. "It's all your fault. Everything would have been fine if you hadn't gotten involved. Because of you, I have to die. And since I need to die, so do you…"

Chapter Thirty-Nine

BEFORE PIET HAD FINISHED his narration of what he knew, which didn't amount to much, he thought, Shannon's Uncle Bob had arrived.

The police detective glared at the whiteboard before turning back to Piet. "I knew she wouldn't leave it alone. And you enabled her with all this nonsense, didn't you?"

Connor had risen for an introduction to Shannon's uncle. "With respect, it can't be nonsense if she's missing, but."

Piet widened his eyes, uncertain if the thunderous look on Bob Miller's face was a result of Connor's defence of Piet and Shannon or his Dublin accent.

"It's nonsense, in my view, when civilians insist on meddling in something they aren't qualified for. That includes my niece and anyone else associated with her and this investigation."

Connor looked like he'd say more, but Piet stepped to his friend's side and gripped his arm to prevent him. "As I just explained to Detective Khan, I've called the few people who might know where she is: Emma, her folks, and Emma called their boss, but no one's heard from her."

Connor turned away and picked up Shannon's portfolio from the table before flopping back into the wing chair.

Piet pointed to the whiteboard. "She planned to explain her latest thinking this evening. I'm sure she believes Chris is somehow involved."

Bob frowned. "Chris Walker? Why?"

Piet shook his head. "I don't know why she believes he's involved, but see how she's circled his name. That's her way of meaning it's important."

Connor held up Shannon's portfolio. "Look. This is where Shannon keeps notes about her work, but after one meeting with someone called Marg Bell, she writes, *'he'd do anything for his father.'* Under that line, she's written Chris Walker."

Bob looked at Khan. "Is there anything to this? I thought Chris Walker was checked out?"

Khan nodded. "He was eliminated because we felt he had no motive. He was at home working the afternoon of Malcolm Walker's death. He doesn't have witnesses who saw him at home; however, equally, no one saw him near the Walker house. People in the neighbourhood know him well and would have recognized him. He was on a Zoom call with two other people at two o'clock, which they validated. All these factors took him off our list."

Connor spoke from his spot in the corner. "You know you can set a virtual background on Zoom, so it looks like you are anywhere you want. If he has a background image of his home office, he could use that while he's sitting in the car or anywhere in the world."

Bob turned to Kal. "Is that true?"

"Yes, it is."

Bob pursed his lips. "Right. Call in Shannon's phone to see if we can track it."

Kal Khan shook his head. "I did that already, Sergeant. No luck.

It's turned off. I also called Violet Walker to see if she knew where Chris might be. She said she had no idea. I left a message for Jennifer, but she hasn't responded yet."

Bob Miller's face flushed. "Send some uniforms to his house. He has to be somewhere."

Kal Khan nodded. "They're on their way now. We should hear back shortly."

Piet yelped. "Wait. I have an idea of how to find Shannon."

Chapter Forty

CHRIS WAVED HIS KNIFE around, and Shannon pressed her back against the door to avoid being slashed.

"Uncle Mal gave me this Bowie knife years ago. Aunt Violet was upset because she didn't think it was a gift for a teenage boy. She was right, but I loved it. It proved how much he trusted me, don't you think?"

"I think I'd be a lot happier if you'd put it back in the holder."

He shook his head in disgust. "*Sheath*. You know so little. I don't know how you came to be such a pain." He took a large swig of whiskey, set the bottle back down and wiped his mouth with the back of his hand.

"You're right. There's so much I don't know about what happened and why we're here. I'd like you to tell me everything. Will you do that?" Her quiet voice helped to settle Dusty down again in the back. The dog turned and stretched out across the seat.

Chris took a deep breath. "Why should I tell you? What's the point?"

"Isn't that why we're here? You need to tell someone, and you picked me."

He shrugged. "You're right about Uncle Mal. He couldn't stand being weak. He was miserable before, but when he started to lose his vision, he decided he wasn't going to just wait for his body to break down, making him a prisoner slowly. He started talking to me after Christmas. No. I said no so many times, but he kept at me. About my responsibility. About how I was the only one he could ask. He wore me down."

Shannon frowned. "If he was so determined, why not just do it himself?"

Chris nodded. "Exactly. Aunt Violet was right when she told the police he'd never commit suicide."

She nodded. "I can understand it. Is it because he felt his life was God's and he didn't have the right to take his own life? Pretty unfair of him to ask you to take it, then."

Chris shrugged. "I owed him. He made that clear."

Shannon saw Chris clench his teeth. *I'll steer him to something safer.* "Tell me how you managed everything. No one saw you. You must have had a boat. I can't believe you pushed him off the dock at the house."

He crooked his mouth in a small smile. "I'm very organized. Once he got me to agree, it was just a matter of planning. It couldn't be too early in the season. A boat on the water in April would attract attention. Too late, and there'd be other boats around."

"The boat? Did you use theirs? I thought the police checked it."

"No. I couldn't use theirs. You know Nate Stevens, right?"

She nodded.

"He has a boat. I should know. I designed the extension of his house in Hall Landing. I have the keys to the house and the boathouse. We're friends by now, even though I didn't talk much about it to Aunt Violet. She took against Nate for some reason. Uncle Mal knew, though. He wanted me to charge Nate a fortune for my work, and I said I did, but he found out from Nate that I fibbed. Mal was furious with Stevens. Said he'd taken advantage of me. That was nonsense, of course. I charged a bit less than the going rate. We were both happy. Anyway, I knew Nate was going away that weekend, so I went and got the boat ready."

Chris had slid his knife back into its sheath as he talked. He shook out several pills and washed them down with the Crown Royal. He seemed to have forgotten about his plan to drug Shannon at the same rate as himself. His eyes were red, and his lids drooped. He turned towards her and frowned as if suddenly recalling his plot.

"But how did you get Mal into the boat?"

"That was the easy part. The only risky thing was picking him up in my car. You've seen the house, though. Surrounded by cedars. Unless someone was there right then, I figured we'd be away before anyone knew anything about it. I called Uncle Mal and told him to walk up the driveway and stand behind the hedge until the moment I drove by. If someone had been there, I'd have cancelled the whole thing, but it went like clockwork. We drove over to Nate's place, which was even more isolated. I had the boat ready. He'd taken a pile of pills already, and we went out in the boat. He had coffee from my thermos and even more pills. I kept asking him if he wanted to change his mind, but he kept repeating, 'Don't let me down, don't let me down.' I knew it was then or never. I couldn't go through all that again."

He subsided into silence, staring out the front window at the darkening sky. Shannon watched Chris's head bob once. *Please let him fall asleep.*

His head snapped up again as he forced himself awake. Fumbling with the pill bottle, he tipped three out and suddenly lunged at Shannon. "Take them. Open your mouth and swallow them."

Shannon pulled her head back and squirmed, but he was strong. He grasped her jaw with his left hand and pried open her mouth, shoving the three pills into her. He held her mouth closed then, not unlike what Shannon herself had done in the past to get pills into Dusty. He glared at her and shoved the open bottle at her. "Drink, or I'll pour it into you."

She took a sip, and the pills went down.

"Open."

She opened her mouth to show him they were gone.

Chris fell back against the driver's door and stared at her. "It went like clockwork." He repeated. "No one should have known what happened. There was no evidence to convict Aunt Violet. Mal and I had talked about that. He knew she'd be suspected, and as much as she irritated him, he didn't want anyone blamed."

"Why was his coat floating around? Did it come off when you pushed him into the water?"

"No. We talked about that, too. He didn't know if his body would sink and disappear, and he didn't want to start a big mystery. He wanted people to know he'd drowned, even if his body was gone. He loved that coat. He wore it that day and almost forgot to take it off." Chris closed his eyes briefly. "I felt like a monster telling him to take it off."

Shannon felt queasy. "The whole thing was awful for you. He had no right to demand you help him."

"Of course, he had the right. I owed him everything."

His head lolled back against the headrest. "And now it's over. If you hadn't gotten involved, Aunt Violet's case would have naturally died from lack of evidence. Instead, you kept poking and prodding until the police figured there was more to the story."

She didn't challenge him on his assumption but suspected it wouldn't have gone away as easily as he imagined. "Chris, I know you're a good person. None of this was fair to you, but you helped your uncle from love. You aren't a killer. Let me go with my poor little dog that's getting so anxious back there."

He focused on her. "Anxious? You've driven me, my aunt, and even Jennifer crazy with your interference. You don't get to go home like nothing's happened. No, sir. You're right, though. The dog is innocent. I'll let the dog go, but you? You're going nowhere."

Chapter Forty-One

ALL EYES TURNED TO Piet.

Bob Miller growled. "Well? What's your idea?"

Piet tapped into his phone. "I have an app here somewhere. I haven't used it yet, but Shannon made me install it."

Bob looked at his detective, Kal, as if he should know what Piet was talking about. "An app?"

Piet held up his phone in triumph. "Here it is."

Kal peered at Piet's phone. "You have a family locator app for Shannon?"

"No. Not exactly. I have one for Dusty."

"The dog?"

Piet nodded to Kal. "Yes. Dusty got away from Shannon once, and after that, she got a GPS tracker that's clipped to the dog's collar. She could share the GPS information with a couple of other people for the same contract price, so she had me install it, thinking I'd be the one most likely helping her find Dusty if she ever escaped again."

Kal nodded. "You find Dusty, you find Shannon."

"Look. She's stationary not far from Port Hope."

They crowded around to peer at the phone." Bob plucked it from Piet's hand. "Right. You come with me and read it out while I drive. Kahn, you follow and, "he waved in the direction of Connor, "you go with Detective Kahn if you need to come along."

Piet glanced at Connor. "Will you come?"

"Try and stop me."

They scrambled from the apartment, and as Bob Miller drove, he called in to give his dispatcher the details of where they were heading and asked for uniform backup.

Piet looked at his phone. "Oh!"

"What is it?"

"Dusty isn't stationery anymore. She's moving around the area slowly like she's just exploring or something."

"If this is a wild goose chase, I'll skin yeh. If Shannon's just strolling around looking for her dog and I'm using police resources to find her, by Jaysus…"

Piet shook his head, eyes glued to his phone. "She isn't. She would have called me, and besides, how would she lose Dusty way out here? Her car's still parked at home."

"Fair enough."

"OK, it's coming up. You'll turn left on Theatre Road. Dusty's still wandering around in the same vicinity at the old drive-in.

Miller made the turn and slowed down. He spoke on the radio to Kal. "I'm driving past. I don't want to spook anyone."

They drove past, going slowly north. "See anything?"

Piet peered into the darkness as they drove by. "I don't know. It's so dark. I don't know if I'm seeing shadows or a car."

Bob drove further and pulled over, out of sight of the drive-in, to wait for Kal. He pointed his finger at Piet. "Stay in the car."

Bob got out and conferred with Kal. "The uniforms are going to be here any minute. You and I better get in there and see what's going on. I'll instruct them to come up here to rendezvous."

Khan nodded. "I'll jog back and then cut across the field. I'll keep my phone open." He composed his sergeant's number, and they both tucked their phones into their shirt pockets.

Connor had walked over, and Bob opened the back door to let Piet out. "You two stay here, and when the uniformed officers arrive, tell them just to stay put until I call them."

Piet pulled out two broken dog biscuits and handed them to Bob. "Just in case Dusty comes at you barking. These are her favourites."

Bob nodded, pocketing the cookies. "Good thinking."

Piet and Connor watched Sergeant Miller U-turn and head back south; his lights turned low.

Connor shivered despite the warm evening. "You think she's here?"

"She's here."

The two of them looked at Piet's phone, watching the small icon of Dusty moving in circles. "She doesn't seem too stressed."

Connor frowned. "How can you tell?"

"She runs around like a dervish when she's excited or upset. She seems to just be nosing around in this one area, which tells me Shannon is close by. Dusty wouldn't wander off too far from her mistress."

"She did run off on her once in the Port Hope Park." Connor pointed out.

"That's different. She knew Shannon was nearby, and she went back to look for her. She couldn't help it Shannon had moved by then."

A marked police car drove up and parked along the shoulder of the road when Piet waved them down. He relayed Bob Miller's message.

"So, what's going on? Something about a missing person?"

"We think Sergeant Miller's niece, Shannon, has been abducted. By a killer."

The police officer straightened up. "Oh, wow. OK."

Piet put his finger to his lips. "Shhh. Sound travels a long way out here in the quiet."

The officer scowled and rolled up his window.

As if to emphasize Piet's point, they all heard a dog bark—a sharp series of yelps and deeper barks. Piet looked at his phone and held it for Connor to see. "Look, she's spotted someone. Either Kal or Bob Miller. See how she's moving fast towards something?"

They waited, their eyes glued to the glowing screen as if it would tell them what was happening a field away from where they stood.

The radio crackled, giving instructions to the police officers in the car. The car squealed in its U-turn, spitting gravel at Piet and Connor, and raced back down the road. Piet watched the brake lights flare when it turned into the theatre's entrance. He had time to think *someone must have moved the barriers* before the car disappeared beyond their range of vision, hidden by the concrete screen structure.

Connor pulled Piet's hand that held the phone towards him to see what Dusty was doing, but before they were able to focus on the screen, a gunshot ruptured the night air.

Chapter Forty-Two

THE MOMENT AFTER SHANNON pleaded with Chris to let her and Dusty go, she wished she'd kept her mouth shut.

He stretched his left arm into the back and opened the rear door. "Go on, doggo. Get out."

Shannon gasped. "No. I'm sorry. She needs to stay with me."

"You wanted to save her. Get her out of this car, or I'm going to stuff a couple of pills down her gullet, and we'll all go together. You choose."

Tears streamed down Shannon's cheeks. "I'll have to get out to lift her down."

"You stay right where you are."

Chris slid his knife from its sheath again and leaned back to tap Dusty's rump with the broad, flat side. "Out. Go on. Go."

Dusty edged her way toward the fresh evening air and lifted her nose to the unfamiliar scents. She looked up to her mistress.

Shannon tried to keep her voice calm. "Off you go, Dusty. Go pee."

With that permission, the spaniel scooted out of the car and slipped into the dark.

Chris pulled the door closed. "See? I'm not a bad guy."

Shannon swallowed. "I know that. You don't need to do any of this, Chris. Prove to the world you aren't evil. If you and I die here, your Aunt Violet will think the worst of you. Everyone will, and that's not fair. Explain what happened; I'm sure they'll go easy on you. You were put into an impossible position. You need to stay and explain that. This is the very worst thing you can do. Your aunt thinks the world of you. I have a feeling Mal often let her down. Don't you let her down as well."

Chris leaned his head back against the headrest. He shook out two more pills and swallowed them with a mouthful of whiskey. "I'm tired."

Shannon stared out the window, trying to catch a glimpse of Dusty. "I believe you. Stop this now, and you can rest. I'll help you. I'll speak on your behalf."

He had dropped the knife on the floor by his feet after Dusty left. He now held the almost empty pill bottle in one hand and the whiskey in the other. He turned and blinked at her. "You'll help me? You can't help. Don't you get it? No one can help. I thought everything would work out, but that was a fool's errand. I was the fool to listen to him."

He shook the pills. "Almost empty. Almost done." He handed her the bottle. "You take the rest."

Shannon shook her head. "I can't. I'm sick. I'm going to throw up as it is."

"Stop talking. I need to think." He took another gulp of whiskey and then closed his eyes.

She pushed the bottle out of sight between the seat and back. *If I'm quiet, he'll fall asleep. Don't die, Chris. I don't want you to die, but I don't want to, either.*

Chris groaned and dropped the bottle on the floor. What little whiskey was left trickled onto the floor mat, fumes filling the car. He started, as the sharp smell acted in the same way smelling salts might. "What?" He stared groggily at Shannon in the star-filled night.

"It's nothing, Chris. Go to sleep. I'm here to keep watch."

He blinked, confused. "You're supposed to die."

"Sleep now. Everything will work out."

His head lolled back again when suddenly Dusty began barking. Chris snapped upright. He slurred his words. "What's going on?"

He reached down for the knife, opened the car door, and lifted himself from the car, standing in the moonlight, waving his knife around.

Shannon opened her side and stumbled out, calling for Dusty, who had gone quiet, to come to her. "Dusty, come. Where are you? Come." She was disoriented in the dark and felt dizzy after sitting in the cramped car for so long.

A man's voice startled her, shouting, "Put the knife down. Drop the knife, Chris!"

Uncle Bob. I knew you'd find me. She moved away from the car towards the entry drive and then stopped, blinded by the headlights of the police car. She stood still as it passed her and stopped near Chris's car.

She looked back at the scene, now illuminated by the police car lights and the two bright flashlights the officers shone on Chris. Everyone seemed to be shouting at Chris. "Drop it, drop it, drop it."

But he clung tightly to the large knife and seemed to focus on the figure in front of him rather than the police officers with their blinding lights. He lunged forward, stumbling through the tall weeds.

Shannon almost shrieked when she felt a warm body press against her shins. She pulled her eyes away from the scene before her long enough to lean down and scoop Dusty up in her arms. "Good girl, good girl, darling girl."

When she looked back, she sucked in her breath and held it to prevent herself from screaming. Her uncle had his arms raised and extended, holding a gun. He stood with his feet wide, leaning forward as he faced Chris. She heard him speak quietly. "Come on, Chris. It's over, Put the knife down. Drop it."

Dusty growled, and Shannon swivelled to see Kal Khan approaching her out of the darkness. His voice was quiet. "Are you all right?"

She nodded. "I'm OK."

He squeezed her arm. "Move back behind the police car." He pushed her gently away from where she stood, frozen, to a place of safety.

When he was sure she had followed his instructions, Kal looped around, getting closer to Chris while staying out of the line of fire.

From her spot behind the car, she saw Chris abruptly lurch forward, waving the knife and yelling incoherently. He seemed determined to slash her uncle, and Shannon cried out. "No!"

Her words were lost in the sound of the gunshot. She heard Chris scream in pain and crumple to the ground. The two police officers ran towards the fallen man, yelling instructions. Shannon widened her eyes when Uncle Bob handed the weapon to his detective, but it wasn't until Dusty whined that she realized how tight her grip on the small wriggling dog was. She set her pup back on the ground and saw the leash was still attached to Dusty's collar. *It seems like a lifetime ago since we were walking around the park.*

Uncle Bob reached her side while Kal joined the two officers looming over Chris. "Are you all right?"

Shannon threw her arms around him, burying her face against his chest. "I'm fine."

He stroked her hair as she sobbed against him. "Shh. You're all right now, love."

She hiccupped and swallowed her sobs. "I didn't do anything to make him come after me, Uncle Bob. I didn't. I didn't accuse him of anything. I figured out it was him, but I planned to tell you and Kal. Honestly."

"I know, *a stór*."

When Shannon heard him call her his 'treasure' in Irish, she took a deep breath. *He's not angry even though he had to put himself in danger for me.* "How did you find me?"

"Your friends Piet and Connor are waiting up the road. They'll explain everything. You better get to them before that Piet fella has a heart attack. Wait here. I'll have someone take you to them."

She watched her uncle speak with one of the officers who strode over to her.

He nodded to her. "Come on. I'll take you up the road and get someone to take you all home."

She sat quietly in the back seat, holding Dusty on her lap, and listened to the officer give his dispatcher instructions to send another car for witness transport. The calm voice on the radio acknowledged the request and confirmed an ambulance would be at the location momentarily for the injured suspect.

The officer opened the car door to release her, instructing Shannon to stay well off the road until the other car arrived to take her home. Climbing out of the vehicle, Dusty immediately pulled her toward Piet, barking out her joy as she recognized him. Ignoring the dog for a moment, he opened his arms to engulf Shannon in a bone-crushing hug.

When Piet released her, he bent down and scooped up the dog as Connor clasped Shannon in a less vigorous hug. Piet faced Shannon as he cuddled the cocker spaniel. "This is the hero of the hour. She led us to you."

"What? How is that possible?"

Piet grinned while he explained about the tracking device. He was still talking when a second police cruiser pulled up moments later. The three of them, with Dusty perched on Piet's knees, fitted themselves into the back seat as they all spoke at once. They stopped talking to watch an ambulance, lights blazing and siren blaring, turn in front of them into the drive-in entry, and then they were passed. The officers asked questions about what happened, and Piet and Connor interjected to add comments or ask questions. Shannon tried to explain, but her head pounded, and she knew she wasn't making much sense.

She sighed and closed her eyes. "Chris made me take diazepam. I'm sorry. I feel fuzzy."

Piet took her hand. "How many pills? Should we go straight to the hospital?"

"No. Please. I want to go home." She smiled to see Dusty curl up, taking space across Piet's and Connor's knees. "And Dusty wants to go home."

There seemed to be so many questions to ask and answer, but for now, Shannon needed to rest. The adrenalin that had kept her going all these hours drained away, leaving her shaky and sick. She vaguely heard one of the officers speak on the radio and ask for directions about whether they should take her home or to the hospital. She thought she recognized her uncle's voice telling them to take her home, and she sunk into the comfort of Piet, putting his arm around her to hold her close.

Chapter Forty-Three

PIET AND CONNOR LEFT when Uncle Bob arrived to check on her. "Did you call your mammy?"

"I did. She cried and wanted to come right over. I told her not to, but…"

"But she's on her way."

"Yes. Both of them are. I told her I had a shower, and I feel all right, but until Mammy sees me with her own eyes, she isn't buying it."

"I don't blame her."

"I know. I'm sure if the roles were reversed, I'd be on my way to see her, too." She paused. "How's Chris?"

"I barely nicked him. He's fine."

"I'm glad. He's not a bad person."

Her uncle raised his eyebrows. "He killed a man, he left his elderly aunt to take the fall, and he tried to kill you. If that doesn't define a 'bad man,' I'm not sure what does."

She shrugged. "Will you have a wee whiskey? Or a cup of tea?"

"It sounds like enough whiskey's been had for one day unless you're having one?"

"I'm not sure I'll ever have whiskey again. I'll put the kettle on."

"If it had been Jameson's, you might have stomached it better." He joked. "Seriously, though, I wish you'd go to the hospital to get checked over."

She sighed. "By now, the pills are probably just about through my system."

"No. The effects of adrenaline helped to counteract the diazepam for a short while, but it takes a good five or six hours for the sedative to wear off. Even then, the drug stays in your system for about ten days."

She raised her eyebrows. "How do you know so much about it?"

He smiled. "I'm not just a pretty face. I took a course on drug overdoses."

"I only took three, despite Chris's best efforts."

"And how do you feel now?"

"Tired," Shannon admitted.

"I'll stay until your folks get here, but if you want to go to bed, don't fight it. Go ahead."

"I'll have a cup of green tea and see how I feel after that."

He stared at the whiteboard again when they each had a large mug of tea. "Tell me how you figured out it was Chris? He wasn't on our radar at all."

She closed her eyes for an instant and then nodded. "Sir Arthur Conan Doyle said: 'When you have eliminated all which is impossible, whatever remains must be the truth.'" Biting her lip, she shook her head. "That's not exactly right. There's something about, *even if it's improbable,* but that's the gist of it."

Uncle Bob tilted his head, his cup of tea poised halfway to his mouth. "Are you saying you decided it was Chris because no one else made sense?"

"No. Not exactly. I eliminated everyone else because it was clear, one by one, that they couldn't have done it."

"Except for the widow." He countered before taking a drink.

"I eliminated her because I just *knew* from the beginning she couldn't have done it."

"You had a feeling she didn't do it."

"It was more than a feeling. You know what I mean."

"Ah, no. Not the second sight."

"You can call it what you want, but Mammy has it, and I have it. It's a knowing of things." She shrugged. "Of course, I get it wrong sometimes. I was sure Jennifer did this, but when she came to talk to me, it was clearer that she was troubled but didn't do it. I admit I was carried away by Andrew Noble. Once he confessed to stealing the Scriven documents, I assumed it meant he was capable of more."

"So, how did you conclude Chris was yer man?"

"Something one of my clients said struck me. She mentioned that the son of another client was such a good son. She said, 'he'd do anything for his father.' I recognized that phrase. The same thing was said about Chris, and suddenly, I saw the whole thing. It was so obvious once I gave the idea space in my mind."

"Why didn't you call me or Detective Khan right away when you had this epiphany?"

She drained her cup and set it down. "I suppose I should have, but I didn't think anyone would listen to me. I wanted to run it past Piet first to see if it made sense. My theory had so many holes, but now I know how it was all done."

"So, tell me."

Shannon gave her uncle the short version of Chris's explanation, from taking the boat and throwing the coat overboard to the sale of his car to cover his tracks after he struck her.

By the time she finished her story, her parents had arrived. Her mother caught her up in a tight hug while her father thanked his brother-in-law for rescuing his daughter. After that, it was his turn to catch Shannon in his arms.

Her mother didn't want to know all the details. "You're going straight to bed, my girl. Where's your hot water bottle?"

Shannon's smile trembled, and she swallowed down tears of exhaustion. "I don't have one, Mammy."

Her mother dug into the large bag she had brought with her. "I thought as much. It's a good job I brought one, so."

She protested as her mother nudged her down the hall to the bedroom. "It's June, Mammy. I don't need a hot water bottle."

"You're in shock. Get yourself into bed while I get it ready." Her mother ignored Shannon's objections, and the young woman did as her mother instructed.

Before drifting off to sleep, her last words were to inform her mother where Dusty's food was. "You'll feed her, won't you? She's been through so much today, poor little girl."

"Of course we will. And we'll be here when you wake up, so go to sleep."

Leaning over, she tucked the hot water bottle against her daughter's back, and although Shannon was too close to sleep to say anything, she was comforted by the heat and her mother's fragrance.

Chapter Forty-Four

ON SUNDAY, PIET READ the news reports to Shannon as she sat outside in the warm afternoon sunshine. "It mentions you by name. It makes Christopher Walker out to be such an evil guy."

Shannon shook her head. "It's not fair. Malcolm was the evil one here. At least the police have released Violet. I talked to her this morning. The poor woman is devastated that it was Chris. She can't get over that he did this, but worse, he let her take the blame."

Piet closed his phone with the news. "It is awful. She trusted him."

"I know. She trusted him more than she did her own daughter."

"I wonder how Jennifer took the news."

"I asked Violet that. She told me that Jennifer didn't seem surprised."

"It sounds like they didn't get along very well, so I suppose there's some satisfaction in finding out she was justified in her feelings."

"I guess so. It's all so awful."

Piet nodded to her glass of iced tea. "Do you want that topped up?"

"No, I'm good, thanks. Twenty-four hours of Mammy and Da has me filled up with food and drink."

"I suppose you have to go into the station to give your statement?"

"Yes, tomorrow morning first thing."

"What will happen to Chris, do you think?"

"I understand he's in hospital right now. He tried to commit suicide, after all, so they want to keep an eye on him. Once they're sure he's mentally able, I guess he'll be charged with murder. The whole thing was clearly premeditated. A good lawyer will probably argue mitigating circumstances, so that may drop it down to a lesser charge."

Piet flopped down beside her in the other garden chair. "Do you believe him?"

Shannon frowned. "Believe him in what?"

"That he was pushed into this assisted suicide. Wasn't he getting some money through the will?"

She nodded. "The widow gets everything, but according to Violet, she always planned to give Jenn and Chris an equal share of the estate."

He nodded. "Hmm."

She held up her hand. "Don't. I don't want to think there was more to this. I think he did it from a sense of duty. Chris was one of the few people who loved Malcolm just as he was. Violet put up with him. Jennifer disliked him."

"OK. I'll say no more."

※

On Monday morning, at nine o'clock, Shannon met with Kal Khan and a female detective, Anna Rossi, to take her statement. Anna keyed the information into her laptop as they talked. They took a break after an hour.

Her uncle met Shannon in the hallway. "How are you holding up?"

She swallowed. "Honestly, I thought I'd be done in an hour, not taking a break."

"Every detail is important. You can do it."

"I know. I guess I didn't appreciate how every word and movement needs to be recorded."

"Hang in there." He squeezed her arm encouragingly and then strode away.

Detective Rossi brought in a plate with three pastries after the break. "I thought you might need a sugar fix."

Shannon took one of the tubes filled with creamy filling. "Mmm. Cannoli. You didn't get these in the cafeteria."

"No. They came from my mother's kitchen."

"Thank you for sharing. OK. I'm ready to carry on."

An hour and a half later, they finished asking their questions, and Anna Rossi went away to print a copy for Shannon to sign.

As they waited, Shannon thought of her own question to ask Kal. "What happened with Andrew Noble? I hope he was charged after stealing those Scriven documents."

Kal bobbed his head in his yes/maybe no response, which always made Shannon smile. "He's been charged with breaking and entering and theft under $5,000. He's not very happy, though."

Shannon frowned indignantly. "Not happy? He's a thief. Why isn't he happy?"

"The document was fake. We sent it to a forensics documents lab in Mississauga. They use a special imaging device to study the paper, the ink, and several other elements, and they've reported that it's a forgery."

She leaned back in her chair and shook her head. "All that for nothing. He wanted to impress his brethren and prove he was worthy of being part of the congregation. All he did was get himself ostracized forever, probably."

Kal smiled. "Karma."

"Yes."

※

She picked up flowers for Violet at her local shop. The bouquet included black-eyed Susans, blue irises, and violets. When Shannon handed the bunch over to her elderly friend, she explained her choice: "According to the Farmer's Almanac, the black-eyed Susans symbolize justice, and the irises represent hope and faith. It's time to look forward now that this is all behind you. Things will be better. Are you moving to Florida?"

This time, Violet's tears were of gratitude. "No. I've decided I don't want to move south after all. I have everything I need right here. Jennifer needs me, and maybe Chris does too. I have friends who moved to Costa Rica, and I think I'll visit them next winter, but I'm staying put for now. I believed I needed to escape from my old life, but now I feel running away isn't the answer. I can face what the future brings here in Port Hope."

Shannon nodded and sipped on the tea Violet had given her. "That sounds like a great plan. You have friends here who care about you."

Violet nodded, and they talked about gardening. "I might join the community garden here."

Shannon grinned. "Maybe I can convince you to come and look at my back garden. It's a disaster and needs some love and tender care."

Before she left, Shannon made a date for Violet to look at her garden.

Epilogue

THEY AGREED TO TAKE her car versus his motorbike.

"I always take Dusty when I visit the family. I can't leave her behind, and I'm not quite prepared for the adventure of having her on the bike with us yet."

Kal Khan agreed, even though Shannon saw the disappointment on his face. "We can take my car. I don't mind driving."

She smiled. "It's not that you want to be in control, right?"

He subsided with a sheepish smile. "I will be happy to be a passenger with you and enjoy the passing view."

"That's settled, then."

The events of the past weeks were behind them, and they talked of things other than murder and abduction on this bright, sunny Canada Day.

Shannon glanced over to her passenger. "Thank you for agreeing to come today. It might be daunting to meet my whole family at once on their turf."

Kal shifted in his seat to give her his full attention. "You inspire me, Shannon. You have repeatedly shown me that you are ready to face your fears. You came with me for a bike ride and confronted possible and real villains. If you can do these things, it's only right I face what makes me uneasy."

"Socializing."

"Yes. Also, I fear embarrassing you."

"That won't happen. Although I can't guarantee my family won't embarrass you. They aren't always sensitive. You've met Mammy and Da already. They'll be kind. My sister Meghan will be wrapped up in her fiancé, Declan."

"She's the middle one, right?"

Shannon laughed. "Have you been studying?"

He smiled. "I've been listening."

She continued. "The one who will quiz you the most will be Bernadette. Just don't mind her. If she asks something you don't fancy answering, ask her a question back, and she'll be away to the races."

"Meaning she'll start talking herself."

"That's it. Our Bernie's a great talker."

"I'll remember that tip. Thank you."

"And, of course, Uncle Bob and Aunt Sarah might come by. He knows you'll be there, right?"

"He does. I wanted to be sure he was quite comfortable with my presence before accepting the invitation from your parents."

"Well, I suspect he'll come, and then you'll feel on safer ground."

"I promise not to retreat to work-talk. I am working on my social skills, after all."

"You'll be grand." She cast him another glance. "I'm glad you're coming. Now, you didn't want to stop at the Big Apple, did you?"

"No. I don't want to be late, and I look forward to some homemade apple cider at your family home."

The End

Acknowledgements

I am indebted to Adrian Spiering, who once stopped on a summer bicycle ride with his family to chat with me outside my house. That conversation led him to give me a stack of research on Joseph M. Scriven (1819-1886) since I now live in a renovated church where Joseph Scriven once preached. Thank you so much, Adrian!

Thanks to Cathy Walker (a fellow Canadian author), who sent me an article about the Rice Lake Monster.

I've used the real names of several spots in Port Hope, Cobourg, and Bewdley, Northumberland County, so I'd like to thank the restaurants and shops that help give my stories authenticity:

Toe Beans Café, Port Hope
Dreamer's Café, Port Hope
The Schnitzel Shack, Port Hope
Buttermilk Café, Cobourg
Lakeview Restaurant, Bewdley

Once again, I'm grateful to Dave Wickenden for the first round of edits and Sharron Elkouby for further edits and proofreading.

Thanks to the artistry of Robert Scozzari of Inspiring Design Co. for another gorgeous cover.

As always, thanks to Jimmy Carton for the first read-through and encouragement.

And – most of all – thanks to all my readers for your continued support. I have a big favour to ask. Could you spare a moment to leave a review or a rating? Nothing fancy is needed, but a few words go a long way to help other readers take a chance on new authors. Visit my Amazon book page to leave a sentence or two.

Keep up to date on book news by signing up for my monthly newsletter!

www.rennydegroot.com/newsletter-sign-up

Manufactured by Amazon.ca
Acheson, AB